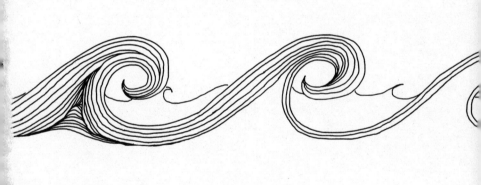

Also by Megan Frazer Blakemore
The Friendship Riddle
The Spy Catchers of Maple Hill
The Water Castle
Secrets of Truth & Beauty

VERY

in Pieces

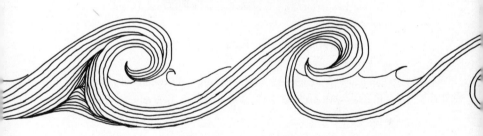

MEGAN FRAZER BLAKEMORE

HARPER TEEN

An Imprint of HarperCollinsPublishers

HarperTeen is an imprint of HarperCollins Publishers.

Very in Pieces
Copyright © 2015 by Megan Frazer Blakemore
For information address HarperCollins Children's Books, a division of HarperCollins Publishers, 195 Broadway, New York, NY 10007.
www.epicreads.com

Library of Congress Cataloging-in-Publication Data
Blakemore, Megan Frazer.
    Very in pieces / Megan Frazer Blakemore. — First edition.
        pages   cm
    Summary: "A straight-A student in a family of free-spirited artists must come to terms with the hard truths about those she loves most"— Provided by publisher.
    ISBN 978-0-06-234839-5 (hardback)
    [1. Family problems—Fiction.]   I. Title.
PZ7.B574Ve   2015   2015005618
[Fic]—dc23   CIP
                                                                              AC

Typography by Kate J. Engbring
15 16 17 18 19   CG/RRDH   10 9 8 7 6 5 4 3 2 1

First Edition

For Sara Crowe

Thank you for sticking by me and by this story.

one

i.

GO GET YOUR SISTER.

It seems like a simple request. Unless, of course, your sister has turned into a raging ball of id, as impulsive and changeable as a summer storm.

Mom is still getting dressed as she says this. She's in her bra and underwear—full, soft curves where I'm all hard lines and angles. I'm lying on her bed trying to pretend that sweat is not soaking the back of my black linen dress and gathering behind my knees. I've never been good at pretending.

"I'm not sure where she is," I tell my mom.

"Smart One, start in her room." That's her pet name for me. *Smart One.* Ramona, my younger sister, has infinite names— Little One, Deep One, Luv—but I am always Smart One. Because I am. Smart, that is.

I hesitate a moment longer as if waiting might make

Ramona materialize like a hologram. I wouldn't put it past her. She doesn't appear, and so I rise, walk down the stairs from my parents' bedroom, and then go up the stairs to the turret that Ramona and I share.

Our house—Nonnie's house—seems to have been designed by a drug-addled architect. From the outside, it looks like a misshapen fortress: golden stucco with red terra-cotta shingles, more suited for California or the Southwest than our small New Hampshire town. There are two sets of stairs inside, one for each of the turrets. From inside, the inspiration is Frank Lloyd Wright, with sunken rooms and wide-open spaces.

At the top of the landing, I stand in front of Ramona's closed door. She'd never been a closed-door person until sometime last spring, maybe six or seven months ago. Over the summer, it got worse. It's like in anticipation of being in high school with me she felt she had to draw a box around herself.

There is the *thump, thump, thump* of a bass line. I knock and hear a moan that could be a yes, so I push open the door. Ramona is sprawled across her bed, face to the ceiling. It's hard to make her out at first, since the entire surface is covered with papers, books, and CDs, pilfered, I am sure, from my father's collection. The floor, too, is similar chaos and if you squint, it all looks like one flat landscape, and finding my sister is a game: *Where's Ramona?*

"You need to get ready for the opening," I tell her.

"What?" she asks without sitting up. "I can't hear you. The music is too loud."

The music is not too loud. If it were too loud, she would not know I had spoken. Still, I raise my voice. "The opening. We're leaving soon. You need to get ready."

She's my sister, my own flesh and blood, so I shouldn't want to kill her, and yet I do. Is there a name for that? *Patricide. Matricide. Fratricide. Sororicide?* It sounds dumb, like a horror movie about a bunch of blond, buxom sorority sisters chasing each other around with knives. Which, come to think of it, would probably make bajillions of dollars.

"I *am* ready," Ramona replies. She is wearing the cutoff jean shorts she's been wearing the past three months. The exact same pair. In June she discovered some old peasant blouses in one of Nonnie's trunks, and those completed her uniform. Sometimes the cutoffs barely peek out from below the blouse. Tonight, though, she has on one of my dad's old concert T-shirts. From this angle it's hard to tell, but it looks like Dinosaur Jr., the one with the girl on the beach, hitching up her pants and smoking a cigarette. Ramona's hair, various shades of golden brown, splays out around her, and even from this distance I can see tangles. Her window faces south, out over the bay behind the house, and the light coming in is just golden enough that it looks like she is fading into a sepia-toned photograph. "You are not ready."

She sits up. "I think it depends on what you mean by ready." She grins merrily. "I mean, emotionally ready, I don't know. I think I am. Aesthetically ready? Well, I haven't researched the artist at all, so I suppose I'm not exactly ready in that sense. Then again, sometimes it's best to go into these things without any preconceived notions."

"Your outfit," I say.

"Nonnie told me that an outfit is actually a set of tools. Isn't that interesting? Where are my tools? *What* are my tools?" She looks around the room. "Remember that old saw that Dad had? The one he kept on his desk as art?"

I rub my thigh where I still have a thick, raised scar from falling on the rusty saw during one of the epic games of hide-and-seek Ramona and I used to play. "Yes."

"He didn't want to get rid of it, you know. He wanted to keep it, just up on a higher shelf. But really, who uses a saw as art? It's like that story—the one about the quilts and the daughter wants to hang them on the wall, but the mom, or maybe it's the grandmother, says they're quilts, they're made for the beds. And the daughter's like, 'No, no, no, they're a piece of our cultural heritage and we need to protect them.' You know, I can't remember what they do with the quilts in the end."

"You need to change," I tell her.

"Into what?"

"Your outfit—your clothing—it's inappropriate." She opens her mouth to speak, but I cut her off. "I don't need an examination of the word inappropriate."

"I was just going to say that keeping a saw as art is inappropriate. Not a thorough examination by any means."

"You know the type of thing you should wear to this. Put it on. And brush your hair."

Her smile falters. "Aye, aye, captain." But she doesn't move.

"We're leaving in twenty minutes."

She flops back onto the bed. By some mix of grace and chance—Ramona, defined—she falls into the exact empty space her body left before, like a cutout doll returning to its paper.

It won't do any good to nag her. She'll be downstairs, or she won't. So I wander into the kitchen, where I open the refrigerator to see what we have to drink. There's about two sips of lemonade left in the bottom of the bottle. I add it to some sparkling water and pretend that's what I wanted all along.

There's a note from my dad on the refrigerator, hung by a magnet shaped like the state of Texas:

VERY, IF YOU SEE THIS, AND OF COURSE IF YOU ARE READING IT, YOU HAVE SEEN IT: HELP! AND, HELLO! I WOULD LIKE TO WEAR MY WATCH TO THE GALLERY OPENING—THE ONE WITH THE COPPER FACE AND THE BROWN BAND—BUT I DON'T WANT TO WEAR IT TO THE OFFICE SINCE I'M GOING TO BE TYPING AND IT ALWAYS GETS IN THE WAY. SO I'LL TAKE IT OFF AND THEN, MORE THAN LIKELY, I'LL FORGET TO PUT IT BACK ON. AND THERE I WILL BE AT THE OPENING, MY WRIST AS NAKED AS THE MODELS IN THE ART

DEPARTMENT (DO YOU KNOW THEY ARE PAID $74 A SITTING? WHAT AN ODD NUMBER!). AT ANY RATE, ALL OF THIS IS TO SAY, WOULD YOU BE A PAL AND BRING THE WATCH FOR ME, VERY? SINCERELY, YOUR FAVORITE FATHER, DALLAS.

ADDENDUM: IT IS POSSIBLE THAT RAMONA OR ANNALIESE MIGHT FIND THIS NOTE. OR EVEN IMOGENE. IF THAT IS THE CASE, PLEASE BRING IT DIRECTLY TO VERY. DO NOT PASS GO. DO NOT STOP FOR A SNACK IN THE PANTRY OR TO PICK A BOOK IN THE LIBRARY. DIRECTLY TO VERY. WE ALL KNOW WHAT WILL HAPPEN OTHERWISE. NAKED WRIST AND NO $74 FOR THE TROUBLE.

I fold the note and put it in my pocket. With a final gulp, I finish my lemon-ish sparkling water and put the cup in the sink, then stop, go back, and put it in the dishwasher, since I'll be the one to load the dishwasher later anyway. Then I go get my dad's watch for him. It tick-tick-ticks with satisfying regularity, like a heartbeat, or soldiers marching onward, onward, onward, not caring where they go.

ii.

Twenty-seven minutes after we were supposed to have arrived, we are in the car.

We crank the AC and listen to mellow music on the way there, and for that bubble of time, it is like when we were little, and Mom and Nonnie would bustle us into the car and just drive. "We're going on an adventure," they'd say. We'd leave Dad behind, working on his book about music—a different attempt each summer, it seemed. Sometimes the trip was just to the town pool or the beach. Often, though, it would be a real journey. We drove to the top of Mount Washington in Nonnie's roadster. It was so windy at the top that Mom's scarf blew into the air like a red keening bird. We went down to Boston to ride in the Swan Boats, gliding along the smooth water while tourists took pictures. Mom and Ramona pretended they were celebrities and the tourists were paparazzi. Once, we went to Bar Harbor to take the ferry to Nova Scotia, but were turned away because Ramona and I didn't have passports. It was the peak of summer and the only place available to spend the night was a cheap hotel on the wrong side of the bridge. I remember the sheets were rough and there was an awful smell of stale cigarettes. Now, though, now that Nonnie is so sick, the memory tastes like warm milk.

We pull into the parking lot and through the glass windows of the gallery I can see people moving around holding their wineglasses and their hors d'oeuvres on tiny napkins.

Mom steps out of the car, gorgeous in a floor-length

turquoise halter dress. She gives herself a once-over in the glass of the car window, touching her fingertips to her hair. I shoot a cursory glance in the rearview mirror, then emerge from the car into the wall of humidity. I've got on my black dress that came from some chain store in the mall, but, in a touch of sartorial creativity I'm quite proud of, I chose a pair of red ballet flats. Most of the time I wear my hair down, but it's so hot, and my hair is long and heavy, so I've twisted it into a bun. I think I look fairly cute, yet sophisticated. Perfect for a gallery opening? I never seem to get these things quite right.

Ramona looks like she is attending a different event entirely. She still has the Dinosaur Jr. shirt on, but swapped her cutoffs for a denim skirt. Long ago she embroidered a rainbow along the hem of the skirt, and now it looks dingy. She's thrown on a couple of strings of Mardi Gras beads in red, pink, and orange. I don't comment because I know that's just what she wants me to do. Or maybe she doesn't care. It's become so hard to tell.

Mom pushes open the glass doors and all eyes swivel to her. It is like they've been waiting for her arrival. Annaliese Woodruff and her two ladies-in-waiting. I bask in the refracted glow. A waiter walks by and offers her a flute of champagne, which she takes with a smile as she floats farther into the room. *Lovely to see you! And you! What a gorgeous dress! Kiss, kiss.*

Mom is on sabbatical this year. She could've gotten the time off just to care for Nonnie, but in her application she promised the chair of the department that she'd create a series of paintings suitable for a gallery exhibition. Work on these, as far as I can tell, is not exactly progressing.

This is the first opening without Nonnie. We usually go into these things together, muttering under our breath about the art and the pretentiousness of everyone there. "This is not how you experience art," she would say. "And oh my, is Professor Ricci still trying to work that comb-over? What a sad, funny man." She once told me that Gertrude Stein stole that famous line from her: "If you can't say anything nice about anyone else, come sit next to me."

My phone buzzes and I pull it out of my pocket to see a text from my best friend Grace: **@ that gallery thing?**

Sadly yes, I text back.

Your assignment: Interview college boys. Find out if they are as woeful as their high school counterparts.

I scan the room full of art-department college boys in ironic T-shirts and faded jeans with chin-length hair and woven bracelets. **Field report: subjects potentially worse. Abort mission.**

I expect a full report tomorrow morning. Graph and determine equation of awfulness if you must.

Hilarious.

Admit it. You're thinking about how to do it.

I was, but instead I type: **Over and out.** Mom doesn't like it when I'm on my phone at the gallery. She thinks it reflects badly on her.

I decide I'll look at the paintings, too. At least then I'll appear occupied. The only problem is that they are all more or less the same: a square of solid paint. They are different colors, sometimes smaller, sometimes larger. Sometimes the canvas is also square, sometimes rectangular. None have frames, so the white edges of the canvas blend into the white of the wall.

"It really exemplifies our society, don't you think?" a middle-aged man asks me. "Always putting boxes around things, putting ourselves in boxes."

"Of course," I say. "Boxes, boxes everywhere." I try to hide a smile, and look around for Ramona. She is on the far side of the room, sitting on a bench and staring at one of the paintings, perfectly still. We used to play this bingo game at the openings. First person to get to five art-gallery clichés won. It was usually her, picking up on the inane things people would say, the way the art students would argue that every painting was about sex or liminal space. Now Ramona is too far away to play the game with me, and anyway, she's not looking at anything but the artwork.

It is a relief when my father comes in. He enters like a dancer, walking in time to the emaciated jazz that plays unobtrusively in the background. He crosses the gallery to my mom and slips his arm around her waist before pulling her close for a kiss. Like moths, Ramona and I are drawn to them, and join them from our opposite corners of the room.

My father, Dallas Sayles, works at Essex College like my mom. He is a music professor—jazz and rhythm and blues and whole seminars on people like Bob Dylan and the Beatles. He was one of the first musicologists in the country to take hip-hop seriously, and he teaches classes in its history, politics, and development. He is the cool professor. I know that his students get crushes on him. I've watched them, read the emails they've sent, trying to be coy. Once people see our mother, though, see the two of them together, well, even those college girls know they don't stand a chance. You can tell just by the way he looks at her that he is infatuated.

I turn to Ramona to share a satisfied smirk, but she's looking at the floor. So I hand my dad the watch and he smiles. "I knew I could count on you, jelly bean." As he slips on the watch, he nods at Ramona and says, "Nice shirt. Dinosaur Jr. Maybe we can get our alt-rock on later."

"Maybe." She slides her hands into her back pockets.

"You," he goes on, talking now to my mother, "look stunning as always. I could ravish you right here."

Mom sips her champagne and plucks at a stray thread on his tan suit. "Thank you, love."

He glances at me next. I shift in my ballet flats. "And you, my dear, reliable Very. She who actually reads the notes left on the refrigerator. Thank you for getting them all here."

"No problem." Suddenly my outfit makes me feel like a child playing dress-up.

"So this is your visiting artist?" he asks with a frown at the colored squares.

Oh thank God. I'm not the only one who thinks these paintings are ridiculous.

"Marcus Schmidt," Mom says. "All the way from Germany."

Dad nods, then says, "It's really daring work."

I look again at the nearest painting. This one is a blue square on a square canvas.

"What do you think of it?" Mom asks Ramona.

She sucks in her cheeks. "It's like the ocean. Like just one small square of it, right up close."

"Ah," Mom says. "The essence of abstraction."

"Nice," Dad says. He puts his hand on my shoulder, bare except for the thin straps of my dress. "A second opinion?"

I pause, and feel myself starting to sweat again, even in this heavily air-conditioned room. There is a small group of people around us, students, mostly, and a few other professors. My parents being who they are means that the crowd is listening, even if they don't want to appear to be eavesdropping on the magnetic couple and their children. It's like I am being called upon to perform, only the expectation is that I will *not* perform, not be up to the task of commenting on the art.

I clear my throat. "I guess I don't think it's the ocean."

Olivia Knotts, a potter who's been the junior member of the art faculty for seven years, is fiercely chewing on her lip while the department chair, Melora Wilkins, swirls her champagne.

"I mean," I go on, "the paint is too even. The ocean, though, it's made up of hundreds and hundreds of colors."

"That is true," Mom says, "about the actual ocean."

Isn't that what Ramona was talking about? A few heads in the small crowd nod—Olivia Knotts looks about ready to sob for me—and I wonder what I am missing. They can't all see the blue of the ocean. It isn't even the right shade: it is royal, not dark like our ocean, or turquoise like the Caribbean.

"Well, I just think there might be other interpretations."

"There are always *other* interpretations," Dad says. His hand slips from my shoulder.

"Some people argue that's the beauty of art," Mom says.

"You'll still be having your party, won't you?" Melora asks Mom, and just like that I'm forgotten.

"Oh yes, of course," Mom says, placing a hand on her boss's arm. Every year Mom invites the whole art department up to our house for cocktails, food, and more cocktails.

"Perhaps you'll show us some of your new work there?"

Mom smiles slightly, a bewitching twist of the lips. "We'll see. You know how these things go, Melora. It's coming along, but—well, the best way to say it is that I'm evolving along with it."

"As long as we can see it on these walls, Annaliese, that's what matters." They begin walking toward another canvas. "Be sure to send me the date so I can get it on the department calendar."

When they move on, I look at the small typed description.

Oceanic.
Acrylic on canvas.

It's possible that Ramona checked the title, but I doubt she ever looks at those gallery labels. She would consider that cheating.

Yet she knew. She knew without hesitation, as if the knowledge had been deposited in her brain before birth. Nonnie always says that if everyone in the family were an artist, we'd never eat or have clean clothes. "Everyone has their role to play, Very."

I'm sick of mine.

iii.

The gallery is too much. Too bright, too square, too white, too many bubbly champagne-drinking sycophants.

I slip out a side door of the main room and descend the stairs to the lower level of the gallery. The walls down here are gray and there's no light jazz playing, just the sound of the air conditioner whirring.

The New Hampshire High School Art Exposition is on display. This art, at least, makes sense to me. There are paintings of vases of flowers or landscapes—the White Mountains, mostly. Silver gelatin print photographs of buildings or blurry people. Crooked ceramic mugs.

A wall at the back is reserved for the best of the best, and as I walk toward it, my eye is drawn to a large-format photograph of two girls. They are sitting with their bodies twisted into each other and their faces pressed together. They are both white girls, like me, and the photographer has made them even paler, as white as the dresses they are wearing. One is a brunette, the other a redhead, and the color of their hair seems to pop against all the white. Their lips and eyes, too, are unnaturally saturated.

They are beautiful. Like angels or fairies or ghosts. They are not real girls.

Only they are real, and I know them. Callie and Serena. They're in my grade at school, going into our senior year. I look at the attribution, and I recognize the name of the photographer: Hunter Osprey. The three of them are inseparable, a triumvirate, and I never felt that I really knew anything about them. Callie, Serena, and Hunter. Now, though, I want to touch the picture and feel if their skin is as cool and smooth as it seems.

I want someone to see me as Hunter sees these girls. Unnaturally beautiful. Tempting as the quince in Eden. Dangerous.

I don't have to go far for a reminder of how I'm really seen, for there, on the adjoining wall, nestled among the also-rans, is Christian's portrait of me. Christian, my steady-in-every-sense-of-the-word boyfriend, and I had taken Intro to Art to fulfill our arts requirement. I was terrible, which delighted Mr. Solloway, but Christian was decent. We had to pair up and sketch portraits. Mine of him looked like some demented cross between Albert Einstein and Yo-Yo Ma. He sketched me leaning forward, pencil in hand, sucking on my lower lip as I worked through a math problem. Everyone said it captured me entirely: driven, studious, intense, blah, blah, blah. I used to love it, but now seeing the gray lines on small white paper compared to the glorious photograph of the girls, I want to tear it from the wall and smash the frame.

Behind me a man clears his throat. I imagine that I'm not supposed to be down here, and I wonder if I should explain who I am—Annaliese Woodruff and Dallas Sayles's daughter, Imogene Woodruff's granddaughter—but when I turn, I don't see a docent or a security guard or a man at all. It's Dominic Meyers, the closest thing my high school has to a juvenile delinquent. The rumors are that he's a small-time drug dealer, pot mostly. He's standing there looking the part in dark jeans, white T-shirt, and black Doc Martens.

He stares at me with deep green eyes and I wonder if he even knows who I am, that I go to his school, that we're both seniors. Our school is small, only 130 people in our graduating class, and yet I can't recall a single time we've interacted. Our lives slip by on lines that don't intersect, and it's possible he's never even noticed me.

"Quite the photograph." He nods toward the picture of Callie and Serena.

I glance back as if I hadn't even noticed it, at the same time sidestepping to put myself between him and Christian's sketch. "I guess so."

"People say that Serena's slept with half the hockey team."

So at least he seems to know that we go to the same school. I heard the rumor, too, as it ricocheted around the halls. I thought it was disgusting, and not just because Christian was on the half of the team she hadn't slept with. There is something in the way Dominic looks at me—the glint of his eyes, the twitch of his lips, even the curl of his dark brown hair—that seems like a challenge. *Good girls don't talk about sex.* So I say, "It seems to me that it's the hockey team that has the problem, not Serena."

"What's their problem?" he asks.

"A lack of imagination."

He laughs at this, which makes my body relax and shiver at the same time. He looks past my shoulder and I turn to block his view, hot in my cheeks at the thought of him seeing Christian's portrait of me.

"A general laziness," he agrees, "like lions jumping on the gazelle once one of them has already brought her to the ground."

"It's not like they've devoured her. She's still there."

He raises an eyebrow. I've never really looked at him before. I mean, I know his general outlines, the way I know everyone in school, but I couldn't have said before this moment, for example, that there seems to be a faint scar in that raised eyebrow, a thin line where no hair grows.

"There's something I've always wanted to ask you, Very Woodruff." Hearing him say my name is a small thrill, a question answered: he *knows* me. His voice is low and almost like a whisper. Instinctively, I lean in to hear him better.

"What's that?"

"Why do they call you Very? What is it that you are very—very what?"

My name is number two on my own personal list of frequently asked questions, right after "What's it like to be Imogene Woodruff's granddaughter?"

"It's short for Veronica," I explain. "I'm named after the Elvis Costello song."

He looks at me blankly.

"You know, 'Veronica.'" Usually people either have no idea what I'm talking about when I explain my name, or they fawn all over Elvis Costello like he's God's gift to pop music. But Dominic just shakes his head. I sing my own name back to him, off-key and warbling.

He grins crookedly, of course, and I can't help but wonder if he practices the rakish expression. I can just see him standing in front of a bathroom mirror: *Too cocky. Too sly. Too menacing. Ahh, just right!*

The air-conditioning is cranked up in the lower gallery, and I'm suddenly very, very cold, goose pimples and everything.

"For what it's worth, I like that one better." He points to Christian's sketch behind me.

"That's not me."

"It seems a pretty fair representation."

"No. I mean that's not who I am."

"Well then, who are you?"

"This gallery isn't open." The voice comes from behind Dominic: a security guard.

"We're here for the exhibit opening," I say.

"Upstairs," he replies. "This floor is closed for the evening." His eyes shift from Dominic to me, back and forth, as if we're up to something illicit down here. Hardly.

"Right," Dominic says. "Our mistake. Sorry."

The security guard waits for us to move. Dominic holds the door open for me like he's a proper gentleman. Just as I'm walking through, he leans in close enough for me to feel his breath on my neck, and asks again: "Who are you, Very? Very what?"

I step around him. "See you around, Dominic."

He laughs so loud it dances through the empty gallery. "Sure you will."

iv.

"Sylvia Plath had the right idea sticking her head in that oven," Nonnie declares.

"Nonnie." I'm perched on a wingback chair pulled up next to my grandmother's bed, where she sits with pillows propped behind her like some sort of Middle Eastern royalty in a storybook.

"It's true. Sylvia, Anne, they're both famous as much for their deaths as their poetry. *Oh that beautiful, sad Sylvia. Oh that sexy, psychotic Anne.* If I had known it was all going to end like this, I would have done it myself long ago. I should have just walked into the ocean with stones in my pockets like Virginia Woolf."

She coughs and I tilt toward her, ready to—what? Catch her falling body?

"Yes, I should have let go back when I was lithe and beautiful like you. I thought about doing it. Before them. After them.

19

It wasn't like I was jumping on the bandwagon. Bandwagon. God-awful word. Things were different then for women. Women writers especially. You're lucky to live now."

"I know." Sitting here across from my fading grandmother, I don't feel fortunate. Seven months ago, she was diagnosed with adenocarcinoma of the lungs. She is dying.

She wipes her thin wrist on her forehead. "At least couldn't I be dying of something gorgeous like consumption?"

"Consumption is tuberculosis," I tell her. "You would die coughing up blood."

"I would die pale as ivory with rose-red cheeks and lips. Snow White in the flesh."

"Snow White in the ground."

Nonnie's room is cast in shadows, the only light coming in through slim gaps in the curtains. The radiation treatments bring on migraines, and she's never been one for bright light anyway. Still it seems I can see every angle in her face. Everyone knows the iconic pictures of her: dark brown hair in a pixie cut, white blouse, tailored black pants. Like Audrey Hepburn only sharper, and the cancer has made her edgier. In contrast, her hair is growing back soft as a baby's and is starting to curl over her ears. "You need a haircut. Do you want to go to the salon or just have the woman come here?"

"That woman is so dreary. I much prefer the gay man."

"Carl."

"Yes, Carl."

She doesn't precisely answer my question and instead returns to her perennial topic: her impending death. "No one else will talk about my death with me, Very. Not your mother. Not your father, though that would hardly be worth trying. Ramona won't talk to me at all."

Mom says Ramona is like a snake in its old, dusty skin, but when she sheds it and emerges full of brightly colored scales, watch out. I say she's being a petulant little brat who's breaking our grandmother's heart every day. *Po-tay-to, po-tah-to.*

"I'll talk about whatever you want, Nonnie."

She raises her penciled-in eyebrows. The radiation treatment stole those along with the hair on her head and hasn't returned them yet. She doesn't take the bait, though. Instead she says, "It's coming. Sooner and sooner."

I don't tell her that doesn't make sense, that time doesn't bend like a function that curves up toward the axis of the graph but never quite reaches it.

"Professor Winslow visits from time to time," she says, picking up our old line of conversation. "He just sits and drums his fingers on his pants as if they were his piano." Professor Winslow is in the music department with my father and had a brief, unsuccessful stint as my piano teacher. "And Anton came by a few days ago." Professor Anton Dixon is the chair of the English department at Essex College, where my grandmother has been poet in residence for ages. He's been her nemesis since the day she started at the school, at least from her perspective. She says his class is where poetry goes to die. And his breath smells of liver and onions. "He said, 'We need to talk about your death.

How you want it handled.'"

"You should have told him you plan to go into his class and perish there just like all the poets he's killed before you."

She laughs, which turns into a cough. "I said I wanted a museum in my honor. The Imogene Woodruff Museum. Has a nice ring to it, doesn't it?" She lies back against the pillows and closes her eyes as if she is dreaming of that museum.

"Are you tired?"

"I'm always tired." Her eyes are still closed but I can see them moving underneath her eyelids. "It's strange, Very, to watch yourself decay. I hope it never happens to you. When I was young my girlfriends and I would ask each other if we'd rather be pretty or smart. I always said pretty because pretty girls might not realize they aren't smart, but smart girls always know they aren't pretty."

"Can't you be both, Nonnie?"

"A bit of both, perhaps, but not devastatingly both."

"You are," I tell her. "You and Mom."

"Don't be a sycophant, Very."

I yawn.

"Boring you?" she asks.

"I had that thing last night. Mom's gallery opening."

"I wish you wouldn't use the word *thing*, Veronica. Banish it from your vocabulary." Nonnie always uses my full name when admonishing me about language. "It's my dying wish," she adds.

I roll my eyes at her. "I wish you had been there. I had no one to talk with, and nothing exciting happened."

"You know how I hate those parties."

I agree, but I know she's lying. Nonnie loves any event with wine and admirers.

"Mom and Dad quizzed me about the art. I got it wrong."

"There is no wrong and right with art," Nonnie says. "It's not like your mathematics."

"Mom and Dad don't seem to think so. Or Ramona. But Nonnie, you should have seen it. It was just squares painted on canvas."

"Now I'm doubly glad I missed it."

"Ramona said it looked like the ocean."

"She did always love the ocean."

"So you see what you love in paintings like that?" I ask. And if so, what would I have said? The bay behind our house? The blue of Nonnie's veins as they shine up through her skin, letting me know that she's still alive?

The seconds tick by on the clock.

She moans and resettles herself on her pillows. I think she has fallen asleep: her breaths are coming ragged but even.

"You know, there was only one art opening to which I ever looked forward. One of Andy Warhol's. He used one of my poems in a painting. 'Word Art,' he called it. All the words were silk-screened onto the canvas in different colors and sizes. I thought it was a bit gaudy, but he adored it. It was going to be a fantastic party." She opens her eyes and they are glinting. "Mick Jagger was going to be there. But then that crazy woman shot Andy and the opening was closed, and the paintings never saw the light of day."

"So sad for the paintings," I say.

"Sad for the crazy woman. Valerie something. Solanas. Ugly name."

"Valerie sounds like Very to me."

"You have a lovely last name. One of them anyway. She was a pretty woman in her way. Interesting-looking. She wanted to get rid of all men. Andy was as good as any to start with. He was a bit of a prick. That's a good slang word. Sounds just like what it is." Then she says, "This is the last day of summer vacation, isn't it?"

"Yes."

"So what are you doing spending it with me?"

"You're who I want to be with, Nonnie."

"What about that boyfriend of yours?"

"He just got back from Lake Winnipesaukee yesterday."

"Ha! There is someplace else you would rather be. I'm your fallback." She coughs. "And that was yesterday. Where is he today?"

"He had to go to some leadership seminar this morning, and then I had my math class at the college, and then he had to take his sister to get her clarinet fixed." We had joked about it on the phone: *Well then I guess I'll pencil you in for three months from next Tuesday.*

"Sounds like he leads a thrilling life."

"I would rather be with you anyway." It's true and I try not to think too much about what that means for our relationship.

"Can't we call him Chris? Christian is just so . . . Christian. That's not even his religion, is it? He ought to be called Buddhism or something."

"Just because he's Korean doesn't mean he's Buddhist." I wonder what she would think of a boy named Dominic. "I like the name Christian. It suits him."

Nonnie snorts. She has never thought much of Christian. It took me a while to come around, too. Christian pursued me in a sweet, almost quaint way—writing me notes, leaving a daisy taped to my locker, telling me that he had scored a goal in a hockey game just for me—but I kept putting him off. Nonnie had been diagnosed the month before. I was tired. And there was Christian, day after day, with his daisies and his sweet smile. So, I had given in to him, and we'd been together ever since. It was the first real relationship for either of us, and we prided ourselves on doing it so well.

Nonnie waves her hand at me. "You find me dull." Before I can reply, she says, "And you should. You should have something better to do than hang around your dying grandmother."

It's not Christian I think of. Or Britta and Grace. Instead it's Dominic's annoying, sexy smile that fills my mind. "Oh I do. I'm just sucking up to you for the inheritance."

Nonnie waves her arms around at the shelves of books. "There it is. Take it now for all I care."

The books, I know, are all that really matters to her, not the money she's amassed. They say poetry doesn't pay, but my grandmother made it work. She and my mom had this boho existence in New York City. They shared a one-bedroom apartment and got themselves invited to fancy parties for their meals. I guess Nonnie was socking money away the whole time, right from when she first came up from West Virginia and got a job as a chambermaid at the Chelsea Hotel. By the time they moved up to New Hampshire, she had a huge stash. Nonnie took the job at Essex College and had this big house built, designed by some famous architect too esoteric for any common person to have ever heard of. It's ridiculous and over-the-top, and if anyone but Nonnie had built it, I would probably hate it. But I love it.

"I remember being seventeen. On the Tuesday after my confirmation I went down to the pawnshop and sold my rosary beads for seven dollars. Seven dollars! And you know what I bought with it? A copy of *On the Road*, Emily Dickinson's collected works in this little paperback edition, and a pair of pedal pushers. Then I went and got my hair cut just like this. I wanted to look like Jean Seberg, the girl in *Breathless*."

I don't know who she means, and anyway, my mind is half somewhere else, thinking about what I still need to get ready for the first day of school. "So what were you like before that?" I ask because I have to ask something.

"Well, Veronica, I suppose I was just like you."

Nonnie might as well have picked me up in her frail arms and turned me over, like I'm an hourglass that she flipped before all the sand had finished passing through.

v.

Well, Veronica, I suppose I was just like you.

I'm trying to trace the path backward from the woman who writes poems about sex, who won't tell anyone who my mother's father is, who once climbed over the fence at the top of the Chrysler Building to raise a New Year's toast to all of New York City, how to get from there all the way back to a girl like me. Or for a girl like me to get there.

Just the thought of someone knowing I'm having sex makes me want to burrow under the house never to come out.

As I walk down the stairs from her room above our garage, I try to picture Nonnie with longer hair, maybe even with a ribbon in it, going to the store, doing her homework, studying for tests, sitting with a boy in the movie theater and moving his hand when he tried to put it on her knee.

Ramona is loitering at the bottom of the stairs. She's slouched against the wall of the garage like some hood outside of a convenience store. A rake hangs above her head, giving her a menacing look.

"Going to see Nonnie?"

She shakes her head. "I'm looking for something."

Looking generally requires moving about, but I don't feel like calling her on this point. "She would like it if you went to see her."

Ramona glances toward the garage door as if she's considering running away from me. Instead she kicks her toe into the ground, sending an ant scurrying. "I'm busy."

"Oh yes." I keep my voice as serious as possible. "That's quite clear. So busy standing in the garage. I don't know how you even have time for this conversation."

"I don't," she replies. "Actually."

"Why won't you go see her?"

"I didn't say I wouldn't."

"But you haven't."

Another glance at the garage door. She tugs on her long hair. "I will, though."

I don't tell her what we both know: that there isn't a whole lot of time left. "Fine, Ramona. Dinner's at six."

We both know this is wishful thinking at best. We haven't had a family dinner in forever. Dad used to bring things home from the market—ready-to-go meals that he would dress up to feel homemade—but somewhere along the way he just stopped, and now we all fend for ourselves.

"I'm not hungry."

"You sure look hungry." Her wispy frame seems to be getting slighter by the day.

"Drop it, Very." Her voice is hard.

"Suit yourself."

"And I don't think I'll need a ride to school tomorrow," she tells me.

"Someone else going to pick you up?" I wonder who this might be. None of Ramona's friends are old enough to drive yet.

"Maybe I'll walk."

"It's over five miles."

"That's not so far." She's still wearing that same T-shirt of Dad's, and her Mardi Gras beads, which she pulls from side to side as she speaks.

"I don't mind driving you."

"I know."

"It just seems silly," I say.

"Maybe I'll take the bus."

"The bus?" No one voluntarily takes the bus.

"Big. Yellow. The wheels go round and round." She smiles at her joke, but I'm annoyed. Like it's some big imposition on her to get in the car and ride with me to school.

"Whatever."

"Exactly," she answers.

That about sums up the current state of our relationship.

two

i.

WHATEVER IMPULSE LED RAMONA to contemplate walking or taking the bus is gone by the next morning, and she meets me on my way out the door. She hasn't showered, I don't think, or taken off the Dinosaur Jr. shirt. This time she wears it with a pair of jeans.

"It's going to be hot today, you know," I tell her as we get into the car.

"Okay." She answers without looking at me, without looking at anything, really.

I have a basic policy when it comes to first-day-of-school clothes: dressy, but not too dressy. So on this, the first day of my last year of high school, I'm wearing knee-length shorts and a red top that has all sorts of embroidery around the neck. I think it's supposed to look South American.

"Are you sure about that shirt?" I ask.

"I like this shirt."

"Yeah, but, you know, she's smoking on it. I think that might even be against school dress code."

"Huh," she says, as if the idea of dress code is a foreign one.

"This is your first day of high school. You want to make a good impression."

Ramona rolls down her window and lets her hand flop outside in the breeze as we roll down our steep driveway. "I've been thinking about that."

"Have you now?"

"I don't so much want to make a good first impression as an accurate first impression. I mean, I could come to school on the first day in a plaid kilt and collared shirt. I could come that way for the whole week. And the teachers would have one idea of me. But then what happens when I don't match up to that idea? Everyone's annoyed. So I think it's more important that I come dressed as who I am."

I turn onto the road that winds its way down into town. "You should come as the best version of yourself, though."

"The best version of me?" She grabs her hair and twists it into a loose bun at the nape of her neck.

This isn't exactly the first-day-of-school conversation I had planned. I wanted to give her some sisterly advice about starting high school. Like, always do the reading in Mr. Speck's class. Never eat the burritos in the cafeteria. If a senior asks if you're down, the answer is no.

"I just mean you can dress in your own way, but maybe not so aggressively."

"Aggressively." She holds the word in her mouth, sucks on

it like the girl on her shirt sucks the cigarette. "Huh," she says again.

As we drive through town we pass Ruby's Diner. "Do you think we have time for a muffin?" she asks.

I shake my head.

"I really love the muffins there. The way they grill them. And the frappes. Remember how Nonnie used to take us there?"

We're waiting in traffic at the town's one stoplight.

"She stole a mug once."

"What?"

Ramona grins. "I helped!"

"No way." But I know it has to be true.

"I was seven. We put it in that purse I had that looked like a poodle. The one with the legs hanging off and the little bell. She slipped it right in and I carried it out."

"You were an accessory to theft," I laugh.

"Thug for life, Very. Thug. For. Life."

When we pull into the parking lot, Ramona unsnaps her seat belt and lifts her shirt up over her head. She's so quick I can't even say anything. It's just a flash of pink bra and smooth skin and then she has the shirt back on, inside out this time. "The best version of me, I guess."

I grab my bag from the backseat, and when I step from the car, there is Christian. He grabs me around the waist and is kissing me before we even say hello. His lips are soft against mine, and I can taste his toothpaste. He likes the cinnamon kind. "I missed you," he finally whispers. "Stupid sister with her stupid clarinet."

"Yeah," I say. "Stupid sisters."

I turn to look at Ramona, but she has disappeared into the crowd as if swallowed up by a wave.

He takes my hand in his. "Senior year," he says, and hops from foot to foot.

"This time next year, who knows where we'll be."

"Someplace great," he says. His whole body is bouncing, like he's a puppy on his way to obedience school, not a guy ready to start senior year. He got his hair cut at some point in time. It looks recent: there's a thin line of pale skin before his tan starts on his neck.

"I missed you, too," I tell him.

I've forgotten how warm his hand is. Warm and rough. I never expected him to have such callused hands, and it had been a pleasant surprise when he'd first touched me. He reaches to open the school door, but before he can, the door pushes open and Dominic strides out. He sees me, grins, and then brings two fingers to his forehead before tipping them toward me.

"You're going the wrong way," I say.

"Am I?" he replies. And that's it. He keeps on walking toward the parking lot, and we go into the vestibule.

"Leave it to Dominic Meyers to cut on the first day of school," Christian says. "I didn't know you knew him."

"I don't," I say. "That is, I don't know him, know him. But

we've been in school together a long time. And he was going the wrong way."

"Veronica Sayles-Woodruff, hall monitor," he says, laughing.

I push against him with my shoulder. "Hilarious."

"No, really, it's one of the things I love about you. Attention to detail. Follower of rules."

I wrinkle my nose, but he doesn't notice.

"Listen, I have to go pick up my parking pass. I'll see you at assembly, okay?" He kisses me on the cheek and slips into the front office, where the secretaries go all gaga over him. I take a deep breath and start down the hallway toward the senior corridor.

I want it to feel different, but the hallways still smell like cleaning supplies and old milk, the students laugh and holler the same banalities, and the teachers even seem to be wearing the same clothes. The tiles of the hallway crisscross like graph paper. It's the exact same hallway I've walked down the last three years.

Still, I can't deny a shimmer of excitement. Even people who don't like school in general can't help but be excited by that first day back. It's full of potential. There might be some new student to sweep you off your feet. Or maybe that girl who was nebbishy and quiet at the back of the classroom will come back as a bombshell. Maybe that bombshell is you. You never know. It could happen.

But not today. What happens today is a rush of boys on the soccer team come careening around the corner, passing the ball and laughing as Mr. Speck, world's meanest English teacher, yells at them to knock it off. They don't. One boy knees the ball and is about to head it when instead of hitting the ball his skull cracks into mine, just below my eye. My body snaps in half, and I cover my eye.

Juggling. That's what they call it when they kick the ball around like that: foot to knee to head. I don't know why this occurs to me.

"Are you okay?" a boy asks. It's Brooks Weston, an all-around all-star. He and Britta are locked in a dead heat for valedictorian, and Britta says it's our society's latent sexism that means that he can be a cool guy, while she's seen as striving and competitive.

"Yeah," I say, holding my head. "Yeah, I'm fine."

"Bunch of freakin' Neanderthals!" calls a voice behind me. Grace. I try to smile at her, but my head is seizing with pain. "Step away, step away. Nothing to see here." As soon as she says it, I realize a crowd has gathered and they are all staring at me.

"I'm fine," I say again.

"You should go to the nurse," Brooks tells me. "Adam hit you pretty hard. And that kid's head is thick. Like three layers of the earth's crust."

He's joking with me, so I smile, and that makes my whole head shatter.

Grace is lifting me to my feet and Adam Millstein, he of the hard head, is gathering my things. "He's right. My head is extra thick. When they measure it at the doctor's they always do it twice 'cause it's off the charts."

I nod. More pain stars. "Maybe I should go to the nurse," I say. I wonder if it's a record for the first visit to the nurse at the start of the new year. I bet she's sitting in her office in that rolly chair she has, feet up on the desk, thinking she's good for at least another hour.

As we walk, Grace texts Britta, who meets us at the nurse's office. When we go in, there's already a girl there, lying back on the bed. She's a sophomore and I can't remember her name.

Britta takes charge. "There were nine of them, or eight," she begins, as if she had been there. "And Adam Millstein with his oversize head slammed right into her. And he may say that his Ronald McDonald hair meant that she should've seen him coming, but that is trumped by the simple fact that those nine boys—or eight, whichever—were breaking a fundamental school rule."

Fundamental school rule.

Fundamental.

"You put the 'fun' in 'fundamental,' Britta," I say.

"Ha!" Grace says. "Good one."

"Which only proves my point. Very never makes word jokes like that. Something has been knocked loose." She raises her eyebrows at Nurse Kimball, who is busy looking at my face. She shines a light in my eyes, the tiny pin of light going from eye to eye. Eye to eye. Then she gets me an ice pack and a printout on concussions and tells me I can stay in the back room for twenty minutes, but then we need to go to assembly.

"You should have seen it, Britta," Grace tells her. "They were like a pack of hyenas and Very was one of those animals that pokes its head up out of the ground. A lemur? All skinny and straight, and they just knocked her over."

"It wasn't like that," I say.

Britta rearranges the ice pack on my head. "Luckily you have some brain cells to spare."

"Ronald McDonald hair?" I ask.

"Adam Millstein one hundred percent has Ronald McDonald hair," she says. "He'd tell you so himself, I bet."

Grace holds up the handout. "This says that if you have a concussion you can't do anything, like not even read or study."

Britta raises her eyebrows at me. "Yeah, Very will get right on that."

The sparks are lessening and it's more like a dull pain, a blurriness like when one of the older teachers can't get the projector lens to focus right and everything looks wavy and not quite real.

"How many people saw?"

"Everybody!" Grace says gleefully at the same time that Britta says, "Nobody." But, of course, Grace was there and Britta wasn't, so I know who to believe.

I drop my head back so I'm looking at the ceiling. I've never been in this part of the nurse's office before, the back room. I've never been hurt this badly: it's self-preservation. When I was little, and I fell and hurt myself, Mom and Nonnie would be clucking around, not really sure what to do. Once, I fell off of my bike, right out on the driveway. I ripped my favorite shirt at the elbow, and blood oozed out of a scrape on my knee. My wrist hurt from when I'd braced myself, and I couldn't really move it. They'd gone back and forth together. *Is it broken? Do you think it's broken? Well, how am I supposed to know? There's got to be a way for us to tell these things.* They gently poked at my wrist and tried to gauge my reaction. Finally I'd said, "Maybe we should go to the hospital just to check it out." *Right. Of course. Let me just get my coat. And the keys. Don't forget the keys. Or Ramona. Ramona!*

"Does it hurt that bad?" Britta asks.

"Yeah," I sigh. It does. Worse than my head. This memory makes me miss her when she isn't even gone yet.

"I'll go get Nurse Kimball," Britta says. "You need some pain-killers."

"Oh, what do you think she has here? Anything good?" Grace asks, winking at me.

"Yes, she keeps the oxycodone right next to the Vicodin in that cabinet over there."

They quip now, and sometimes I forget it was me who brought them together. Grace and I met in the faculty day care on campus. There's even a picture of the two of us in our baby carriers side by side, holding hands. She's laughing while I stare seriously at the camera. Britta arrived in fourth grade and was in my class, while Grace was down the hall. We became quick friends since we were always in the same levels for group work: the top ones. When I first invited Britta to one of our sleepovers, Grace almost refused to come in protest, but by morning they were discussing the ins and outs of Harry

Potter, a series I had never read.

"I'm fine," I tell Britta. "Let's just go to assembly."

"Are you sure?"

"Those soccer boys just gave you the perfect excuse to miss Mr. Morgan's lost-at-sea speech," Grace adds.

"Does it look okay?" I ask as I reach up and graze my face with my fingertips. I wince.

"Definitely," Britta says.

"You look mahvelous," Grace says. "It's a little pink. You can barely notice it. It will be all the rage by first lunch."

"Let's go," I say.

"I'll hold on to that concussion handout for you just in case," Britta tells me.

Grace picks up my bag and hitches it onto her shoulder. "All I'm saying is that if I ever have a horrible accident on the first day of school, I'm one hundred percent going to let you guys take advantage of it. I mean, I will really milk it. Trip to the ER and everything."

"That's very generous of you," Britta says.

"It is," Grace agrees, and loops her arm through mine.

ii.

The auditorium is mostly full already, but Christian has saved us seats in a row toward the back. I see him and wave. It starts out as this big "Hey, over here!" kind of a wave, but that makes my head throb, so I drop my hand down and wiggle my fingers instead. A coy wave? Let's call it that.

We have to walk all the way up the right-hand aisle, and it's like walking through a telescope as he gets bigger and bigger. His black hair that he fights into a side part every morning (hair which I—and only I—have seen falling down into his golden-brown eyes), the flannel shirt that he's tossed on over his Essex High Hockey shirt in a way that's meant to look casual, his scuffed-up shoes—all of this comes into focus as I make my way up to him. His eyes grow wide as I sit down. "What happened to your face?" he asks.

My hand goes to my cheekbone. "Grace and Britta said it looks fine."

"It *does* look fine," Britta says.

"It's all the rage," adds Grace.

I slump down in my seat. "Is it terrible?" I ask Christian.

"It's pretty red. What happened?" he asks.

"Head-on collision with a soccer jock."

"Which one?"

"All of them," Grace says.

"Adam Millstein," I say. "His head hit my head."

"Was he trying to kiss you?" Christian asks.

"Was who trying to kiss you?" Christian's friend Josh sits down next to him. "Is someone trying to edge in on your lady, Chris? 'Cause I've got your back. Like, name the time and place and I will be there. I'll even bring my brass knuckles."

I shift in my seat. "I'm not his chattel."

Grace punches Josh in the arm. "Enough," she says.

"As you wish," he replies, and he pulls out his iPod and shoves the earbuds into his ears.

Mr. Morgan, our principal, makes the same speech every year, involving an extended ship metaphor. "A school is like a ship at sea."

"As opposed to a ship on land," Grace whispers.

"Every person has a role to play. And let me tell you, before I go on, that I am proud of this ship. It's a good ship. Strong." Our first year he made the mistake of saying he was proud of every seaman. "You all work hard. You should be proud to be from Essex."

A few of the soccer players hoot at that, and Mr. Morgan smiles as if they are cheering for him. "Now, sometimes in school you encounter rough seas. Maybe you're having trouble at home. Or maybe the workload is just a tad too much. Well, let me tell you that all of your teachers, your guidance counselors, even your administration, we're all here to help."

Christian takes my hand in his and squeezes. "It really doesn't look that bad. I'm sure it will fade."

"Thanks." I squeeze his hand back. My stomach is doing the mix of churning and I guess butterflies that I feel when I'm around him.

The side door opens and a girl walks in. She has black hair that's chopped unevenly at the chin and she's wearing a flowing black skirt and blue tank top. She looks familiar but also not, and for a moment I think it's another transformation of

Ramona. But then I say, "Is that Kayla Winters?"

Britta looks up. "It's Dru now," she says.

"Dru?"

"Yeah. She said Kayla was too much of the 'white-bread patriarchy that pervades our town.' So she decided she would be Dru instead."

"You can't just do that," I say. "You can't just change your name and who you are."

"Well, she did." Britta doesn't sound especially interested. Then again, she was the one who came back to school last year saying she was a lesbian. So maybe she doesn't think metamorphosis is a big deal.

"How do you know all this?" I whisper. Someone in the row in front of us turns around and shushes us, and Grace scowls at him.

"She played tennis at the club. One day she was Kayla. The next day she was Dru. And the day after that she was gone. Tennis is just too chichi, I guess."

I don't mean to stare at Dru, who's taken a seat by the aisle a row ahead of us, but I can't help it. She was one of those girls who wore jeans that were never quite the right shade of blue with polos from the uniform department at Sears, but that look has been jettisoned. Instead she wears a choker with a bright blue stone on it right in the center of her neck, which she flicks at with her ragged fingernails.

Mr. Morgan says something that has the audience laughing, bordering on losing control. Josh laughs so hard he isn't even making a sound. Grace mutters, "Oh my God."

"What?" I ask.

"Remind me to thank you for not letting me miss this year."

I turn to Christian, and he just squeezes my hand again a few times as if he's trying to send me a Morse code message. Whatever it is, I'm not receiving it.

Up on stage, Mr. Morgan is getting into his speech. "You all need to toe the line!"

"How are you doing?" Christian asks. I'm wondering if he means my face, but he adds, "About your grandmother, I mean."

My body tenses. Everyone else seems to have forgotten. This isn't the place I want to talk about it. "Okay."

Josh leans toward us, pulling an earbud out of his ear. "Excuse me, but I am trying to listen to our brave sea captain, and you two are disturbing me."

"Put your earbud back in and turn up the music," Christian tells him.

"Yes, master."

Josh turns his music up so high that we are all able to hear the bass and heavy beats of the hip-hop he likes. Britta sighs heavily, but he, of course, cannot hear her.

Christian brushes my hair off my shoulder. "So you're holding up okay?"

"Yeah," I say. And then repeat myself as if that will make it true. "Yeah."

"That's my strong girl," he says, then immediately corrects himself. "Woman. That's my strong woman."

It's like he has a checklist in his head, all the right things to do and say, and the right words to use so as not to offend anyone. He's that kind of good guy. Maybe that's why Nonnie doesn't like him. My gaze flicks down to our interlaced fingers and I notice that he is wearing a bracelet of corded leather, and I wonder where he got it, and why, and if he thought I would like it. I nuzzle closer to him, knowing that he will put his arm around me, and that will be enough. He won't have to keep talking to try to make me feel better.

Mr. Morgan is wrapping up his speech. "So go forth, young sailors. The world is your oyster! Explore."

"Go forth and multiply, young seamen!" someone calls out.

Mr. Morgan frowns but then tries to pretend he didn't hear it, which is probably a pretty good way to deal with the situation. Public high school principal is high on my list of jobs I never, ever want to have. "Good luck and have a great year. Thank you."

From the assembly, we all go to our homerooms. When we reach a bend in the hall, I need to break off with Grace to go to our homeroom on the second floor. Christian pulls me to him for another hug. "See you at lunch," he says. And then he whispers into my hair, "I love you."

"Yep," I say. "See you at lunch!"

Grace takes her schedule and places it on my desk on top of my own.

"Notice anything?" she demands.

We've been in homeroom advisory together all through high school, since for some reason my last name is alphabetized under the *W* instead of the *S*, and her last name is Yang. Our adviser is Mr. Tompkins, who was also my math teacher last year and convinced me to take his AP Chemistry class this year by promising it would be absolute candy to college admissions officers. That's when I was still thinking about Stanford—before Nonnie got sick.

Mr. Tompkins is busy handing out schedules and checking in with kids, and doesn't seem to care that Grace is perched on her desk, her feet on her chair.

"Chinese," she says. "My mother is making me take Chinese. She heard they were offering it and even though I'm a senior, now I need to learn a whole new language. With a bunch of freshmen, I bet."

"She's making you?" Grace's mom subscribes to a theory of parenting we like to call "The Power of Suggestion." She never tells Grace and her brother to do anything. She makes suggestions based on her own experience, but ultimately "supports" her children in their choices. Like, "Grace, getting a perm is going to make you look like a French poodle, but if you really must do it, let's go to the salon."

"She's going through another renaissance. And this one is all about getting in touch with her Chinese side."

"But your mother isn't Chinese." Grace's parents' families have both been in America for generations. Her mom can trace her family back to Spain, and her dad to China. Grace likes to say that unless people still have splinters from the Mayflower in their asses, her family was probably here first, so stop asking her where she's from. Her father is a professor in the sociology department, and her mother, well, dabbles, I guess.

"You know how you can marry someone Jewish and then convert? I think she's trying to convert to being Chinese. And she's not just going regular Chinese like my dad. She's going ultraorthodox Chinese. It's her latest thing. She's learning how to do Chinese calligraphy. And she's started ordering all these clothes from Chinese companies. I mean, like clothes that they wear in China, not like clothes we wear that are made there. Like she's walking around in these tunics and flat canvas Mary Janes. Anyway, I thought it would all blow over by the time school started, but here we are and I'm signed up for Chinese. And I'll bet you that the teacher is going to see my face and he's going to break out into this big grin and probably even start talking to me in Chinese right away, and I'll have to be like, 'No hablo Chinese, dude.'"

"It could be fun."

She sticks her finger in her mouth.

"A lot of people try to reclaim their culture. My dad talks about it all the time. Like, people come to America, and it's all melting pot, and then a generation or two goes by and they want to get back their culture. Music is often the first place they start."

"Well, maybe your dad could convince my mom to let me take some sort of Chinese music class, but Chinese the language? I don't even know which Chinese language it is."

"Probably Mandarin," I tell her.

"I'm supposed to be in French four," she says. "You know what they do in French four? Crepes. Crepes, crepes, crepes. Every day is just a big crepe party in French four, but will I be having tasty Nutella and whipped cream? No, I will not."

"Maybe you'll make dumplings or something."

"It's bad enough being half Chinese and friends with you and Britta. The expectations are like—" She waves her hand above her head.

"Wait, what's bad about being friends with me and Britta?"

"Not bad, exactly." Her voice is calm, but I swear I see a slight eye roll. "It's just, like, I walk into a new classroom and the teacher does a little math. Model minority plus friends with two geniuses. Must be übergenius. And then when I'm my mediocre self, it's like I fall down into the negatives."

Her math doesn't make sense, but I think I understand what she's trying to say. "You're not mediocre," I tell her.

"But I'm not a genius. The only way I could make the setup worse is if I dated Brooks Weston."

"Britta would flip."

"She would filet me. And flay me. And flambé me."

The bell rings, and we grab our stuff. In the hall, she chirps, "Make good choices, honey!" before disappearing into the throng of people.

iv.

Our petite, elfish English teacher, Ms. Staples, is already seated in a chair-desk at the front of the room with an array of books stacked up in front of her. Britta and I take seats in the circle with our backs facing the windows. Once I'm settled with my notebook open and my pen ready, I look across the circle and see Dominic Meyers. He's the last person I would have expected to see in this class. Officially there's no tracking at Essex High School, but everyone knows which English electives are puff-balls and which are the tough ones. Ms. Staples's American Literature class is definitely one of the toughest, harder even than AP English. Dominic is definitely not in the college-bound set: he's the type of kid to whom the phrase "up to no good" is often applied. Surprising, also, is the way he is staring at me. His dark green eyes watch me intently from beneath a shag of brown hair. He gives a sly smile, and I remember his hot breath on my neck in the cold gallery and I realize that now I am the one who is staring. I avert my gaze.

"You don't have to be so nervous," Britta says.

"What?" I blush harder.

"I know it's an advanced-level class, and we'll be doing

scansion and all that. But you know, scanning a line of poetry is just like doing a math problem. There are symbols. Balance."

"If you say so." Even if I work my hardest, I'll be lucky to end up with another A minus from Ms. Staples—which was better than the B I got from Mr. Speck. But Mr. Linz, my guidance counselor, assured me that colleges would like that a math genius—his words, of course, not mine—would challenge herself with difficult humanities classes.

My gaze flicks to Dominic, then over the rest of the class. Hunter, the photographer, and his hockey-loving model Serena are sitting next to each other. She is sketching in her notebook with her red hair falling onto the paper while he talks to the guy next to him.

As soon as the bell rings, Ms. Staples jumps to her feet in a stunning display of agility for someone her age and says, "Welcome!" She quickly circles the room, passing out a syllabus printed on pale purple paper. "I'm so glad to have you here, and to see some of you again."

Britta and I had Ms. Staples for freshman English, and probably that comment is directed at Britta, who is a crazy-good English student.

"And," she goes on, "of course I'm happy to meet some of you for the first time. I don't believe much in the getting-to-know-you activities that so many teachers do. Waste of time as far as I'm concerned. You all know each other, and I'll know you soon enough, as well as any teacher knows any student."

I like Ms. Staples because she's a fan of Nonnie's but never makes a big deal of it to me. I've had other English teachers who expect me to be like the second coming or something, and are inevitably disappointed in my work, which isn't bad, just not ready for the anthology of Best American anything. I guess that's the same feeling Grace was talking about.

"The English department has done some rearranging, and we've decided to approach material thematically rather than chronologically." She has made her way back to her desk and now picks up another stack of papers, these ones printed on green. "We're going to start with some poetry. Specifically, women's poetry." She pauses and glances at me. I wonder if she knows how sick Nonnie is.

As soon as the packet lands on my desk, I begin to flip through it to see what poems are included. Past Emily Dickinson, past Elizabeth Bishop, past Plath. There she is.

I exhale: none of the sex poems she's so famous for. Nonnie's exploits are okay by me, but I really don't want to discuss her sex life in English class.

Ms. Staples folds herself back into her chair. "To say good-bye to summer, I'd like to start off with one of Imogene Woodruff's poems. Page seventeen of your packet. Now then," she says cheerily. "Why don't we read it aloud?" She surveys the room, looking for a reader, and I feel people's eyes on me. I make a show of looking away so that Ms. Staples knows that I really, really don't want to read.

Dominic saves me by raising his hand. Ms. Staples claps joyfully. "A volunteer!"

He clears his throat and holds up his paper. "Fireflies." He
reads the title, nods at Ms. Staples, and begins reading:

I shed my cardigan sweater
Slip out of my sensible shoes
Leave them on the sun-charred grass
And march
Past the summer garden
Gone to waste,
Past the pine tree garlanded
By student words
—Always words, words, words—
Past the puddles of feint praise.

I go to join the pixies
In their
Polyester nightgowns.

(You scoff.
The wry smile tells me you
think I'm telling you tales.
Yet this time it's
Truth.)

They hold glass jars
And capture tiny lights
Detain dancing fireflies

Until their light fades.

(And what I want to say to you is:
You cannot catch my lightning in glass.)

Dominic lowers his paper, and, once again, looks right at me. He has figured out, I am sure, that I am one of the pixies. I shift in my seat, and stare at the poem, trying to reread it, but the words just swim in front of me.

I know the cardigan she mentions. It's army green and she wore it rolled up because the sleeves were too long. A moth ate a small hole through the front pocket. The polyester nightgowns, too: mine had a rainbow, Ramona's a winged unicorn.

These are details that people would like to know. They would like me to share my insider view of the poem, but I won't.

The class discusses the poem's meter (could one be discerned, and the places where it broke it, and why), the allusions and metaphors, and the emotion underlying it.

In town, you can buy her books everywhere, even at the grocery store. The college store sells postcards proclaiming Essex to be "Woodruff Country." Every year, we have to attend the Woodruff Festival, where Nonnie gives an award to some aspiring poet who proceeds to read one of his or her (usually dreadful and quite long) poems. Everyone thinks they know her. I just want my memories of the woman who braided my hair and brought me down to the large outdoor swimming pool—which was really more of a swimming hole—and sipped gin from a water bottle while she watched me and Ramona splash around. She always traveled with gumdrops, and would pick out the white ones for me because she knew they were my favorite. She told me that men weren't worth the bother, unless they were particularly handsome, and then they'd be worth it for only a week or two, which made me giggle and say, "What about Daddy?" To which she replied, "I suppose we can keep Dallas around. He makes a good Manhattan." Analyzing her poems in class made her less my grandmother, and more of the world.

"Ms. Staples, I take issue with this whole unit." It is Hunter's voice that breaks into my reverie. "Separating the women out like this is a form of ghettoization."

"Ah, yes!" Ms. Staples says. "A common argument. Now here's my retort: if we didn't celebrate them separately, they might not get included at all."

"Okay, but why these particular women? I mean, like, Sylvia Plath, she's most famous for killing herself. And Imogene Woodruff. I know she's like our local pride or whatever, but I just don't think she's worth all the fuss." Hunter sucks on the end of his pen for a moment. "I mean, she's an okay poet, but she's really more famous for who she slept with. She couldn't even write a pastoral without talking about taking off her clothes."

Britta glances at me sideways and makes a frowning, uncomfortable face.

It is Dominic, though, who says something: "Watch yourself."

Hunter smirks. "I mean, no offense, Very, but when someone

puts themselves out there, they open themselves up to criticism."

It's not like I go around harshing on their grandmothers' cookies or knitting or whatever a typical grandma does. Sure, she had affairs, and it isn't like that's something I would recommend as a general course of action, but people do it all the time. At least she's honest about it. "Whatever," I say. I want it to come out icy, but I just sound cowed.

"So far you've only criticized the author, not the poem," Dominic says. "You still haven't offered up any reason why we shouldn't be studying her work."

"Well, this one, for instance, it's all Robert Frost–y. Like all we do in New Hampshire is sit outside and enjoy nature, don't you think?"

Which is hilarious because "nature" and "enjoy" aren't really two things Nonnie puts together. We went out and caught fireflies; that was true. Ramona never punched enough holes in the lid of her jar, so eager to get collecting, and typically hers all died by the morning.

Serena has her desk pressed right up against Hunter's, and his arm is resting on the back of her chair. Her legs are pulled up into her desk, and she curls over it, sketching. She almost never speaks in classes. But today she unwinds herself and says, "I like her poetry. I like the way it moves over you like a river. You don't always know where you're going, but it's good to be carried along."

Hunter smirks, but Serena gives me a small smile before she coils herself back up, like a snail retreating into its shell.

v.

As Mr. Tompkins wrote in his letter to Essex College, "The limits of the Essex High math program have been reached by Very. In fact, I used L'Hopital's rule because her mathematical limits are at this point indeterminate." Despite that awful pun, I still got into the college's Advanced Calculus class that meets right smack-dab in the middle of our day.

I jostle my bag in the hopes of shaking out my car keys, which always seem to find the wasteland in the bottom of the pocket, when someone falls into stride with me. "You don't seem like the playing-hooky type." Dominic. Fabulous. Absolutely, precisely what I do not need.

"I'm not playing hooky. I've got a class up at the college."

"That's right. I'd heard you were some sort of prodigy."

"Not exactly." A prodigy is a child who is able to perform at the level of a highly trained adult. "Gifted is more precise."

"Is that modesty?"

"It's accuracy."

He grins his wolf grin.

My hands close around my car keys and I click on the fob to unlock the door.

"Give me a ride, then," he says.

"Where?"

"To campus."

"Why?"

"Maybe I've got class, too."

"In what? Badass posturing?"

"Oh, she wounds me," he says, and places his hand over his heart. "I'm enough of a badass that I was the only one who stuck up for you in class. Everyone else was going to let that prick stomp all over your grandmother's reputation. Are you going to thank me?"

Prick. That's a good slang word. Sounds just like what it is.

"Maybe I didn't need you to stick up for me. And it wasn't me, by the way. It was my grandmother you were defending, and Serena was the one who actually said something nice about her poetry."

"A thank-you would be nice either way."

"Thank you." I want to get in my car, but he's standing between me and my door. "I'm going to be late."

"So drive me."

"Maybe I don't want to be an accessory to truancy."

"It's your first time," he says, still grinning. His right canine overlaps the tooth next to it just a little bit. "You'll get off with a wrist slap." I start to protest and he leans back against my car. "I'll tell them I forced you to do it."

"How did you force me?"

He cocks his head to the side and examines me. "How?" he repeats.

"If we're going to go into this criminal partnership, I want to know what my alibi is going to be."

"I'll say I told you that my mother teaches at the college and I just got a call that she's fall-down drunk in front of the class."

"Implausible."

"There's always the classic carjacking. How about we say that I pulled a knife on you? Oh! Or that I smacked you upside the head. Look, you're already getting a bruise!"

I rub the sore spot on the side of my head and wince. "You'd wind up in prison for that."

"Would you miss me?"

This game is getting old. "I really do need to be going."

He doesn't move. "I'm stubborn. Truculent, even."

I raise my eyebrows. How does he know the word that tripped me up on the SATs? Coincidence, I decide. "Fine," I say, because I'm late and it's already a big enough deal that there's a high school student in this math class. Every single head turns when I walk in the door, so I try to be early. "Let's go."

He hops up and around to the other side of the car. "I knew you'd let me in. You're a good egg, Very."

"A good egg? What does that even mean?"

"You're nice. You like to help people. We're alike in that way."

I slip the key into the ignition. His sweet pot smell is filling my car and I wonder if he's high right now. But that would mean he'd also been high during English class. "I don't think we're very much alike at all," I say, backing out of the parking place.

He reaches for the handle that reclines the seat and lets himself drop way back. "But we are, Very. You help people by being friendly and joining clubs and doing community service. I help people forget their problems."

I'd laugh if I weren't so annoyed. And shocked that he's

more or less admitted that the rumors are true: Dominic Meyers is a small-time drug dealer. "What do you know about my extracurriculars?"

"You almost make it sound dirty, Very."

I roll my eyes.

"Athlete. Student council. Yadda yadda."

Yadda yadda. That about sums me up in most people's minds. Very Sayles-Woodruff doing the things she needs to do to round out her application to Stanford or MIT or wherever. And I will swear to you up and down that I don't do the things I do to fluff up my apps. But the deeper, darker, coalish center of me wonders if people are right. I'm on the Community Service Committee (president, actually) and in the peer counseling group, not that anyone ever comes to us for counseling. I swim in the winter and play doubles tennis with Britta in the spring. And the math team, of course, not that I'd ever bring that up to Dominic Meyers.

"How do you know all this about me anyway? You seem too cool to care." I almost said too cool for school, which would have been on par with, say, crashing the car in terms of embarrassing things to do.

"I watch. I observe. Like today in English class. I noticed that you were deeply uncomfortable—"

"Because you were staring at me."

"Uncomfortable once we got the poetry packet. You flipped right through it and then your whole body just relaxed. You were looking for your grandmother's poems, right?"

Instead of answering, I spray the windshield washer fluid on the glass and let the wipers sluice it away.

"And after I read, you smiled this minuscule hint of a smile. And then Hunter started being a dick and—"

"Why do you even care?"

He blinks his green eyes and looks offended. "I'm just making conversation."

"Why?" I demand.

He laughs. His head tilts back and the sun catches his face in a way that almost makes his pale skin look both translucent and angelic: a jellyfish angel. "You're funny, Very," he says. "I never would have guessed you were so funny."

I'm not sure what he found so amusing. "Whatever," I say. "Thanks."

It's a straight shot to the college now. Right through town and then there's the campus. I pull into the lot closest to the math building. He leans closer to me. "That's going to be a hell of a bruise."

I reach up and graze the spot on my face where the soccer boy's head hit. "You should see the other guy."

"Good one. Classic."

"What are you even going to do here, anyway?"

"It's not where we are, Very. It's where we aren't."

"How profound," I say, reaching around for my bag on the backseat. "Any more platitudes you want to spill?"

He puts his hand on my forearm. His palms are smooth where Christian's are rough. "I think you take things for granted."

"I don't—"

"I don't mean like you're entitled or anything. I mean that things are the way they are and they're pretty good for you, so you don't question it. But things could be different. That's all I'm saying."

There are always other interpretations.

I tug my arm away, bumping him with my bag.

I shove the door open and step out into the hot sun, doubly warm after the air-conditioning in the car. I hear him shut his door and I turn to face him. "I'll talk to you later, Very." His repetition of my name is getting annoying.

"Sure, okay," I reply. *Sure, okay?* He grins again and lopes off into the parking lot, and I am left with the unshakable feeling that Dominic Meyers is not through with me. What's worse: I'm pretty sure I don't want him to be.

three

i.

THREE DAYS LATER MY bruise is purple and tinged with blue. Nonnie says it looks like a mottled plum. I say it looks like hell. *A hell of a bruise.* I've figured out that if I part my hair more severely to the right it hangs down and mostly covers it, or at least puts it into shadow. My head still rings, which convinces Britta that I have a concussion, so she makes me promise to go see the nurse twice a day to get checked for continuing symptoms—sleepiness, headache, irritability, and a bunch of other things that seem fairly common among the general high school population.

Christian takes me for my first check before chemistry class, and then we head toward Mr. Tompkins's room. "If you still have the bruise for Halloween," he says, "You could be Gorbachev and I could be Ronald Reagan."

"I think Gorbachev's mark was more on his forehead, wasn't it?"

"And Reagan was white," Christian says with a shrug. "I just want to do something clever. Something unusual. Guys are always so lame about it, and girls just use it to be trampy."

"I could be sexy Gorbachev," I tell him.

"That's an image I really don't need in my head."

He holds the door to the classroom open for me. We share a lab table in the first row. Nurse's orders that I sit up front in all my classes, not like I would've been sitting in the back anyway.

Mr. Tompkins is writing a chemical equation on the board when we arrive. He wears khaki pants and a button-down shirt with a pink tie. He seems to have cut himself shaving—he has a nick right on his jawline, still red with blood. The smile he gives me when I come into the room is a mix of hope and guilt, like maybe he's realized it was a bad idea to convince me to take this AP chem class. "How's the head?" he asks.

"Prognosis is good," I tell him.

"I think she's holding back this concussion by force of will," Christian adds.

Mr. Tompkins slides his dry-erase pen into one of the loops on a tray that he wears, no joke, like a holster on his hip. Total nerd squad. But Mr. Tompkins is not a geek. He's young and handsome in a sort of hipstery way—heavy-framed glasses, grandpa cardigans—and more than one girl has professed her undying love for him on the stalls of the second-floor bathroom.

Adam Millstein comes in and nods at both of us. He's on the hockey team with Christian, but they don't really hang out much, and now that Adam has maybe given me a concussion, I think he's too embarrassed to even talk to Christian.

Once class starts, some of the guys get Mr. Tompkins off-topic by asking about relativity and space travel and if you went out in a spaceship at the speed of light, when you came back, would anyone else even still be alive?

One time Ramona declared that she was on a solo space mission and we had to walk like we were in spacesuits, fighting zero gravity.

"If it's a solo space mission, then I wouldn't be there," I told her.

She looked at me strangely. "Well of course you'd be there."

We walked side by side. I'm sure we looked more like lumbering giants than weightless explorers. Mom saw us out on the lawn and she and Dad came out to the patio to watch. Mom held a hand up to shield her eyes. We floated over to them.

"We're on the moon," I told her.

"Mercury's moon," Ramona added.

"Mercury doesn't have a moon," I corrected.

"Jupiter's moon," she said, unfazed.

"I hear it's nice there this time of year," Mom said.

"Oh it is!" Ramona agreed.

"Well then, I just may have to get in my rocket and join you. Coming, dear?" she asked Dad.

"Am I properly dressed?" Dad pointed at his bare feet.

"Oh, the moons of Jupiter are very casual," Mom replied.

They buzzed around the lawn, and then, throwing open the

door of the imaginary spaceship, she called out, "Would you look at that view!"

They began to spacewalk with us. It was Ramona who got the giggles first. Little titters.

"Astronauts don't laugh," Mom told her, straight-faced. "This is serious work."

"It is," Ramona agreed, and pressed her lips together.

It was no use, though. The titters boiled up in her again, and the next thing we knew, the four of us were on the ground, holding our stomachs. Dad rolled over to Mom and grabbed her in his arms so they were tumbling together across the lawn. "We have to rescue her!" Ramona called out. We leaped to our feet and ran over to them, trying to loosen Dad's arms from around her waist, but his arms were long, and we were ticklish. He embraced Mom with one arm while tickling each of us in turn until we all collapsed tangled together like mice in a nest.

We came inside and Nonnie had gone to the fish market and brought home lobster and steamers because "what's the point of living in New England if you don't get fresh seafood?" She got oysters, too, and we watched as she shucked them, jamming the knife between the lips of the shell and prying them open. Ramona's eyes grew wide. "Doesn't that hurt them?"

"Yes," Nonnie said. "But we're going to eat them, which will hurt them even more."

"And maybe we'll find a pearl," Mom said.

Nonnie handed us each a shell. We slurped the oyster out of it; I don't think I even chewed before swallowing the slippery mollusk. Ramona and I exchanged a glance as if deciding together what we thought. The flavor was salty and smooth and even a bit sweet. "I think I like it," I said.

"Me, too," Ramona agreed.

"Good," Nonnie said. "I never trusted anyone who refused to eat an oyster."

Looking back I wonder if she was teasing us somehow. Still, it was such a lovely day. We ate the lobsters out on the patio and Mom said it always felt like you should be hosed down after lobster, so Dad pulled out the hose and chased her all around. Then he set up the sprinkler, and Ramona and I ran through it just in the clothes we were wearing.

I should have collected these moments—pinned them down so they wouldn't slip away like nymphs disappearing back into the forest. But maybe Nonnie is right and you can't catch the light of fireflies in jars.

ii.

Why do you divide sin by tan?

Just cos.

We spend our first math team practice of the year telling math jokes. That's mine.

Ramona takes the bus home and I don't see her until I pull my car up the driveway. She's crouched on a large rock in a half circle of trees. It's like she is that space explorer again, investigating the surface of a moon. I practically bound from the car and start lumbering toward her. "It's very nice on Jupiter's moon this time of year, wouldn't you say?"

She looks up, frowning. "What are you talking about?"

"Remember the day with the space walking?"

She shakes her head. I guess maybe to her all of the imaginary games ran together.

"Nonnie got us lobsters and oysters," I prompt.

"I don't remember." She looks into the trees. Her profile seems etched against the sky. Her narrow nose and her pouting lips are both pronounced. She's grown so thin it's like she isn't even there. The dark circles under her eyes are the only thing about her with any gravity.

"You really don't remember the oysters? We ate raw oysters for the first time." She has to remember, doesn't she? It had been her game, her idea.

"I just don't, okay?"

Her tone is as sharp as a January icicle, so I say, "Okay," and back away. Ramona grabs a low limb of an oak tree and begins hauling herself up and away from me.

Inside the house, I cross through our sunken living room and head for the library. It's a dark room, with floor-to-ceiling bookshelves on every wall and an old leather chair next to an ashtray stand.

From the library I can see into the sunroom. The plants are looking yellowish, and I think that I should water them, but I always seem to do it wrong. Too much. Too little. Even the plants that can withstand some benign neglect can't seem to withstand me. Dad tried to teach me how to care for them. I remember hot Sundays in here as he told me the names of the plants—their scientific names as well as the ones he had created for them: *Bonnie, Buster, Thelonious.*

The plants are better off without me, and I can't decide on a book from the library, so I go to the kitchen. There, I can see my mother through the window. She's sitting in the hammock. One long leg hangs down off the side, while the other is extended. She wears oversize sunglasses, like Jackie O, and the blond highlights in her hair catch the sun.

It's almost five o'clock, which Nonnie has always taken as a dictate for a cocktail, rather than a mere guideline. This is a lesson my mom has taken to heart. So I take out a glass, pour her some blueberry juice, and add a splash of vodka. *Summer's Twilight* is a good name for it, or *Power Punch.* I pour myself juice and water it down. Virgin. With a glass in each hand, I kick off my sandals and head out across the lawn. The air is heavy, and I feel like I'm swimming more than walking.

As I approach, she tucks her sketchbook against her side as if she doesn't want me to see it. When my sister and I were younger, she used to draw stories for us in her sketchbooks. Fairy tales in which the princesses wore haute couture gowns and the balls were high-society soirees.

"I made you a cocktail," I say when I get close enough for her to hear me. "Cocktail" sounds so much more sophisticated than "drink." "It's a Power Punch. Blueberries have those good antioxidants, you know."

"Hmmm. Thank you," she says, raising her sunglasses. I should have gone with Summer's Twilight. I hand her the glass and she takes a sip as I lower myself to the ground. She uses her foot to rock herself back and forth.

"It's almost five," I tell her.

"Mm-hmm," she replies.

"I wasn't sure if you knew how late it had gotten." It is possible that she's been in the hammock all day, her studio left empty, her paintings unpainted. I know better than to ask if she has anything planned for dinner.

"Slow summer days. That's what hammocks were made for." She lets a smile drift across her lips like the brush of a kiss.

"Do you remember the day we pretended to be astronauts and then we had oysters with Nonnie?"

She takes a long sip and considers the question. "I think so." She continues to rock in the hammock. "Why?"

I look down into my juice, blue like the lines on graph paper. "I just thought of it today, and I asked Ramona about it, and she didn't remember at all."

"Well, our little one has an active mind. I'm sure some things just get tumbled together."

"Are you worried about her at all?"

"Because she didn't remember one afternoon back when you were kids?"

"No, it's more than that, it's like—" But I'm not sure what it's like, because it's not like anything. And it's not just one thing. "It's like she's slipping away from us. She's, I don't know, drifting." As I say it, I can see her: we are back in space again, and she has cut the line that ties her to our ship. She floats away with her arms reaching back to me.

Mom lifts her sunglasses up and nestles them in her hair. It's a familiar gesture; she does it with her regular glasses, too, and I know it means she's really thinking about things. "Some girls just go through this emotional, creative phase. I'm sure I went through something similar."

"What if it's more than that? What if it's—" But my worries about her are as nebulous as Ramona herself. There one minute and then, somehow, not.

"You don't need to worry about Ramona, Very. She's fine."

We look at each other for a moment, and then I say, "Okay, you're probably right."

I gaze down the slope of our lawn toward the bay and the water there.

"I ought to take a shower. This air is so sticky, I feel like caramel. Can you pull together something for dinner?"

"I'm going to Christian's," I say, a decision made in that moment. I finish my blueberry juice in one big gulp, and then stand, expecting my mom to extricate herself from the hammock and come inside with me. Instead she lowers her sunglasses back down over her eyes and tilts her head up toward the sky.

Halfway back across the lawn, I turn around to see if she might be standing up, or looking at me, but her gaze is still trained upward. I wonder what she sees there in the clouds. I wonder if she's looking at anything at all.

iii.

Christian's family always has way too much food for dinner. His father subscribes to all these cooking magazines and is constantly trying new dishes. More often than not, they flop. It's better when his mom cooks. She knows all these great Korean recipes, but most of them take a long time, and she's got a job as a high-powered divorce attorney, so she only cooks for special occasions.

I check on Nonnie before I go. She's sleeping, but her mini-fridge is stocked with healthy heat-and-eat meals that her doctor recommended, probably because she realized how hopeless we all were. They're basically TV dinners and milk shakes, and Nonnie calls them her prison food, but she can make them herself, which seems to please her.

When I arrive, Christian and his parents are just sitting down to dinner. His little sister, he's told me, is at some band rehearsal. I slip into a chair next to Christian, wondering if he might lean over and whisper that he loves me again, right here in front of his parents. It wouldn't shock me. That's the kind of relationship he has with them. I bet he's even told them that we're having sex. I'm trying to figure out how I would respond to a public declaration of love. Would I repeat it back, affirming him like a woman who receives a proposal on the Jumbotron at a baseball game? Or would I make some silly joke? Quote Shakespeare to confound the table? *Love is not love which alters when it alteration finds.* What would Nonnie do? Probably just laugh it off. He doesn't say it, though, which is oddly disappointing. Instead he tucks his foot under my ankle so it's like our feet are hugging.

His dad made stuffed peppers. "It's quinoa! Quinoa is the perfect protein, you know."

The stuffed peppers, though, are not perfect. More like mush with the sides of the peppers collapsing in on themselves.

"That's some bruise you have there," his dad says as he passes me the tray.

"It doesn't hurt much anymore," I tell them. I untuck my hair from behind my ear so it falls down to cover the contusion. As I do, the ends swing down and brush across Christian's arm.

"I hope the nurse kept a good record of the incident," Christian's mom says. "If you need to take legal action, it's good to have a paper trail."

"Mom," Christian says. "It was an accident. Very is not going to take legal action."

"I might," I say. "Stanford's tuition is over fifty thousand dollars a year. Not to mention books. A big fat lawsuit could really help." I don't know why I keep saying Stanford is my top choice college. Once Nonnie got sick, I knew I would need to stay closer to home.

"Very, don't encourage her."

I push the pepper plate away from me. "Do you think I should go after just the one guy, or the whole team?"

"You start with the school," Mrs. Yoo says. "They'll have the biggest insurance policy. If you can't get enough from them, then go after the kid's family."

"How much do you think I could make?"

Christian rolls his eyes.

"Well, it all depends on how you play it. If you can provide some evidence that your intelligence was somehow diminished—you are a smart girl, after all, that is your greatest asset—you could make a claim that the injury hurt your future livelihood. With your youth and potential, that could be quite the windfall."

Indeterminate limit.

It gets me thinking, though. What if Adam had hit me harder, had jostled my brain with such force that I really did lose my intelligence? Not that it would make me stupid, just average. Or what if it had changed me completely? There was a boy in our class, Logan Whelcher, who had been in a car accident. He'd been kind before, the type of kid who said thank you to teachers at the end of class. When he came back he was surly and mean and had a whole new group of friends. It wasn't just that the accident shocked him or anything. It flicked a switch in his brain and made him this alternate, inverse version of himself. What if that had happened to me? Who would that girl be?

"I can put you in touch with one of the personal injury lawyers in our firm if you'd like," Mrs. Yoo tells me.

"I'll hold off on that for now. I think maybe the injuries weren't so bad after all."

"I wish you'd come to the lake with us," Mr. Yoo says. I can't tell if he's simply turning the conversation away from his wife's litigiousness, but I do know that he's sincere. Christian asked me to go. His mom asked me. His dad asked me. His sister offered to play taps every evening on her clarinet. Christian once held his phone up to the dog, whose whine crackled across the ether to me. I said I wasn't able to go because I was taking a Latin class at the college over the summer, but that was only a half truth, one that Christian and his family would approve of. I could've gone up for a weekend, but I didn't want to leave Nonnie. And there was something terrifying about being alone with Christian in the silence of a still lake and heavy trees.

"Maybe next summer," I say.

"Maybe," Mrs. Yoo says. "That will be the summer everything changes, though."

"Mom," Christian says.

"Well, you'll both be going off to college. They don't call it the Turkey Dump for nothing."

"Turkey Dump?" I ask.

"Mom," Christian says again. His voice spikes like he's dropped back into his puberty days, when he was chubby-faced and his voice cracked so much he almost never talked in class.

"It's basic statistics. If you look at when most relationships end, it's around Thanksgiving, and the rates are especially high for college freshmen. Tell them, Jin."

Mr. Yoo does a hefty fake chuckle and says, "That's not exactly my area of expertise. How's your pepper, Very?"

"Delicious," I lie. I take another bite and the quinoa is mush in my mouth. I don't think he cooked it right. Christian stares down at his own half-eaten pepper like his mom just grounded him or something, but I feel a bit of relief, like she has given us an expiration date. Not that we have to break up next Thanksgiving, but if we make it that long, that's good enough.

iv.

After dinner Christian and I go down into his finished basement and lie side by side on the carpeted floor, books open in front of us.

This was where we did it the first time. It. An imprecise pronoun, Nonnie would say, but everyone knows what "it" means.

When we first started dating we would kiss and kiss and kiss and kiss until our lips were sore—so sore they'd be raw the next day. It was good. It was fine. He really seemed to like it. Not surprisingly, given the way we got into it, we moved up the chain—around the bases, so to speak—fairly quickly. Shirt off, pants off, oral sex. It was like we were ticking things off of a syllabus, racing to get through the course work. Then we made it to the final: sex itself.

So I lost my virginity in his basement rec room while his parents were at a neighbor's playing bridge. We got to the point where I normally said, "Okay, stop"—me sitting astride him, his hands on the bare skin of my breasts. I didn't tell him to stop, though, and he kept going, helping me to slip off my underpants, struggling to put on a condom (Why did he have it with him? Did he know that was the day I wouldn't say no? Did he always have one with him?) and then just pushing himself inside of me. He didn't say anything. I don't know what I expected him to say. It's not like he was going to yell, "Incoming!" I guess I just expected there to be some acknowledgment of what we were about to do, but instead it was like he snuck in, like he thought if he just went ahead and did it, I wouldn't notice. That makes him sound like he's a bad guy, and he's not. And I did want it, so I don't know why I'm making such a big deal out of it.

Moments after it started, it was over. He left to go throw out the condom in the bathroom—wrapped, I'm sure, in layers and layers of toilet paper to hide the evidence—and I lay there sticky and stung. It had hurt, but, of course, I'd known it was going to hurt, just not how—sharp at first and then dull burning. I figured that was the problem. The next time, though, was less painful and no more exciting. I wondered if maybe we were doing it wrong. But no, all the parts went into the places they were supposed to—just like Coach B. had explained in health class. Maybe sex was overrated. He left for a summer at his lake house soon after that. So we'd had sex two times. Two and a half if you counted a misguided attempt on my part at a second go-round that second time. Trying to do it better. Trying to do it right. It had been nine weeks, not that I was counting.

"I've been thinking about college," Christian says.

"Have you? What an odd thing for a young man just starting his senior year to be thinking about." I laugh and he doesn't.

"I'm going out to Minnesota for Columbus Day weekend, to look at Macalester College, and I thought—"

"Minnesota? Land of a Thousand Lakes?"

"Actually it's Land of Ten Thousand Lakes, but who's counting, right? Macalester has a great political science department and I could focus on foreign relations. They don't have a varsity hockey team, but they play in a club league that's really good." I am nodding my head in agreement. So he's going to go to the arctic tundra of Minnesota. Good for him. But then he says, "I thought maybe you could come with us. We're going to go see Carleton, too, and maybe St. Olaf. They're all pretty close to each other—maybe a little more than an hour. It's like going down to Boston. No big deal."

I'm having a hard time making the gears in my head fit together. Why, exactly, would he want me to visit a college he may or may not attend? Although, now that he's said it, it seems a perfect fit for him. Maybe Macalester has one of those lumber-jack teams, and after we break up next Thanksgiving, he'd join it to try to find some solace. He'd learn how to walk on a log as it went down a river. He could fell a pine tree with a manual saw. He'd come back after freshman year with even broader shoulders, and I'd shake my head and say, "I can't believe I let you get away." And then maybe he would kiss me and it would be just like in the romantic comedies that Britta watches, the ones where there's all sorts of missed connections, but everyone winds up paired off in the end. *Just like a Shakespearean comedy* is what she says.

"I was looking online and I think the math department at Carleton—well, I mean, I think it's worth your time to look at it."

"Wait, what?"

"You should look at it. I know you have your heart set on Stanford."

"I don't necessarily—"

"Or MIT, I know, but sometimes at small liberal arts colleges you can get more attention, and the faculty is just as strong. And I know it's stupid, I mean totally stupid for us to plan on going to the same school, but I also think my mom is wrong about that Turkey Dump thing. And it's just that all these schools around Minnesota are really good, and then we'd still be close to one another."

"In Minnesota, ya? Do you really think I'm a Minnesota kind of a person?" I say the state's name again, the way I think people there do—*Minny-soh-tah*—although I imagine this would sound as false to them as someone attempting a New Hampshire accent does to me (*wicked smaht, ayuh!*).

"You could be a Minnesota person. With effort and support, you can be whomever you want to be, right?"

It's one of the corny sayings we had to learn at the training to be a peer counselor. My personal favorite was, "You're the best at being you." Britta and I remind each other of this regularly.

"Even with effort and support, I don't think I want to be a Minnesota person. You'd be great there. I'll buy you a lumber-jack hat."

"It could be someplace else. Like if you really want to go to

California, there are the five colleges out in Claremont. I could go to Pomona, and you could go to Harvey Mudd."

"There's a college called Harvey Mudd?"

Christian sighs and starts turning through the pages in his chemistry textbook.

"I'm not sure we're Southern California people, Christian. And anyway, I doubt they have a hockey team."

"There's roller hockey."

He's still looking down at the book, but he goes past the chapter we're studying. I don't stop him.

"There are lots of college towns. I mean, lots of places with lots of colleges. Chicago. Philadelphia. You could go to Penn and I could go to Haverford or Swarthmore."

"It's just that everything's all up in the air right now," I say. "With Nonnie, I mean. I don't want to leave her."

"But that's why you should go look now. I mean she might not even—" He stops himself, but we both know what he's about to say. She might not even be alive.

Now it's my turn to look through the textbook, at all the diagrams of molecules and atoms and electrons flying by.

"Very, I'm sorry."

"It's fine."

Our pages make a fluttering sound as we turn through them.

"Here," he says, and flattens his page. I turn mine to match his.

I pick up my pencil and start copying down the formula from the book.

Christian's dog comes padding down the stairs and into the room. She sniffs and then, seeing that we have no food, turns and leaves again.

I should be angry, but he's right. Nonnie might not be here. And then where will I be?

Well, Very, I suppose I was just like you. What if Nonnie had taken the train northwest to Minnesota instead of up to New York City? Would she have still re-created herself in the same way?

"I really don't think I could be a Minnesota person," I tell him.

"Fine, Very," he says.

"No, seriously, do you really think I could become a Minnesota person?"

"I'm not even sure what that means."

"Earnest, affable, kindhearted. Not a sarcastic bone in the body. Maybe I could do that. I just wonder how much people can really change, without some, like, Logan Whelcher–type accident."

"Logan Whelcher?"

"Yeah. Like, do you think the person he was before was who he really was? Or the person he is now?"

"Is this about Adam and your head?"

"Not really. It just had me thinking. Like maybe it sucks for Logan, this new version of him. But what if for some people their other version is better. Like—" I pause. "I mean, do you think people just are who they are and there's no changing it?

Or do you think we get to determine who we are? Could I make myself into a Minnesota person for you?"

I wish I hadn't said the "for you" part, but it seems to relax his body. He stops picking at the corners of the pages in his book. I stare at him with wide eyes, like if he can answer this question, then maybe we won't have an expiration date. If he could just tell me yes, then maybe I will visit Minnesota with him and consider the arctic tundra. I want to shake him so he will tell me all his truths, all that he believes. I want him to give me my answers. "What do you think?"

"I dunno, Very. Seems like people have been struggling with that question for ages, though I think 'Can I be a Minnesota person' is a new approach." He grins at me. "Maybe there isn't an answer." And then I swear to God he chucks me under the chin like he's my grandpa or something. "I know you don't like a world without concrete answers."

I sit up and pull my textbook onto my lap. That's what people don't understand about math. They think it's all concrete and right or wrong. And yes, there are right and wrong answers, but it's how you get there, how you derive the answer, that matters. You can be plain and pedestrian, or you can meander around, or, in the case of the best mathematicians, you can be elegant. It's not poetry, I know that. But it can be far more satisfying in its beauty.

"Are you mad?"

I shake my head, but of course I am.

"I know I shouldn't have said what I did about your grandmother."

"I'm not mad about Nonnie. I'm mad because you aren't answering the question. All I'm trying to figure out is if you think personalities are set in stone."

He chews on the metal part of his pencil where the eraser is attached to the wood. I can practically taste the aluminum just watching him. "Well, there's what you do and who you are."

I nod. Now we're getting someplace.

"And I know who you are, Very. You're my girl."

This should be the final straw. *You're my girl.* Who says that? It's like we're caught in this old movie where guys and gals went steady and shared sodas. It's a world that never existed. I cast my glance toward the carpet, the place we first had sex. "What I'm saying is that who we are, maybe it's all constructed for us. By genes and our families and people's expectations, and it all gets built up around us. What if none of it is real?"

"Genes are real," he tells me.

"But they aren't everything. All that other stuff. The stuff other people put on us right from the start. We might not even know it happened. People get this sense of us and it's hard to tell if that's really who we are or if we've just been told it so many times we have to believe it. We're certain it's true. But then maybe someday someone lifts a curtain. Or there's a hairline crack. And we decide to just throw off the whole cape, and underneath there's a new us all pink and raw like the skin beneath a blister when it pops."

Christian wrinkles his nose at that. "I think you'd better leave the poetry to your grandmother."

I sigh and lie back down.

"What?"

"Nothing. Let's just get this done."

I go back to writing out the chemical equation in my notebook. I bet Nonnie never even took chemistry. She would call it ghastly, a real bore. She would be right. Who cares about atoms and molecules?

"I'm two problems ahead of you," he says, grinning. "Keep up!"

This is not normal flirting. I have a hard time imagining Hunter and Serena sitting around doing their homework, and I'm pretty certain that joking about it doesn't constitute their pillow talk.

I slide over so our sides all the way down our bodies are touching; not just shoulders but hips and thighs, too.

"Hey, you can't copy my work."

I tilt my head in toward his neck. I'm doing an experiment of my own. I'm more interested in how he will react to my coming closer than I am in actually doing the deed. A few months ago, my meaning would have been clear. A few months ago, he would have tilted his head to mine, kissing would have commenced, and our homework would have been forgotten.

"That should be a negative charge, Very," he says, pointing at my paper with his pencil tip. "You have it as a positive."

"Right." I slide away and erase the work I had done on the problem.

It doesn't feel like a rejection. Maybe it should. It's more like a nagging. A pit in my stomach telling me that things are not quite right. This feeling rises and falls throughout our relationship, and each time I have to convince myself I'm being foolish. Because I am.

Maybe, I've decided, maybe this is what love feels like. Comfortable. Because I am comfortable with Christian—not as comfortable as I am with Britta and Grace, but close. And he is good-looking, even with his skinny, hairless legs. His eyes are deep and brown and comforting as a chocolate Lab. He can calm me down when I get riled up about school or life. He doesn't even have to say anything. He just wraps his arms around me, and I feel better. So maybe that's what love is. Or perhaps passion is limited to a select group of people—people like Ramona who seem to approach their entire life with intense emotion. Maybe wild, passionate love just isn't in my personality. Maybe it's not who I am. Or what I do.

v.

Back at home I follow the sound of laughter to find Mom and Dad on the sofa, and I stop short. The light on them is perfect. It filters around them from the Tiffany-style lamps that dot the room, casting a glow on them like the world's softest spotlight. It makes their skin look golden. Mom puts her drink down on the floor beside her. "Is everything okay?" she asks.

"You look like a painting," I say, and they both laugh.

"Middle Age, At Rest," Dad suggests for a title.

"Speak for yourself, old man," Mom jokes back. "I prefer something like Interior Domestic, Number Two."

"What was number one?" he asks.

She raises her eyebrows and they giggle.

"Ew," I say, because that's what's expected of me. "But you should paint the two of you like this, Mom. As part of your sabbatical project."

Mom picks up her glass and shakes the ice cubes. "Pour me another, love?"

I take the glass from her and go to the bar cart, where I pour gin over the melting ice cubes, but the tonic bottle is empty. "We're out of tonic," I tell her.

"I guess I'll drink it straight," she says. "You know I've heard that tonic has more sugar than just about any soda. I'm better off without it."

Dad strokes her arm. "You don't need to worry about that."

I hand her the glass. "Did you know that gin and tonics came from when the British were in India and they took quinine to prevent malaria? They thought it was so disgusting that they added gin to cover the taste. And limes."

"Now, that is an interesting bit of history," Mom says. "That is history I can get behind. They teach you that in school?"

Grace had told me, though I wasn't sure where she had learned it. I shook my head. "I'm a woman of endless trivia," I say. "A trivial woman." That's something I'll have to tell Nonnie: she'll be proud of me. It's just the type of word coiling she so admires. "Do you want anything, Dad?"

He holds up his microbrew. "Still have plenty here."

"Move over," Mom says. "Make room for Very."

Dad slides over, pushing the old, red afghan out of the way, and I sit down between them. Dad throws his arm over the back of the sofa so it's behind my shoulders, and I tilt my head and look up at the exposed beams of the ceiling.

After a long sip out of his bottle, Dad says, "I was looking at the Stanford website for you today, jelly bean. You couldn't do much better than that school. I got lost in some of the pictures. The campus just dwarfs Essex College's."

"Everything dwarfs Essex," Mom says.

"Their music department sounds amazing. Their webpage says they're 'vigorously engaged with the technological and artistic evolution of sound.' I wrote that down. 'Vigorously engaged with the artistic evolution of sound.' Got me thinking about how sound does evolve, and tastes, too. It really got my head spinning."

"If I end up going, I'll be sure to take a class."

"Are you sure everything's okay?" Mom asks. "You look—" She waves her hand and doesn't finish the thought, as if the gesture is enough. Evidently I look like a flitting hand feels: disconnected and purposeless.

I could tell them that I'm not so sure about Stanford anymore, but that's not what's bothering me. It would be impossible to explain the lingering sensation to them, the feeling left behind after seeing Christian. Their love is not typical. It's storybook. They met, of course, at a New York

City gallery. They bonded over the art—early-twentieth-century minimalists—and went from the gallery to a bar to dinner to another bar and closed the place down. Long ago I realized that most likely the night had not ended with a kiss on the cheek and the exchanging of phone numbers.

It's a Manhattan fairy tale through and through. They went for walks in Central Park. They visited the galleries in SoHo. They went to the Metropolitan Museum of Art and Smalls Jazz Club. Each day they fell more in love, though it seemed impossible that their love could get any bigger. At the end of the summer, Dad started working at, coincidentally, Essex College. Mom came home to do her art and, eventually, began to teach at the college, too. It all fell into place so easily it was as if it were fated.

And the love hasn't faded. All these years later, and it's just as intense.

"How long have you been together?" I ask.

Dad stares up and to the right, and Mom looks down at her hands, counting on her fingers.

"Twenty-three years," Dad says.

"No, Dallas, it's nineteen."

"Right," Dad says. "I never was good with math. That's your strength, Very, though who knows where you got it."

It doesn't matter if it's nineteen years or twenty-three. It's a miracle that they still have so much to talk and laugh about. It's Guinness World Records book worthy. It's not normal, but it's beautiful. Nothing like what Christian and I have. Or

Christian's parents, who seem like partners in Mrs. Yoo's law firm. Or Grace's parents: her father watches each of Grace's mom's transformations with bewilderment.

"And you knew right away?"

They exchange a look.

"Not right away, right away," Mom says.

"Well, I knew right away. I knew before we even spoke. There you were standing in the doorway, books in your hand."

Mom stretches her legs across me to kick Dad. "Dallas," she says in a singsongy way. "I had an inclination," she says to me. "I had a hope."

"I knew," Dad assures me. "And by the end of the night, she knew, too."

Mom giggles, and this time I don't say "ew" because it's too perfect, too lovely. And at the same time it makes my stomach turn because it has been six months with Christian—six months!—and as much as I tell myself it's just an arbitrary number (186 days, more or less) it does mean something. It means something that after six months I still don't know what my parents knew after six hours and continue to know after nineteen years. Or twenty-three. Whichever.

four

i.

IN ANOTHER WEEK, MY bruise has faded to a bluish green with yellow around the edges. Now Nonnie says it's like a banana bruise and this scares me more than her coughing: that she would resort to fruit analogies twice in row, one of them actually using the word *bruise*. That her words are slipping away from her seems the cruelest twist of all.

It's after school on Thursday and I'm waiting for Ramona. I'm always waiting for Ramona. We've been in school for two weeks now. School time is funny that way. It feels like we've been back for months. The weather is nice now, not as hot, so as I wait, I sit outside on the low wall that leads up to the building. I have my English packet out, and I'm struggling through some Emily Dickinson: "Hope is the thing with feathers"? Hope is hope. The thing with feathers is a bird. And I don't think birds are particularly hopeful. They're practical. Mercurial even.

When Dominic sits down beside me, smelling not quite of smoke, but of something smoky, like he's been spending time in front of a campfire, it reminds me of my grandmother, although she has never been camping, that's for certain. "Hey, Rapunzel," he says. My hair goes halfway down my back, and I've gotten the Rapunzel comment before.

"Hey, Big Bad Wolf," I reply, and immediately wish I hadn't.

He laughs. "Truthfully I think of myself more as the woodsman."

"In some versions the woodsman is no better than the wolf."

"Fairy tales were all just ways to keep young women in line in the Victorian era. Don't stray too far from the path, little girl, a wolf might get you. Or a woodsman. Don't go poking around the castle, a spinning needle might prick you and make you fall asleep. If you're pregnant and have weird cravings, don't send your husband off to steal lettuce from a witch's garden."

"What are you talking about?" I put my packet down on my lap and squint over at him.

"Rapunzel. That's how she got into the tower. Her mother wanted leafy greens when she was pregnant, so her dad went to steal them, and when the witch caught him, he promised her the baby. Then years later the prince came along to Rapunzel's tower and figured out that he could call out 'Rapunzel, Rapunzel, let down your hair,' and she'd invite him up. So then they had lots of sex and she got pregnant and the witch figured it all out and chopped off her hair and banished her. Then the witch tricked the prince and when he came up to see Rapunzel, instead he found the witch, and he jumped off the tower and landed in the thorns that blinded him—"

"You're making this up." This is nothing like the version I remember.

"No. This is the original. Don't worry. It ends happily. Eventually they find each other in the woods and her tears of joy make it so he can see again."

"That's the stupidest thing I ever heard."

"That's love for you," he replies.

A group of freshmen come tumbling out of the school, howling and giggling. I recognize some of them as Ramona's friends, but she's not with them. One of them looks over at us, elbows another girl, who turns to look, too. I know what they are staring at. Very Woodruff sitting with Dominic Meyers: that was a combination they'd never expected.

"So, what, you just sit at home reading fairy tales?"

"Beats sitting on this wall."

"I'm waiting for my sister. She's late. As usual."

"So why don't you go?" he asks.

"I can't leave her here."

"Why not?"

"She needs a ride home."

"I'm sure she'll figure something out," he says in a way that makes me wonder if he knows Ramona. "And if you leave her, you'll be teaching her a lesson."

I smirk. Teaching Ramona a lesson is a feat worthy of Hercules, or maybe Sisyphus. Few have tried, none have succeeded.

"It's easier to wait. I have homework I can do anyway." I hold up the packet and hope he gets the hint that I want to get back to reading it.

"Emily Dickinson. I like her."

Of course. Everybody but Very gets Emily Dickinson.

"She was a shut-in, you know," he tells me. "This guy in town broke her heart and she locked herself in her house."

Nonnie had mentioned this to me, how it was starting to seem like a good plan. But Nonnie could never shut herself away like that. "Sounds pretty stupid to me."

"It was a real waste," he agrees. "She was kind of a dish."

I think of the pictures I've seen of her: narrow face, hair in a bun. "That's not what I meant. I meant she was smart. She should've just gotten over him and out into the world."

"Well, now I know who to come to for a sympathetic ear when I need relationship advice."

I didn't realize that Dominic had a girlfriend, and I'm embarrassed at how this makes me feel.

"Though it would be cool to be that guy—the one she packed it all in for."

"Ah, yes, every guy's dream—to be the guy that makes a girl lose her mind."

"Not that. I meant how it would feel to inspire greatness."

He slips the packet from my hands, flips to the next page, then returns it to me. "This one is my favorite."

I read the poem, "Wild Nights—Wild Nights!" Only three short stanzas. It's more subtle than Nonnie's poems, but even I can understand the imagery of a ship seeking a mooring. "It's funny though—" I begin. Then stop. For what I was about to point out was that the poem is from the perspective of the ship, seeking the mooring "in thee." So the speaker seems masculine. I can practically hear Grace yelling. "Insertion! This poem is about inserting a penis into a vagina!"

But of course I can't talk about that with Dominic.

"Never mind."

I pick up the packet again and turn back to the hope poem.

> *"Hope" is the thing with feathers—*
> *That perches in the soul—*
> *And sings the tune without the words—*
> *And never stops—at all—*

God, that stupid bird. Would it just shut up already? (But in my mind I'm picturing a tiny boat, rocking itself loose at sea.)

"You're not easy to get to know," he tells me. It feels like an insult. Or a promise. Both, really.

"You're not giving me much choice," I reply.

"I can go," he says. He stands up and I'm eye level with the hips of his worn-in jeans.

"I'll see you around, then," I say. I'm just as bad as that bird.

"Sure you will." He grins again and strides off into the parking lot, where he gets into a beat-up black sedan and drives away.

I'm trying to figure out why he needed me to drive him to campus if he has his own car when Ramona appears. "You're late."

"So shoot me."

"I could just leave you here, you know. Teach you a lesson."

That makes her grin. "Do what you have to do." Then she just stands there looking at me like she thinks I might actually leave her behind.

ii.

I ease the car into my parking spot in the driveway. As the engine noise dies down, Ramona coughs.

"Yes?" I ask.

"What?" she demands.

"Did you want to say something?"

"It was just a cough. God." She coughs again as if I'm unclear on the concept.

"Sorry, Your Phlegminess. I won't make that mistake again."

Her hair is in a bun, and she lets it down as she gets out of the car, like Rapunzel unraveling her tresses. I wonder if Dominic was telling the truth with that whole lettuce thing. It seems so absurd, but I guess most fairy tales are. I mean, a glass slipper that fits only one woman in the whole town—not to mention the impracticality of dancing in a shoe made of glass. I'm glad Dominic didn't bring that one up. I know the original story there, with the stepsisters cutting off their toes and all that gruesome stuff. Or the Little Mermaid walking on shards of glass. Then again, Rapunzel is just about the only fairy tale I can think of where the prince gets punished.

I shove my door open and I'm striding toward the house when I see something glinting on the garage, just around the corner from the doors. I walk around to the side of the garage, and about five feet up is a bottle cap jammed into the stucco. It's silver and bright like a beacon. My mind is cycling through possibilities. It fell out of the recycle bin and somehow bounced up there? The wind? Then I see that there's not just one, but many, spotting the outside wall of the house. They fan out from that first silver one I saw, just a few close to it, but more and more as they move along the wall, maybe fifty in all. It looks like a spray pattern, but not so even. Like someone had a jar full of them and threw them at the wall and they just stuck. The twist-off tops are flat and perfectly round, but the ones you need an opener for are bent and scratched. Some are faceup, showing their brands to the world, but others are bottom up, their sharp teeth like mouths ready to bite. By far the most prevalent are the orange caps of Moxie soda, Nonnie's favorite.

"What the hell," I mutter. I pick at the shiny one, but it holds fast. It's not just shoved in, it's glued.

I look over my shoulder at Ramona, who is watching me. "There are bottle caps. On the house."

"Yes," she replies, matter-of-factly. And I'm not sure if she's so blasé because she's so far divorced from reality that she thinks bottle caps attached to the house are perfectly normal. I mean, she is wearing that same Dinosaur Jr. T-shirt, right side out, with a cardigan that covers the offending cigarette, and a pair of jeans, even though it's in the seventies. And she's standing on one foot. So maybe in whatever new reality Ramona has constructed for herself, bottle caps on buildings are just the way things are done.

"Go get Mom," I tell her.

I use my fingernail to pick at a cap from a bottle of Moxie just to test again that they are really, truly stuck, and it holds.

Ramona steps forward. "I don't think they're going to come off."

"It looks like they used hot glue," I agree.

She peers closely. "Maybe. Or some sort of caulking."

"Why would someone glue bottle caps to our house?" I ask.

"Why do people do any number of things?"

If you were going to go through life with the attitude that people's actions couldn't be explained—well, it's exasperating to think about. I just accept that she's not going to go in and get Mom, so I do it myself. Inside, I find my mother sitting at the kitchen table, working on the *New York Times* crossword puzzle. She looks up and says, "Good day?"

"Sure. Listen, have you—"

"I need your help with this one: mathematics branch that deals with limits." She taps her pencil on the paper. "Eight letters."

"Calculus."

"That works! This is why we have children, to complete the *Times* puzzle."

"Have you seen the bottle caps?" I ask.

"Bottle caps?" she echoes.

"On the garage? Glued there?"

Mom throws down her newspaper. Once outside, she bends over and tries to pry off a cap, just as I had. "Those little shits," she mutters. She says it like she knows specifically which shits are responsible.

"You know who did this?"

"It has to be one of Imogene's fans. There's that poem"—she waves her hand in the air—"about the bottles never being with their caps?"

"'Detritus'?" I suggest.

"Nonnie has a poem about bottle caps?" Ramona asks.

"About all sorts of garbage—the things we throw away," Mom says with another wave of her hand. "'Piling up, spilling toward entropy, where only dirt can grow.' And there's that section about how nothing ever matches up, and how the bottles can never find their caps." She steps forward and rubs her hand over the bottle caps. "This is vandalism. This is trash on our house. How do they even know she's sick?"

Nonnie hasn't wanted us to tell anyone. She just wants to disappear one day.

"I'm sure it can be fixed," I say, stepping toward my mother. She rakes her hand through her hair. "That's not the point."

"It could be a coincidence," Ramona says. "Maybe it doesn't have anything to do with her. Or maybe Nonnie would like it," she offers, wiping her hands on her jeans.

"All our life people have—" Mom shakes her head. "This

isn't the tribute Nonnie wants."

"It's just a little thing," Ramona says. "Don't be upset."

"How the hell did they get them to stick to stone?" Mom mutters.

"It looks like hot glue to me, but Ramona thinks it's caulking," I say. "Either way, we'll have to take them off carefully, or we could ruin the stucco."

"This is going to make the resale value plummet." Mom looks heavenward, as if an answer might come from above. "You think we can get it off? We'll hire someone. I'm not messing up the house for a bunch of crazy wannabes. What are they even thinking? Imogene would never vandalize someone else's property. Not someone's private property, anyway, not unless she had some political motivation for it, and what motivation would there be for putting bottle caps on our house? You know I believe in free expression, but this isn't art or politics or creativity."

"Maybe—" Ramona begins, but Mom pivots on her heel and goes back inside the house. "I'm going up to my studio," she calls over her shoulder, as if the destruction has inspired her to be creative.

"Wait," I call after her. She hesitates before turning back to me. "What do you mean about the resale value?" I ask.

"Once Nonnie's gone, what is there to tie us to this place?" She's looking at the ground at my feet, not at me.

"Well," I begin, but she doesn't let me say anything.

"We'll sell this place, get something more reasonable. Maybe a condo in Portsmouth, that's almost like a city."

"But that's a different school," I say, then bite my lip. Nonnie will survive through this school year. She has to.

"I'm sure we can work something out if you really want to stay at Essex High School. You know I moved my senior year and I survived."

"But you *hated* it."

"Yes. I hated it here."

I can tell the conversation is over. Ramona has been watching us like a Ping-Pong match, and now she starts slowly retreating. Mom spins and heads again toward the house. Her mind is not on the bottle caps, but on oils and brushes in her locked studio.

I stay outside in the warm afternoon air. The sky is dotted with big, white puffy clouds—like something out of a child's drawing. As one of them moves across the sun, the light hits the bottle caps just so and makes them look like they are moving. Like the wall is alive.

I turn to say something to Ramona, to point it out to her, but she is gone.

iii.

I had to explain it three times to Britta on the phone, and then she finally said, "I'm coming over. Call Grace and tell her I'll pick her up."

Now we all stand and stare at the side wall of the garage. The big oak tree casts a shadow on the house, and the bottle caps have lost their shine.

"So someone snuck up to your house and glued them on?" Britta asks. "You realize that's creepy, don't you?"

"You have no sense of adventure." Grace squats down and looks at the ground as if there might be more bottle caps there.

Britta inspects the wall more closely. "I wonder who would do something like this. I mean, to sneak up here and put bottle caps on your house, either the person is crazy, or it's personal."

"My mom thinks it's a message to Nonnie. Because of her 'Detritus' poem."

"Right, of course," Britta says. "It's like all the lost caps are showing up here."

"She's not too happy about it. My mom, I mean."

"What does Nonnie think?" Britta asks.

"I haven't told her yet."

"We should tell her now," Britta says.

"I think she's sleeping."

Britta has always been nervous around Nonnie, even when we were younger. It's like just hearing that Nonnie was a poet— a writer of books—made Britta's mind reel, and she always mumbles and bumbles around Nonnie, which Nonnie both loves and hates.

Grace hops up. "What we need to do is have a stakeout. I mean, clearly that's the proper course of action here."

"Where are we going to stake out?" Britta asks.

"Very's house, of course. We can hide out back behind the garage there. We'll take turns sleeping. We'll need binoculars. I've already started looking for clues, and I can say with some assurance that the perpetrator left no footprints."

"On the paved driveway?" Britta asks.

"Correct. You know, I'm realizing that on cop shows, there's an awful lot of soft dirt ground for the criminals to leave their rare and unusual footprints in." She regards her own shoes, sparkling Converse that she purchased in the children's department of Target. "You know, maybe Nonnie did it herself."

"That is a ridiculous idea," Britta says. "Imogene Woodruff would not have stuck bottle caps onto her own house."

It would not have been such a ridiculous idea if it weren't for the fact that Nonnie couldn't get up and down the stairs to her room by herself. We tried to move her into the main house, but she refused.

Grace is undeterred. "Maybe she's trying to tell you something, or leave a message for when she's gone. It could be hints that will lead you to some big discovery. Like maybe it will reveal who your mother's father was. Oh! Or maybe your grandmother, like, arranged for all of this, like, what's that book? *The Westing Game*? And she's left you your inheritance to find."

"Stop," Britta says. "Slow down. Okay, now let's step back onto the conveyor belt of reality."

"I don't like conveyor belts. Like those moving walkways— I'm always afraid I'm going to get sucked down into them somehow. Escalators, too."

"I don't think a stakeout is the best idea," I tell them. "We don't know if whoever did this is going to come back, and anyway in the dark we might not see them."

"Fine," Grace sighs.

"Very's right. We need a more organized approach. If we could figure out what they are trying to say, then we could maybe figure out who would want to say it," Britta suggests.

"Dude, we are totally like Nancy Drew," Grace says.

"You are not Nancy," Britta tells her.

"Why not? Because I'm Chinese?"

Britta sighs. "No. Because this is Very's house. And Very's grandmother."

"Nancy Drew solved crimes at other people's houses."

"Nancy had Ned Nickerson, who's an awful lot like Christian."

"Fine," Grace says. "But then I'm being George. I'm not going to be wimpy-ass Bess."

"All right," Britta says. "When you're done being twelve, we need to help Very figure this out."

"You know," Grace says, tucking her arm through Britta's, "some people thought that George and Bess were a lesbian couple."

"You wish," Britta replies, and laughs. "Focus on the details. We'll figure this out. We're smart girls."

Smart girls, all right, but those bottle caps glinting in the sun were not about to give up any secrets.

iv.

"Bottle caps?" Nonnie asks. "On the house?"

"Glued there, I think." I'm holding a bottle of pink nail polish, my toes spread out, and I'm trying not to slip and paint my skin.

"Just right on the stucco?"

"Yep. Scattered around. I don't see any pattern. All different kinds, too, but mostly Moxie."

"How strange," she says. I can tell she is pleased. The Moxie is the clue: this is in her honor.

"Mom's pissed."

"Livid," Nonnie corrects. "Or irritated. Affronted, perhaps. But surely she is neither drunk nor urinating on the house." She pauses. "Well, certainly not urinating."

"Livid," I choose. I've done the right side, and now it's time to put the second coat on the left.

"Do mine," she says.

"Your what?"

"My toes," she says. "Though pink is not my first choice. Have you got any other colors?"

I shake my head.

"Pink, then." She sits up and throws the covers off her legs. She's still wearing her trademark black narrow pants. She folds her body in half to peel her socks off her feet and when she moves like this—graceful as a bird—it's hard to believe she's so ill.

Her skin is white with lines of sharp blue like rivers through ice. Her toenails have a yellow hue. "Ghastly," she says, shaking her head.

"They're the most beautiful feet I've ever seen," I tell her.

She carefully repositions her body so her feet are at the edge of the bed. I begin with her right foot. I cup the heel in one hand as I paint the toes. The pink looks like cotton candy next to her pale, pale skin.

"Did I ever tell you about the young film director?" she asks. "The one who wanted to cast me in his movie."

Her foot twitches and I paint a bit on her toe, but she doesn't seem to notice.

"Such a bad boy he thought he was. I told him *Rebel without a Cause* had already been made so he might as well just go curl up and die." She laughs. I think of Dominic in his jeans and black Doc Martens. I can't imagine telling him to just go curl up and die. He would probably laugh and tell me I was funny again. "Are you sure you don't have any other colors? Red, perhaps? Or orange? My skin did always look nice with a touch of orange nearby."

"I've got six different shades of pink, Nonnie. What can I say?"

"The first thing I'll do when I can get out of this bed is go get you some red nail polish. Red nail polish and red lipstick. Every girl should know the precise shade of red lipstick that's right for her face. If you have red lips, you don't need any other makeup. Especially with eyes like yours."

"Red lipstick is garish." I want to tell her that she can get out of this bed, can go downstairs. I'll even drive her into town. We still need to make that appointment for a haircut. But I know that she means something more than just getting out of bed, something bigger, something that just isn't going to happen.

"Don't try to distract me with perfect words. This pink makes me feel like a little girl. And not in a good way."

"Next time I'll bring fuchsia. Other foot."

She lifts her other foot and I hold it in my hand. She has a small bruise under the nail of her big toe. It's black and more solid-looking than the mottled green-and-blue one on my face. She gets bruises so easily now because of one of her medications.

"As I was saying, the film director. He used to paint my toenails for me. I think he had a bit of a foot fetish, though of course I never said anything about that to him."

This was unlike her, not to name a thing. "Why not?"

"Why, he might have stopped painting my nails. He was quite good at it. In fact, I'd wager he enjoyed it more than the other thing we did together."

Wink, wink, nudge, nudge.

"Nonnie."

"You are seventeen; your prudishness alarms me. At any rate, all I'm saying is that I wouldn't be surprised if his interests lay elsewhere, as it were. His rebelliousness could have been a front he put up to hide his homosexuality."

"Nonnie, just because a man likes nail polish doesn't make him gay."

"No. But not enjoying sex with a woman is quite the clue."

I drop the brush back into the bottle. "Done."

Nonnie tilts her head back and looks at the job I've done. "Thank you. Of course it's not as good a job as the James Dean impostor did, but I'll forgive you."

"You're very kind," I say. I look down at my own feet. The right toes are a shade darker than the left.

"He was a mistake," she says wistfully.

"Because he was gay? Sounds like he made the mistake when he went after you."

She shakes her head. "It was another notch against me. Arthur Miller can marry Marilyn Monroe and that's all well and dandy, but I go around with a director or a musician, or even silly old Andy Warhol, and my credibility is shot. 'Poet to the Stars,' that's what the *New Yorker* called me once. Only time I ever made it into that rag."

"No one thinks of you that way," I lie.

"People say your choices define you. It's true, but not the way people think. Your choices don't shape you, they shape people's perceptions of you. Even the silliest, most insubstantial decision—someone will use it as evidence of one flaw or another."

"And where are all those people now?" I ask. "Who are they? They're no one, and you're Imogene Woodruff."

"Poet to the Stars," she says. "Queen of the Bottle Cap Mural."

"Jealousy makes people say cruel things."

She's staring out the window, toward the treetops. "I want to see them. The bottle caps. I want to see them."

"Right now?"

"I don't know how long we have."

I tell myself she is talking about my mother, about how she wants to take them down. I tell myself we have no other time limits as I guide her toward the steps and wrap my arm around her waist. She leans on me, and I lean on the railing.

We move in a lurching motion. I step down, then support her as she makes the step.

At the bottom of the stairs, she shakes off my arm and reaches for an old walking stick that's leaning against the wall of the garage. Cobwebs drift off of it and float to the ground. She places it firmly on the concrete, shuffles, places, shuffles her way out of the garage and onto the driveway. She blinks a few times to get used to the natural light and I wonder just how long it's been since she's been out in the fresh air.

The bottle caps are in shadow and they don't look as alive as they did earlier. Still, they captivate Nonnie. She just stares for several minutes before she says, "It's a bit more beautiful than I expected."

"In its way." It looks like a bit of a mess to me, no more sensical than Marcus Schmidt's color squares. "So—"

"I don't want to go back inside," she tells me before I can suggest it. "I made it all the way down those deathtrap stairs, I'm not going to submit myself to a march back up them."

"Dinner, then."

I help her into the house. Mom is sitting on the sofa in the sunken living room, her legs crisscross applesauce, a gin in one hand and a book of Dorothy Parker's poems in the other.

"What's for dinner?" I ask.

She laughs. "Nice to see you out of your room, Mom. Feeling better than this morning?"

"I'm feeling like I have a tumor on my lung," Nonnie replies. "Fix me a whiskey sour?"

Mom doesn't move, so I go to the bar cart, where I hesitate. Nonnie is taking a huge regimen of drugs, and I don't know if she's supposed to be drinking. "I don't think we have any sour mix."

"Brandy, then. Straight up."

"It's in the back," Mom says. "The one with the crystal square on top."

I pour Nonnie some but speak to my mom. "We're all going to have dinner together. Like a family."

"Do families do that anymore?" Mom asks. "We certainly never did when I was a child. Why, I can't remember one family dinner growing up."

"What are you talking about?" Nonnie asks. "We had a million family dinners. Every time we sat down together it was a family meal. Not so light on the pour there, Veronica."

Mom and Nonnie, that was their whole family. Nonnie had become pregnant as a complete surprise at age forty-four and refused to tell anyone who the father was. It would drive me crazy, but Mom found it charming—or rather, she made it part of her own charm.

Ramona trip-trops down the stairs and into the room. One side of her hair is pulled back with a pink feathered clip, and her fingertips are stained with ink. "Nonnie!" she says with surprise.

"We're having a family dinner."

"Really?" she asks. She sits down on the arm of a chair. "What's the special occasion?"

"No occasion," I say. "Just because we're a family."

"Veronica is being dictatorial again," Mom says. "Like the time with the picture place at the mall."

That had been a fiasco. It was in third grade and it seemed like every other kid in the world was going to this new store in the mall for family portraits. It was right in the food court, so everyone eating their lazy food could watch as you grinned at the camera. We wore jeans and white button-down shirts. The photographer, some sort of art-school dropout, directed us with a bored look. Ramona and I sat on the ground, back-to-back, knees to chest. Mom and Dad stood above us, holding hands, each with their other hand on one of our shoulders. The photographer snapped. I grinned like an idiot. The other three looked dead serious. Mom loved it and hung it above the mantel in the library.

"I'm being familial."

Mom holds the book in front of her. "Dorothy was such a wit," she says as she turns the page. "She didn't have any daughters."

"I have heard that daughters drain a woman's wit," I reply.

My mother lowers her book then and arches her eyebrows at me with a wry smile. "You win," she says. "To the victors go the spoils, and all that. We can have a family dinner. Only we don't have anything to cook and your father's at some symposium on campus."

"No one expected him to be here," Ramona says. Mom gives her a sharp look but says nothing.

"I need to sit down," Nonnie tells me.

I help her over to the couch, ease her down, and drape our red afghan over her lap. Once she's settled, I bring her the brandy I poured.

"Dinner will be served in half an hour. Come on, Ramona."

"Me? Why me?"

"Because you're all I've got."

v.

Ramona and I can't find an actual meal, but we manage to pull together enough small dishes to satisfy us: crab Rangoon and spanakopita from the freezer (age indeterminate); pickled herring, almonds, and figs from the pantry; and some mushrooms that we sauté in balsamic vinegar with garlic. We find crackers that are only on the cusp of staleness, and even mango sorbet that isn't freezer-burned that we plan to serve in tiny cups as a palate cleanser.

"It's ooh-la-la fancy, don't you think?" Ramona asks. "We should pretend we are the help and we can stay in here and have catty conversations while they eat."

"What would we have catty conversations about?"

"Oh, all the intrigue of the upstairs folks. Like I hear that young Ramona child is canoodling with the chauffeur."

"Indeed!" I say. I keep arranging the spanakopita on the tray. It's like if I look at her, this old version of Ramona might disappear back into the new model. "George is a nice fellow but if he isn't careful, he'll lose his position."

"They say he's mad for her."

"Mad for her money, I'd say."

"The problem is, she won't get a penny." Ramona takes the crab Rangoon from the toaster oven and drops them onto a plate. "Her dastardly brother is coming back from overseas and he's sure to run this family into the ground. We'll be lucky if any of us have a job."

"It's the ponies," I say. "He's betting the whole fortune away."

"Who's betting on the ponies?" Nonnie asks as she comes in, Mom holding her arm.

"Alistair," Ramona replies. "He's up to his old tricks."

"That rascal!" Mom says. She's always been able to jump right into these games.

"To the dining room!" I tell Mom and Nonnie. "Tonight's meal will be small plates, otherwise known as tapas. It's all the rage."

As Ramona and I finish preparing the food, I say, "You should lay off about Dad. He has a lot going on."

She smirks. "Does he now?"

"Come on, this is turning into a nice night."

Her shoulders ease down and she turns her head a bit to the side. "You know, we could do this every night. Eat as a family."

"You mean like we used to?" I ask. I can't even remember exactly when it was that Dad stopped picking up food at the market for us to have each night. We used to go around the table and share the most amazing thing that had happened that day, only it didn't have to be true. My stories almost always were, though I did once try to claim that Stephen Hawking had visited our school. Ramona would go on and on with her stories of escapees from the buffalo farm on the edge of town, or how it had snowed from one single cloud, a blizzard that covered the playground slide with a layer of white. Nonnie was the best storyteller, though. You could never tell if her stories were true or imagined, or some amalgamation of the two.

"Only we'd make dinner," Ramona says. "Really make it, like, not ready-made stuff. We'd cook it. You and me. We should take a class. Like when we did that bracelet-making class at the library. We could take a cooking class. At that cooking school. In Dover, I think. Or Portsmouth."

"That's for people who want to be chefs. Like instead of going to college, they go there."

"I could want to be a chef."

"You could want to do all sorts of things. But I'm saying that we can't just show up and ask for a Cooking 101 course."

"We could cook dinner every night, though."

"Sure we could. We could also fly to the moon." I use my hip to push the door into the dining room open. "Come on, Ramona, we have to get this onto the table."

While I help Nonnie to fill her plate, Ramona serves our

mother chilled white wine.

"This is my favorite kind of meal," Mom says. "A bit of everything." She breaks a spanakopita in half and manages to eat it without dropping one flake of phyllo dough on herself.

"That's what happens when a girl is raised on cocktail parties," Nonnie says. "It was the cheapest way to feed her—just bring her along with me."

"And if they said no children, I'd do a little dog and pony show for them," Mom says.

"What do you mean?" Ramona asks.

"She'd recite T. S. Eliot and then insult their wine selection."

"Come one, come all, see the poetess's daughter perform!"

"It wasn't like that," Nonnie says. "Your wine talks were a public service."

"That's true," Mom says. "Half the time those folks didn't know the first thing about good wine."

"How did you know?" Ramona asks.

"I read a lot of magazines," Mom replies. "Remember that awful Mrs. Finnegan, who said you were teaching me to be a drunken harlot?"

Nonnie tilts her head back. "Lorraine Elizabeth Finnegan, patroness of the arts. So long as said arts were clean, predictable, and not at all appealing to her husband."

Ramona giggles beside me and helps herself to a crab Rangoon. "Hey, Mom, after dinner can I go up to your studio to look at some of your art books? We're doing self-portraits and I want to get some ideas."

"I'll get one for you," Mom replies.

"I don't know which one I want."

"Sorry. Studio's closed. Take it up with management." She forces a smile before taking a sip from her wine.

Ramona turns a spanakopita at a right angle. "I don't know why you like working alone. I like being in the art room at school, seeing all the other pieces, the buzz, you know?"

Mom doesn't answer.

"Let's talk about something Very can relate to," Nonnie suggests.

"I can relate. It's like my math class at the college. You're sitting around discussing solutions. You see how someone else came at it. Maybe you won't use it on that problem, but you tuck it away for another."

"Artworks aren't exactly problems to be solved, dear," Mom says.

"Don't you think so?" Ramona asks. "You have your goal, the outcome you see in your head, and you have to figure out the best medium and techniques to use."

"That's for assigned art: art you have to do. Real art comes from someplace else, someplace within you, and you follow it."

"What about commissions?" Ramona asks.

"What about them?" Mom's starting to get an edge in her voice.

"Now we *are* talking about something outside of my realm," I say, desperate to pull us back.

Nonnie glances at me over her wine and nods.

Mom picks up a fig between her thumb and forefinger and drops it into her mouth.

"You know how figs are pollinated?" I ask.

"How?" Mom asks.

"Fig wasps. The female wasp goes into the well, the sort of the bud of the fig, and she lays her eggs. She's the one that pollinates the fig flowers, too, when she lays her eggs. But getting in, she loses her wings. It doesn't matter, though, because as soon as she lays her eggs, she dies. The very act of giving birth kills her."

"This is not the happy story I was expecting," Mom says. She has her foot drawn up onto her chair, her wineglass held lightly between her fingers.

"It gets worse. So then the nonpollinating females come in and are basically hitching a ride on her work. They lay their eggs, too. When they hatch, the male wasps immediately search for a mate. Then they dig their way out of the fig, and all the female wasps can escape and go lay their eggs in other figs."

"That's better. I've always liked a hero, even a wasp."

"But," I say, "once the male gets out, he dies, too."

Mom holds the fig up and regards it. "Love, birth, tragedy, death. It's like this fig contains the works of Shakespeare." Then she bites it in half. She lifts her wineglass. "To the male wasp, who saves us all."

"How about a toast to the wasp who gives her life to lay her eggs?" I ask.

"Of course, her, too," Mom says.

"And to the wasps who get away," Nonnie adds.

And we all clink our glasses together.

Cheers!

five

i.

WHEN I GET TO school, I find that someone has graffitied my locker. I say *someone*, but who else but Dominic could have written the lyrics to "Veronica" in red Sharpie on the fire-hydrant-yellow door? The words swirl together like they are ants trailing their queen in a May Day dance.

I'm just standing there staring at it when Haylie, one of Ramona's friends, comes up beside me. She's wearing canvas sneakers with sparkling cherries on them. "Is that where your name comes from?" she asks.

I nod.

"Weird," she says. "That someone would write it on your locker. I mean, like, yeah?"

Haylie always seems to be starting sentences and then finishing them with a string of words that don't quite make sense.

"You haven't been around much lately," I tell her. "You

should come by the house. I could drive you and Ramona home if you want."

She kicks her toe into the linoleum tile and the sparkles on her shoes cast glimmering, dancing red light onto the floor. "So, yeah? I mean, maybe, if you want?"

"Of course. You and Ramona work it out."

"Right. Okay?"

The bell rings.

"Great. See you later, Haylie."

"See ya?"

Down the hall in his classroom, Mr. Tompkins seems to be waiting for me. "I have exciting news for you!" He doesn't give me enough time to prompt him with a *What?* before he bursts out with "Professor Singh is coming to the Math Around U conference!"

Last year Mr. Tompkins submitted one of my math solutions and explanations as part of a proposal for a session at a conference. It has a hokey name: Math Around U, and it focuses on teaching math to kids about to enter college, in college, and in graduate school. Anyway, they chose his proposal, and in a few weeks, he's going to present his methods, and I get to go along.

"Professor Singh was my favorite prof at MIT. She's brilliant. Brilliant! And I think the kind of math she does will fascinate you. So . . ." He drums his fingers on his desk. "I've arranged for the two of you to have coffee. Her schedule is jam-packed, but I explained how very smart you are—"

"Please tell me you didn't use the L'Hopital's rule pun again."

He shrugs and then says, "This is a big deal, Very. She is a big deal. And listen, I'm not trying to pressure you to go to MIT, even though that's where I went and even though it's quite simply the best institution in the world for mathematicians, especially one of your caliber, but if you did decide to apply, and Professor Singh put in a good word for you, well, that would be about as close to a shoo-in as you get there."

"Thank you," I say. I can picture myself sitting there with Professor Singh, two women mathematicians, in that old vein of student and teacher, like Plato and Aristotle, only with better hair. In my imagination, Professor Singh has waves of dark hair with copper highlights, and we are laughing about a clever proof I've done. Laughing, and my soul is at peace because now I'm settled. It's not so much MIT—or Stanford or even Minnesota—it's knowing. In this imaginary future world I am happy because at least one huge, looming decision is taken care of.

He hands me a manila envelope. "Here are some of her articles. I was going to give them to you earlier, but I wanted to make sure she was able to come and could meet with you."

"Thanks."

"Of course, we'll have to get a better handle on this silly chemistry stuff for you."

I take my seat center front, as if being right there will somehow make the information get into my head more easily. Christian comes in a moment later and slides into the seat next to me. He moves like he's going to kiss me on the cheek, and I duck away. Kisses don't belong in classrooms.

Mr. Tompkins starts to explain the symbols he's drawn on the board. There are plus signs. I'm comfortable with plus signs. It's that arrow instead of an equals sign that gives me trouble. What goes on in that arrow, the invisible transformation of molecules from one thing into something entirely different, always seems just out of reach to me.

Still, I copy down everything from the board just as he has written it. I even use his oddly shaped J for joules. When I look up from my paper, Mr. Tompkins is standing by the door. Just beyond him, on the other side of the glass, Dominic stands in the hallway. He's staring right at me, and when he notices I'm looking at him, he starts to gesture at me to come out and meet him. I frown and glance at Christian, who, as if the glance has weight, looks up, first at me, then to Dominic in the hallway, then back at me. In the hallway, Dominic smirks. But then he beckons again, softer this time. I trace over the letters of the equation.

"So, let's start working through this thing." Mr. Tompkins claps his hands together. "Come on, guys, show me what you've got."

Adam, he of the hard but evidently scientifically inclined head, raises his hand.

"Adam, awesome. You're going to take a break from tackling girls in the hallway to help us solve the mysteries of chemistry."

I run my hand over my bruise, which is more green now than blue.

"Actually I need to go to the bathroom," Adam says, blushing.

"Rookie move there, Adam."

"As soon as I get back, Mr. Tompkins, I'll be all over the problem."

On the way out, he taps my desk and mouths the word "Sorry," which is, by my estimation, his seventeenth apology.

I look down at my paper. I know I can figure this out. It's not that hard. My attention is drawn back to the hallway, but when I look out the window, Dominic is gone.

"Any actual volunteer who wants to explain his or her process?"

Stupid Dominic. I didn't even get a chance to think about the problem with him out there waving his arms around. Mr. Tompkins calls on Christian, who explains that when the sodium hydroxide is mixed with the hydrogen chloride, it neutralizes the hydrogen chloride.

Neutralizes. It's like that sodium hydroxide comes in and just takes over all the spicy acidity of the hydrogen chloride. I'm not one for personifying inanimate objects—Nonnie would call that sentimentality—but I almost feel bad for that hydrogen chloride, giving up all its personality in the arrow.

"So," Christian goes on, "we take our specific heat capacity equation and plug in the known values."

Our specific heat capacity. What is our specific heat capacity, Christian? Have we reached it? I smile for a moment, catch myself, then frown at my paper. I can't help but feel like Christian is explaining this in a slow and deliberate manner for my benefit. I'm not used to feeling this way, left behind in a science class. I can't say that I like it.

ii.

Ms. Pickering is waiting for me at my locker. Frowning. This is not normally the way I am greeted by the assistant principal and it makes me feel about as uncomfortable as my floundering in chemistry class. "I had hoped this was a mix-up," she says, pointing to my locker.

"I didn't write it there," I tell her.

"Of course you didn't. I just wondered if perhaps you might have some idea who did."

"No," I lie, annoyed with Ms. Pickering for finding it completely impossible to believe that I might have written on the locker myself.

She nods her head. "Well, if you could clean it up, that would be grand."

"I think it was done with a Sharpie. It might need new paint."

She sighs. Sighing is something else I've never gotten from an assistant principal. "Just do the best you can, okay?"

This seems like especially poor leadership on her part. She just told me that she knew I hadn't done it. *Of course* not. What other court requires the victim to clean up the crime scene? Next thing you know the police or whoever are going to be making Nonnie clean the bottle caps off our house with a toothbrush. Maybe if Ms. Pickering were doing a better job looking after the school, Dominic wouldn't have had a chance to write on my locker in the first place.

She starts to go, but then says, "How's the class up at the college going?"

"Great." Now we are back on familiar territory.

"We're awfully proud of you, Veronica."

"Thanks."

As she walks away, Christian arrives from his locker on the other end of the hall. When he gets close, he gives me the peck on the cheek that I avoided during chemistry. "What's up with your locker?"

"I don't know, but it's the topic du jour."

He grins. "I love when you speak French to me."

I giggle. Isn't that what girls are supposed to do in these situations? Giggle? Sometimes it's exhausting just trying to get it right. He looks away from me, and at my locker, reading the lyrics. "Depressing song."

"I don't know. It grows on you."

He wraps his arm around my shoulder and says, "We got Portugal for Model UN. Can you believe it? Portugal!"

"I can't think of anything wrong with Portugal."

"Can you think of anything right?"

"Um, I can't say that I know that much about Portugal. Modern Portugal anyway."

"Exactly. It's a nonentity. We will have no pull. We might as well be nonvoting members." He shakes his head. "I was hoping for Pakistan this year."

"Portugal used to be a huge power. They had all those colonies."

"Hundreds of years ago."

"It could change back. You never know."

"Somehow I doubt that they're going to get back on top in the next three months, but I admire your optimism." He starts going on about the economic situation and debt ratios and the utter hopelessness of Portugal being anything but a second- or third-rate country.

I try to listen to him, but instead I'm thinking about Ms. Pickering's assumption. Okay, sure, it would be tremendously stupid to scrawl graffiti on my own locker—especially song lyrics about my own name—and everyone knows that I'm not stupid. But someone like Dominic or Ramona, they aren't stupid, and if there was graffiti on their lockers, no one would doubt that they could have done it themselves.

"Why do you think Ms. Pickering was so sure I didn't write on my locker?"

"What?" Christian asks, breaking off his monologue. "Well, because that's just not something you'd do."

"I might. If I had a good reason." I think of the bottle caps glued to our house: there has to be some reason for them. Someone is trying to say something about Nonnie—or to her. Whatever it is, the message is unclear. I glance at my locker. Two acts of graffiti in two days. Maybe the bottle caps aren't about Nonnie.

"What would be a good reason for writing on a locker?"

"Well, maybe not writing on a locker per se, but some act of graffiti maybe."

Christian shakes his head. "What type of vandalism is acceptable?"

"I don't know. Something artistic. Or political."

He wrinkles his nose. "There are more effective means of political expression."

We've gone way off course from my original question. All I want to know is what would happen if I just ignored people's expectations. What if, for just one day, I didn't want that to be me? What if I decided to be like Ramona and only focus on math the way she focuses on art? Or like Dru, and come to school with a new look and a new name and just expect everyone to play along? What if I did want to glue bottle caps to my house? My mind is reeling. I'm like a little kid on the playground who's just been pushed off the swing by a bigger kid, one old enough to know better, stunned and sore at the unfairness of it all.

Christian is back to griping about Portugal, and I'm nodding, but I guess not in the right places, because finally he says, "Is everything okay?"

"Sure, of course," I say hastily.

"I thought maybe your grandmother had taken a turn for the worse or something. You're just not quite all here."

I shake my head. "It's nothing."

"In chemistry, too. You kept looking out in the hall like you were expecting someone to come in. So I thought maybe you were anticipating bad news. But the only person I saw out there was Dominic Meyers."

"Who?" I ask, the word escaping from my lips like a bubble from a wand.

"Dominic Meyers. It kind of looked like he was waving at you. Again."

"I didn't notice. I was trying to figure out that specific heat capacity problem. How the sodium hydroxide neutralizes the hydrogen chloride."

"Actually, they neutralize each other. I'll help you with it later."

"Thanks." I lace my fingers through his. "And I'm fine."

"Good." He nods as if we've settled something. "I like your outfit."

This is one of the things that perplexes me about Christian. I'm wearing capri-length jeans and a pink T-shirt. It's pretty similar to what I wear most days, not worth commenting about. "Oh, thanks." And then, because it seems only right to balance things, I add, "I like your shirt," though he, too, is wearing just a simple T-shirt. "The color, it looks nice with your eyes." There. At least I added a detail to make it more personal, more plausible. And he does have beautiful eyes.

He seems to blush. "Thanks, Very. That's sweet."

I'm walking on a tightrope. Every day. A little too far one way or the other and I'll come crashing down to the pavement.

iii.

That night, with time I've set aside for looking up college information online, I instead research graffiti. Sitting in the living room with my laptop resting on my knees, I read about Banksy, who painted murals of peace around the West Bank, gorgeous silhouettes against crumbling walls. And Keith Haring, whose brightly colored figures ended up being used to increase awareness about AIDS. It's not all just people scribbling to leave a mark.

As I'm bouncing around the web I find a page about the Guerrilla Girls. The website has a woman with a gorilla mask on holding up her arm like Rosie the Riveter. They're a group of woman artists who've been around since the 1980s and they do all this art, almost like pranks, to counter the sexism they find.

My phone buzzes with a text from Britta: **Any more bottle caps?**

When I'd looked at the house after school, there had seemed to be more caps. They were starting to fill in the spaces in the fan.

It's definitely growing. Do you know anything about the Guerrilla Girls?

Do I???

Then, another bubble of text: **FWIW, as rad as they are, I don't think they're the ones gluing things to your house.**

I know. I just thought it could be something like that.

If only Essex was cool enough to have a group of renegade artists.

Maybe not a group? I thought of the words on my locker. One renegade artist. Dominic. I still wasn't sure what he was trying to say, though.

True. I'll come take a look soon, and maybe Google up some other ideas.

Thanks.

See you tomorrow. Dickinson day!

Emily Dickinson can, as Grace would say, suck it. And take her stupid bird with her.

You just need some more feathers, dear.

I click off my phone and look back at the computer. The Guerrilla Girls are all political, a single mission. I take out a piece of paper and draw the T of a geometric proof.

STATEMENT	REASON
1. Dominic wrote the lyrics to "Veronica" on my locker.	Given.
2. Bottle caps appeared on our house one day prior.	Given.
3. Therefore, Dominic put the bottle caps on our house.	Transitive property.

It wouldn't hold up. There's not enough evidence. I have hunches. I have Dominic's sudden interest in me, but I don't have proof. I need to find out more about graffiti and renegade artists, and maybe even Dominic himself.

Ramona and Dad come in as I'm looking at the site. "Nice,"

he says. "That's what I'm talking about. That's the type of stuff you should be studying."

"It's not really for a class. Just something Christian and I were talking about—graffiti and street art and their role in society."

"You and Christian were talking about graffiti?" He scratches at his stubble. "It's not for debate team or anything?"

"Let's call it a friendly disagreement."

He grins. "What side were you on?"

"That occasionally there is a purpose for this type of vandalism. Like with the bottle caps on our house."

And writing song lyrics on someone's locker.

Ramona looks up from the orange she is peeling. "Do you think the bottle caps have a meaning?"

"Maybe."

"Like what?"

"You tell me," I say. "You're the one who knew that square of blue was the ocean. I'd say these things were open to interpretation."

Ramona drops a whole, perfect spiral of orange peel onto the coffee table. "But what's your interpretation, that's what I'm asking."

"That's what I'm trying to research. I'm trying to find information about more personal messages."

"That is way cool, Very. I'm impressed." Dad sits down in a chair across from me. "I mean, a lot of people think graffiti is just young men screaming to be heard. After all, that is why the tag is so important."

"The tag?"

"Like a signature, but stylized."

"Does all graffiti have a tag?"

He laughs. "It's not like there are rules, Very."

"Oh, there are totally rules," Ramona says. "Like all graffiti must be completed between one thirty and four thirty a.m., local time. And all graffiti must have a tag, though said tag may not be obvious or ornate."

"It would be easier if people just came out and said what they wanted to say," I muse.

Dad slaps the table. "You'll like this. Way back when I first came to Essex, there was this bridge in Portsmouth. An overpass, actually. And there was a message that had been spray-painted there forever, it seemed. 'Pam I love you sorry Julio.' But you see, there was no punctuation. So it was always a question: was the person who wrote the message apologizing to Julio for stealing Pam away? Or was it Julio himself who wrote the message and he was apologizing for loving her? And then over time I guess it faded or maybe was painted over. But then probably ten years later, a new message came up: 'How do you like me now Julio?'"

"So Pam wrote back?" I ask.

"Maybe. Or maybe it was someone else who knew the message—and knew that everyone in the area would know it, too—and he was playing with it."

"Or she," Ramona says.

"Right. Or she. That's what's cool about graffiti—about any art really—the conversation, the dialogue that can go on." He stands up. "I'm proud of you, Very. It's nice to see you branching out, breaking out of your shell."

I shut my laptop. Dad gave me some important information, like that stuff about tagging. I'll have to check my locker and the house to see if I can find anything that looks like a tag.

It's the story of Pam, though, and Julio that I think of when I'm brushing my teeth, because I've got a picture lodged in my mind: Dominic scaling the overpass, can of spray paint in his hands.

Very, I love you. Sorry. Dominic.

iv.

There are no tags.

I mean, unless there is something hidden in the bottle caps, like some secret code. There's no name, no signature, no symbol. And the words on my locker are just the lyrics. Nothing to tie either of them to an artist or an underlying message. Nothing to support my theory that Dominic had something to do with the bottle caps.

I am sitting on the wall again after school, contemplating the lack of tags and wondering if Dominic will show up, when Ramona emerges from the school. She looks like she has ants crawling all over her legs. When she gets closer, I realize she has completely covered her right pant leg in drawings.

"Not drawings," she says as I back the car out of the shady spot I always choose. "Draw*ing*. See, it starts down here with under the ground." She holds her leg up on the dashboard and points toward the cuff of her jeans, where vines tangle together. "Then it comes up to the earth, and we've got trees, and flowers." She turns onto her side and looks at her butt. "Back here I did some birds, but I couldn't reach all the way around."

"Put your seat belt on."

"Yes, Mom," she replies, and we both kind of laugh since it's more likely we'd have to remind Mom to buckle up.

"Anyway," she says, "if you would actually look you'd see it's a whole scene."

"I'm driving, Ramona. I can't look right now."

"You could stop the car."

"I'll look when we get home. How long did that take you to do anyway?"

"I started third period. I had to stop to go from class to class."

"You did that in class?"

"It keeps me focused." She trails her finger along the window.

"Focused on class?"

"On life." She clenches her hand into a fist and then straightens out her fingers. "It's like sometimes my brain gets going and going and drawing lets me slow it down."

I glance at her sideways: she's adding leafy details onto her knee.

"I love this time of year," she says. "I love the way the light starts to clarify. Everything is crisp and perfect and you think that maybe the world is a beautiful place after all."

"Maybe," I agree. "Oh, hey, I forgot to tell you that I ran into Haylie. I told her that if you guys want to hang out, I can drive you both home."

"Haylie?"

"Yeah, Haylie, or anyone you want. Rose. Mika. We can squeeze at least three of your friends back there."

"Three of my friends. Sounds great." I figure that's as close to a commitment as I'm going to get from her these days.

We reach a stop sign and wait for a day care group to cross the street. The teacher holds a long rope, and each child has his or her hand through a loop. "Look at that." Ramona points. "It's like a multiheaded toddler dragon. They're marching off to fight the evil sorcerer that lives up in the mountains."

"I didn't realize the scourge of child soldiers was so prevalent in the dragon world."

"You'd be a good dragon army leader."

"Uh-huh," I say, and navigate down Main Street. It's tricky. You never know when a student might lurch out into the road.

"Oh sure. Organized. Capable. Patient. Maybe a little ruthless."

"If you say so."

"I don't want to be the princess in the tower. And I can't be a dragon. I'm not the sorcerer. What's left?"

"I don't know, Ramona."

"Let's go to the library. I need to get some fairy-tale books."

"We already passed the library."

"So turn around."

"Not today, Ramona, okay? I have things I need to get done." I've promised myself that today I will go online and read up about Minnesota colleges.

She nods, and her body is still for a moment, but then she sees a collection of balloons tied to a street sign. "Oh, do you think it's a birthday party?"

And so it goes the whole ride home. Every tiny detail elicits a comment from her, from a leaf spiraling in the center of the road to an off-kilter mailbox. It's the same things we pass every day, but suddenly they are alive with meaning for her.

When we get home I forget to look at her jeans. We both bolt out of the car: she heads into the living room and I toward the kitchen for a snack, stopping to look at the bottle caps on my way. The sculpture has grown more detailed. There are maybe three times as many bottle caps, and they are starting to form patterns and shapes: swirls like a night sky.

I wonder when and how the artist added to the sculpture. It must be one of the students at the college. He or she could know Nonnie is sick and would have the free time to do something like this. I walk forward and touch the bottle caps, hot in the sun.

With a shake of my head, I go inside to the kitchen, where I open up the walk-in pantry. All I want is crackers or maybe a granola bar, but we have no typical American family snacks.

We have condiments and sauces: three different kinds of mustard; seven varieties of salad dressing; gourmet pasta sauce; mild, medium, and hot barbecue sauce. We also have things that came in cans: anchovies, marinated artichokes, something pink and slimy-looking. But after Ramona and I cleared out the kitchen for the family dinner, we have nothing that I can just sit down and eat.

Mom has probably forgotten to send in the grocery order. Now that Dad has stopped picking up meals, the responsibility for food falls on her. She never goes to the store, but orders online and has it delivered. Only she rarely remembers to place the order, even though you can set it up to send you the exact same thing every week—*Oh, but we need variety, Very!* It is a wonder we aren't all emaciated and writhing on the floor from hunger.

v.

"I'm going to the store," I announce on my way through the living room.

Mom and Ramona are sitting on the couch, their legs all tangled up. "Wonderful, I'll come along," Mom says. She's not the best shopping companion, but I agree. It's not like I can say no.

"Me, too?" Ramona asks.

There's this market in town that used to be a glorified convenience store but then decided it wanted to be all gourmet, so now you pay twice as much for so-so food. Ramona disappears while Mom loads up at the ready-made section, Dad's old stomping grounds: rotisserie chicken, half-baked eggplant Parmesan, mashed sweet potatoes, macaroni and cheese, baby-size pork dumplings. "When are we going to eat all this?" I ask.

"This week," she says. "Sometime."

She heads off to the olive bar, carefully selecting the most ovaline of the varieties. "I'm buying a pound of these. I haven't decided yet if I'm going to eat them or paint them in a still life. Look at that color and shine!"

I peek down the baking aisle and see Ramona standing in front of the cake decorations. She's holding a jar of rainbow sprinkles, the kind that look like they should taste good but feel like wax in your mouth.

Moving on, I round the corner into the cereal aisle and pick up some of the Cocoa Krispies Nonnie likes, and some granola for the rest of us. I'm reading the labels trying to decide between Golden Berry Almond and Autumn Honey Harvest when I hear an all-too-familiar clomping.

"Very Sayles-Woodruff," Dominic says.

I turn and face him, a bag of granola in each hand. "This is getting ridiculous," I tell him.

"I know. It's like fate stepping in, isn't it?"

"I was thinking more along the lines of stalking."

"You're stalking me?"

I raise my eyebrows, but he taps at a name tag and I realize that on top of his jeans and white T-shirt, he's wearing a green apron. DOMINIC, his name tag reads. MEAT.

"Meat?"

"I'm a butcher."

"Seriously? Isn't that like a specialized skill?"

"A butcher in training. An apprentice butcher. At your service." He looks into my cart. "Not much of a cook, huh?"

I put both bags of granola into the cart next to the Cocoa Krispies. "We're busy, and this is easy."

"You know what's easy? Brisket. Just pop it in the oven for a couple of hours. Or pork loin. Put a pork loin in a slow cooker."

It's like he's speaking another language. "I don't think we have one of those."

"An oven?"

"Funny."

"I tell you what, you invite me over some night and I'll cook you something. I make a mean set of spare ribs."

"That sounds like a line."

"A line would be me telling you I make a mean French toast." Dominic leans in. "Which, by the way, I do."

"What's this all about, anyway?" I ask.

"I thought it was witty banter."

"No. I mean all of this. You and me."

"There's a you and me?" he asks, leaning on my cart with his wolf smile in full effect.

"You know what I mean. Chatting me up, writing on my locker—"

"When was I chatting you up?"

"Right now as a for instance. And then trying to get me to come out of chemistry class."

He looks confused for a moment, and then he says, "Oh, that. I wasn't waving to you."

Immediately my cheeks are turning pink and warm: my stupid body betraying me.

"I mean, I did wave at you once you saw me, but I wasn't trying to get you to come out of class. I've got a"—he pauses—"a friend in that class."

"Who?" I demand.

"Never mind."

"Yeah, right. I'm sure you've got lots of friends in AP Chem."

He smirks. "You don't think I'm smart enough to have friends who take AP classes?"

"It doesn't seem like your circle, that's all."

"Maybe I don't believe in the narrow boxes of the typical high school experience."

"You don't have to believe in them, but they're there."

"Says you."

I frown.

"You know, if you want me to come and get you out of class, I can."

"You wish." Not a witty comeback, but I'm unnerved by him—his smile, of course, but also the casual way his body leans into mine. I turn away from him, hoping my face isn't too pink, but I know I am flushed all over. His hand is right next to mine on the shopping cart handle, our pinkies touching. My mother chooses that moment to come around the corner. Her peasant skirt is trailing behind her and she's holding a box of Twinkies. She looks at Dominic and she looks at me and then she looks at Dominic again and a slow smile spreads across her lips. "Why hello," she says.

"Hello," Dominic replies without moving his hand off of the shopping cart.

"I'm Annaliese Woodruff," she introduces herself.

"I know," he says. "Very's mother. I'm Dominic Meyers."

"Are you a friend of Very's from school?" she asks. Nicely played, Mom.

Dominic turns to me. "I don't know, Very. Am I?"

"We have English together," I say.

"How nice," Mom says. "You know I had Ms. Staples, too. She was practically a brand-new teacher back then."

"You did?" I ask.

"Didn't I ever tell you that? We didn't start off on the right foot. It was my fault. I walked into that classroom and before she even said a word I told her my name and that she shouldn't expect me to write any poetry ever. She told me that was a shame. And I said it's not like poetry was genetic. And she said, I'll always remember this, 'Of course not. But it is bloody. And it is essential. Everyone should try it at least once.'"

"So did you?" Dominic asks.

"Did I what?"

"Try poetry."

My mom cocks her head to the side. "Never."

"Never too late, right?" Dominic asks her, and gives her a softer version of his wolf smile, which of course she just eats up.

"You're right. Though I think you're better off working on Very. Get her to try writing poetry, maybe make a little art."

Dominic looks at me with eyebrows raised. "Something tells me that she'd be just as stubborn about it as you were."

This makes my mom laugh. Not a belly laugh, but a tinkling, trilling laugh. She says, "Oh, Very and I aren't much alike." She looks him up and down. "But then, girls are ever-changeable, aren't they?"

"I can't say I've ever tried," Dominic replies.

"Oh, but you ought to. Everybody should try it at least once."

"Mom."

She shrugs.

"Well, I should get back to the meat," Dominic says.

"Do you cater?" she asks him.

"Me or the store?"

"Either." She's still holding the Twinkies in one hand.

"The store doesn't, and I've never thought about it before. I was just telling Very that I'm a whiz in the kitchen. Maybe with her help I could whip something up for you."

"It's a college event, and I haven't been too happy with the company we've been using."

"Mom."

"Right. It was nice meeting you," my mom tells him. She holds out her hand. I half expect him to take it and give it a kiss, but he just shakes it. Mom looks at his hand, his face, then back at me, and then she, honest to God, gives me a wink, which of course he can see. "I'll be in the next aisle. When you're ready."

We watch her push the cart away, and I expect him to say good-bye and head back to the meat section, but instead he says, "Hey, are you going to the party Saturday?"

The party. My mom's party? "Whose party do you mean?"

"I don't know. Nobody's party. Everybody's party. Up in the woods behind the ice rink."

"Well, that's a dumb place for a party. It's bound to get broken up."

He gives me a funny look. "There's a party there every year at the start of school. Everyone goes."

Not everyone, evidently. "I hadn't really decided."

"You should go. It'll be cool."

"Are you asking me to go with you?" I ask. He laughs, but I say, "Because I have a boyfriend, you know."

"Christian Yoo, right? Bring him along."

"Maybe I'll talk to him and see if he wants to go."

"You do that."

I can tell he doesn't believe me. "Or maybe I'll just go on my own."

He raises his eyebrows. "Good. I'll see you there."

"Okay," I agree.

He grins and shakes his head. He's probably figuring I'll never show, and he's probably right. A party up in the woods doesn't sound like a good time to me, and anyway, I need to help with my mom's art-department shindig. "I need to finish my shopping."

But before I can go, he takes a step closer and says, "You, me, brisket."

"I prefer French toast," I tell him.

And for the first time, I end the conversation with the upper hand.

Mom of course cannot let the appearance of Dominic slide. I try to distract her by asking her about the Twinkies, and this works momentarily. "Lard!" she exclaims. "Did you know that the filling is made with lard? It says 'animal shortening,' but I can read between the lines." She shakes her head as if disgusted, but throws the box in the cart all the same.

Ramona appears carrying the rainbow sprinkles, a notebook with a kitten on the front, and a bag of frozen mangoes. "We should make smoothies," she says.

"We should. Do you know Very's friend who works here?" Mom asks.

Ramona looks around. "Britta works here? Or Grace?"

"A boy. Dominic."

"Dominic Meyers?"

Mom looks at me. "We need to get going," I say.

She manages to keep quiet while we check out, but as I drive us home, she reclines in the passenger seat and peppers me with questions about Dominic. Who he is and where he lives and how long I've known him and what he says in English class and doesn't he have a devious smile, but in a good way. Mom puts her feet on the dashboard and begins to pluck the stem and leaves from an oversize strawberry. "Tell me about him, Ramona."

"Ramona doesn't know him," I say.

"I know *of* him."

I imagine her telling Mom about Dominic's side job selling pot. She could tell Mom about the graffiti on my locker. She could tell her how he cuts class and hangs out in the library. She could tell her any number of things, but all she says is, "He seems nice enough. He's a good artist, too. I hear he's wicked smart."

I've never heard this about him, but hearing Ramona say it, I realize it's probably true.

Mom turns around in her seat to look at Ramona. "Book-smart or smart-smart?"

"He reads a lot, but I think he's more smart-smart."

"What's the difference?" I ask.

"The difference?" Mom replies. "The difference is everything. I'm certainly glad to hear he's smart-smart. That's what you need in your life."

"Am I not smart-smart?" I ask.

"Oh, of course you are."

"You're more book-smart," Ramona says.

"You're both, Smart One. Don't worry about it."

"I don't know why you're making such a big deal out of this. It was just me talking to a guy I know from school."

Ramona digs through one of the grocery bags. "It's not a big deal. It's just, you know, I've never seen you interested in, like, reaching out before."

"What's that supposed to mean?"

"Just what I said. You've got your friends, and you stick with them." She pulls the sprinkles out of the bag and gives them a gentle shake. It's a neutral thing to say—most people, after all, have their friends and stick with them—but the way she says it makes it seem like an insult. "Dominic Meyers doesn't seem like your kind of person."

"What kind of person is that?" I ask, as if I hadn't just challenged Dominic with the same argument.

"You're just you, Very. That's all."

That's all.

And in that moment, I decide I'm going to that party.

six

i.

OVER THE WEEK, THE sculpture grows. Each day I note the changes. The bottle caps are closest together in the lowest right-hand corner of the garage—the one nearest the front of the house—then spread out so they look like points on a scatter graph. There are some aluminum cans, too, cut open and splayed out, though they peel back from the wall like birds' wings. Some are label up, but others show their silvery insides. Most of those are on the bottom of the garage, layered on one another and the building like shingles, with a few bending around to the front of the house. When the sun hits them, the glare is intense.

Wednesday, stems of copper pipe twist from the ground up the side of the house, stiff as toy soldiers. It is a false step, I think, these harsh lines against the soft contours of the rest of the piece, but by Thursday, they have been moved back against the garage, and their arcs have been taken in by the curves of the sculpture.

A bird begins building a nest inside one of the crooks, weaving the sticks through with yarn.

And all the while, more and more and more bottle caps. They are growing into clusters. Hundreds of them. Where do they all come from?

Britta says that soon the artist will slip up and leave some salient detail, but I hope he won't. Maybe it's Dominic, and maybe it isn't, but I think that once we know one way or the other, the sculpture will stop. The mystery is as much the point as the piece itself.

Grace still thinks we should have a stakeout. "I'm going to wear a beret and dark sunglasses and be incognito as an artiste."

The pace of the development seems to be gaining. It's like the bigger it gets the faster it can change: an exponential function. It's living things that usually chart that way. Yeast expanding or a field of flowers blooming. And so it seems that the sculpture, too, is not so much being constructed as being cultivated, the gardener in shadows.

ii.

Only four people are allowed to sit at each table in the library. Ms. Blythe has semipatiently explained to us more than once that there have been actual studies done that show that productivity goes down and volume goes up once you get more than four students together at a library table. So we clump together on the floor on the far side of the stacks, by floor-to-ceiling windows that look out over the playing fields.

Christian and I have our chemistry problem set out, Britta is working on her early-action essay for Brown, and Grace and Josh are supposed to be working on Chinese. Only they each grabbed a copy of this Christian teen magazine that the library subscribes to. It sits on the shelf between *Teen People* and *Fish & Game*. Grace laughs. "Okay, so this girl writes in that her boyfriend keeps pressuring her to have sex. She doesn't want to lose him, but she knows it would be wrong to give in and have premarital sex."

Next to me, Christian regrips his pencil. We still haven't had sex since he came back. Maybe he discovered the Bible while he was up at his lake house.

"And?" Britta prompts.

"Well, their advice: 'This young man has been led off of the Lord's path and now he's trying to take you with him. You've done the right thing by resisting. Now, try to help him. Invite him to youth group meetings at your church or offer to read the Bible with him. If he's strayed too far, you might not be able to help him. Leave him to fall into the hands of our Lord, Jesus Christ. Remember: God is always testing us. If you give in to this boy, you will fail God's test.'"

"That'll go over well," I say. "No sex, thanks, let's read some scripture instead."

"I'm sure he'd respect her decision if he really loved her," Christian says.

Does Christian think I don't want to have sex with him? I sort of tried that night we were studying in the basement, but he was focused on trying to get me to go to Minnesota with him, and anyway, I doubt he would ever do it when his parents were home. We could go to my house. Dad's never around, and Mom is always on the couch or in her studio.

Josh interrupts my thoughts. "Not a chance."

The problem with my house is Nonnie. Not that she'd care that I was having sex. It's just that it's hard to be home without wanting to be with her.

Outside, someone is walking across the field in faded jeans and black boots. Dominic.

"Where's that hoodlum going?" Christian asks.

"He's not—" I start to say. But maybe I shouldn't draw attention to my friendship, or whatever it is, with Dominic. "Wait, am I doing this right?"

"Hold up," Josh says. "Did you honestly just use the word *hoodlum*? What is this, 1953?"

"Hoodlum. It's a word."

"Are we going to the soda counter after school? Maybe to a sock hop?"

"It's a word."

"So is *greaser*. But I'm not saying, 'Hey, look, there goes that greaser Dominic Meyers cutting class again.'"

Britta looks out the window. "You don't know that he's cutting class."

"Sure. He's just heading out across the field as part of an independent study," Christian says.

"I have the elements all lined up, I think, but it doesn't look right." I slide my notebook over toward Christian.

"An independent study in economics," Josh snickers. "You know, supply and demand, price points, that sort of thing."

Christian laughs.

"Knock it off, guys," I say.

"What?" Josh asks. "He can't even hear us, seeing as he is outside and we are inside."

"What happened to hall-monitor Very? You were ready to bust him on the first day of school," Christian reminds me, but it doesn't feel like a joke anymore.

"If you guys don't start focusing, Britta's not going to get her essay done and she won't get into Brown, and I won't pass chemistry, and I won't get in anywhere, even with Mr. Tompkins's punny recommendations."

"Sorry," Christian murmurs.

"Right, Grace," Josh says. "Let's get back to this Chinese stuff."

"By the way, my parents were wondering if you were going to come to Minnesota with us or not."

"Oh . . . I haven't really had a chance to think about it."

"Hey, Very, isn't that your sister?" Josh asks.

"No, she has art right now," I say. But as I look over my shoulder, back through the stacks, I see Ramona sitting in one of the carrels. She has a couple volumes of *Encyclopaedia Britannica* in front of her and is carefully tearing out pages. "Oh crap," I mutter.

"What's she doing?" Christian asks.

"Oh man, is she a little cuckoo for Cocoa Puffs?" Josh asks. "That is so sexy. Is she seeing anyone?"

"You know, 'crazy' isn't usually at the top of the list of things to look for in a potential girlfriend," Grace tells him.

"Do you think you should go talk to her?" Britta asks me.

"Yeah," I say, still watching Ramona. She has a small pile of pages in front of her. Grace taps my back as if pushing a button to start me walking toward Ramona. "Stop," I hiss when I get to the study carrel.

Ramona looks up and doesn't seem surprised—nor does she stop. With a raspy *shriffft* she tears out a page from the *V* volume.

"You can't do that," I say.

"Nobody will even notice," she replies.

"It's a library book."

"At least I'm using it."

"This isn't using; this is destroying."

"You should have seen the dust on these. No one has touched them in years." She adds the page to her stack before closing the volume and picking up another. "I'm saving them."

"It's vandalism."

"That's your opinion," she says.

"No, I'm pretty sure that's a fact. Hey, you've got the *V* volume right there. Why don't we look it up?"

"Your friends are staring at us."

I look over my shoulder. Grace lifts up her magazine, and

Christian tugs on Josh's shirtsleeve, but Britta keeps looking right at us. "Stop," I say again.

"Don't worry, Very. It won't rub off."

"What are you talking about?"

She pushes the books to the back of the carrel and picks up her stack of pages, which she shoves into her bag. Sidestepping me, she says, "See you later." And that is that. I pick up the encyclopedias and put them back on the shelf, right where they belong.

"What just happened?" Josh asks when I get back to them.

"Nothing. I don't know." My face is hot, and I am sure the whole library is watching us. Ms. Blythe will be coming around the corner any minute, and I'll have to try to explain something that has no explanation.

Christian takes my hand in his and gives it a squeeze. "What did she say?"

"She said she was using them."

"Maybe it was an art project. Mr. Solloway loves that sort of thing," Grace suggests.

"Right," Britta agrees. "And it's possible that Ms. Blythe actually set those books aside for kids to use. You know, old books she was going to get rid of anyway."

"And Ramona was probably just messing with you, letting you think she was actually tearing up a library book," Grace finishes for her.

"Exactly," Christian says, giving it a stamp of finality. "It was just Ramona being Ramona. It was nothing."

"It sure didn't seem like nothing to me," Josh says.

"Drop it," Grace tells him.

And for once he does.

In the car that afternoon Ramona doesn't mention it and neither do I. I think about telling Mom, but when we get inside she's up in her studio actually working, and I don't want to disturb her. Anyway, everyone said it was nothing. Everyone except Josh, who, let's face it, is not the best judge for this sort of thing. So it's nothing. Just Ramona being Ramona and messing with me.

She slips out the back door and makes her way across the lawn, where she disappears into a stand of trees, as nimble and insubstantial as the pixie she was in Nonnie's poem.

iii.

Britta, Grace, and I are in Mr. Tompkins's room after school, making posters for the peer counseling group's Wellness Fair. We've been here for an hour already and the halls are silent. Even Mr. Tompkins is leaving, and he's our club adviser. First, though, he tells me some more about Professor Singh, and asks if I've read any of her articles. "Working on them," I tell him, not exactly truthfully.

He smiles and says good-bye. "Just shut the door when you're done. It'll lock behind you." He claims he needs to get ready for hiking one of the four-thousand-footers tomorrow.

"Total lie," Grace says once he's gone. "He has a date tonight. I can smell it on him. I wonder what kind of girl he dates."

"Not seventeen-year-old students," Britta says.

"The age of consent in New Hampshire is sixteen."

"Good to know you've done your research. So tell me, what is the average length of jail time for a teacher who has sex with a student?"

Outside the window, someone laughs, loud and uncontrolled. I am writing the list of the groups that are coming on a big sheet of blue poster board.

"It's too bad they wouldn't let us have Planned Parenthood come. Or at least someone who would give out condoms."

"Yeah, that would go over real well," Britta says. *Local school gives out condoms, story at eleven.*"

"Hey, you're the one who wants to get into Brown. Spearheading a campaign to bring birth control to your peers seems like something they would love." Grace leans back from her own poster. It's a giant heart and the words *Love Your Body* in curly script.

"Do you guys know about that party tomorrow night?" I ask.

"Whose party?" Britta asks.

"Nobody's party, I guess. It's just out in the woods."

"Oh, one of those crazy keggers," Grace says.

"You know about it?" I ask.

"Well, maybe not specifically that one, but I know people have them out there from time to time. Back by the skating rink, right?"

"How stupid is that?" Britta asks.

"I know, right?" I say. "It's like flashing a light and saying, 'Police! Come arrest us for underage drinking!'"

"Freezing your ass off and drinking cheap beer," Grace says. "No, thanks."

"It's weird that we weren't invited, though, don't you think?" I ask.

"It's not an invitation type of party, Very," Grace says. She sees me writing *Hartley's Homeopathic Healing* and adds, "Ugh. My mom took me there once. They gave me these pills that were the size of grape tomatoes and they always broke in my mouth and were all oily."

"Do you even want to go?" Britta asks me.

"My grandmother thinks I need to get out more. Mom, too."

"Well, your grandmother is dying—" Grace begins.

"Grace!" Britta interrupts.

"What. She is. Your grandmother doesn't have much time left, so she's all carpe diem, and your mom, well, she's your mom."

"Meaning?" I ask.

"Vicarious reenactment? I don't know. I just know she's the only adult who likes me better than Britta and it's because I curse like a fucking sailor."

"It's true," Britta says. "Trust me. You don't want to go to that party. Why don't we all go to my house and have an eighties moviefest instead. Some Brat Pack or maybe *The Princess Bride*."

"Something from this century, and I'm in," Grace says.

"There is no one of our generation who holds a candle to Ally Sheedy or Molly Ringwald."

"Ally and Molly don't interest me," Grace says. "And the boys in those movies have the worst clothes. Popped collars? It's like the whole decade was filled with douches."

"That sounds fun," I say. "I should be with Nonnie, though. And anyway, my mom has her art-department party."

"Didn't you just say she wants you to get out more?" Britta asks me.

A girls' movie night is exactly what both my mom and Nonnie don't want for me.

"Or we could come be waitresses with you," Grace suggests.

"The boys who major in art are woeful, Grace," I tell her. "They're so full of—feelings."

"I'm just trying to help." She's looking down at her poster and adding block letters that read *EHS WELLNESS FAIR*. "Be a good old chap and all that jazz."

"I know."

"Especially since, well, I'm not saying she's useless, but Ramona is probably going to be useless, right?"

"Are you going to talk to her about the library?" Britta asks as she shuffles through her papers, double-checking everything.

"I thought you said it was nothing."

"It *is* nothing," Grace interrupts. "How's this look?" She holds up her poster. The heart is lusciously red.

"Great." I check the time on my cell phone. "I have to go,

actually. I need to bring Nonnie in for a haircut."

"No problem," Grace says. "We've got this. Next up I am going to do Georgia O'Keeffe–style wavy lines. Subliminal messaging. This is going to be the most popular Wellness Fair ever."

"Good luck with that," I say.

"See you tomorrow night?"

"Maybe," I say. "If I can get out of my mom's art-department party."

"You could tell her you were going to a crazy party," Britta says. "Then you can just come and watch movies with us. Everyone wins."

"You're the tiebreaker," Grace says. "Please do not subject me to a night of girls weeping over power ballads."

"I'll see what I can do," I say.

"Love you, Very," Grace calls as I'm heading out the door.

"Love you, too," I call back.

iv.

When I get up to Nonnie's room, she is sitting in her wingback chair wearing her black pants and a white T-shirt. She's put on lipstick, red, of course, and has mostly stayed within the lines of her lips, though it does bleed out into the cracks and wrinkles that surround her mouth. "Looking good, Nonnie."

"We do have our big outing today." She sniffs. "I would have gone on my own but I don't trust myself on the stairs. I'm not going out of this world by falling down a set of garage stairs." She holds out her hand so I can help her to her feet. "And it would be even worse if I fell and *didn't* snap my neck. Good God, I could be laid up in the hospital with a broken hip like a real old lady. I'd probably get stuck with a ghastly roommate who wants to share Crock-Pot recipes with me."

"That's a very specific fear, Nonnie."

Her fingers press hard into my flesh, she's so unsteady on her feet. I push open the door and she regards the stairs that go down to the garage, wooden and open. For sure she can read my thoughts because she says, "There are no bedrooms on the first floor of the house and I'm not going to set up one of those rental hospital beds in the den."

"You could use my dad's office," I tell her. "You know he offered. He said he could take some of his stuff to the college and box up the rest."

"Dallas," she says, shaking her head. "Thanks, but no thanks. I don't want to be stuck surrounded by all those concert posters and album covers. I will stay up here in my garret. And when it all gets to be too much, I'll pitch myself off this landing."

"It might not work. You might wind up with that snoring Crock-Pot-cooking roommate in the hospital." I say this but all the same I'm picturing her broken body on the floor of the garage and I shiver.

It takes us several minutes to get down the stairs. She's

embarrassed. I can tell because she isn't saying anything and she's always saying something. Once onto the concrete floor of the garage, we walk across to the door. I open it for her and she lets go of my arm before stepping out into the sunshine.

I reach for her arm and start guiding her toward my car, but she tugs me around the side of the house to see the bottle cap mural. It has evolved again, and the evening sun makes it sparkle.

"I can't decide if it's beautiful or ugly," I say.

"That is my favorite state, that tipping point between the gorgeous and the grotesque." She leans closer to it. "Your mother asked if we could take it down, but I told her no."

"Why not?"

"Because it's mine."

I look at the ground. Maybe. Or maybe it's mine. And I don't want it taken down, either, I realize. "I guess it's not doing any harm," I say.

She looks at it a moment longer, then says, "I can't go around town in a subcompact. We'll take my car. You'll drive."

Nonnie has a sky-blue Sunbeam Rapier with a soft top. "Your car *is* a subcompact."

"My car is British," she replies, as if that makes all the difference. "The keys are upstairs. I'll get myself situated."

I open the passenger-side door as wide as it goes. There's plenty of room for her to navigate around to the door since Dad's car isn't in its spot in the middle garage bay.

I run up to her room and find the keys on a dresser next

to a picture of Nonnie dressed in safari clothes leaning against a truck and holding a monkey. It's from a photo shoot for an article she did for *Vanity Fair*. She called the monkey Nietzsche and wanted to bring it home, but was told she wouldn't be able to get it through customs.

Downstairs she is sitting in the front passenger seat with her hands folded in her lap. It makes me feel a bit like hired help.

I slide into the driver's seat. I need to let the seat back a few clicks, and then it feels comfortable, like I've been driving it for years. "I'm not the best on stick shift," I tell her.

"Neither was I."

I get the car started and drop it into reverse, and we lurch out of the garage. When I put it into first and try to start, I stall.

"It's a tricky clutch," she says. "You've got to push it in all the way and then ease it out nice and slow. It senses fear."

My second try I get it and we cruise down the driveway and turn onto the road that snakes down the hill to town.

"I was going to leave this car to you, but you might as well take it now. You don't need to be driving around in that tin box anymore."

"Really?" I ask. I turn to look at her and hitch the steering wheel. Nonnie grabs on to the door handle.

"If we make it back alive I'll sell it to you for a dollar so you don't have to pay the estate tax on it."

"Nonnie, don't talk like that."

"A thank-you will suffice."

"Thank you."

I take us to the salon in Essex's lone strip mall: A Cut Above. The salon's owner is Carl and he's been cutting Nonnie's hair since she moved to Essex. When we come in the door, he throws his hands up like a southern preacher and says, "Imogene, what have you done to your hair?"

"Nothing," she says.

"I can see that."

He spins a chair around for her and I help her step up into it. Her body relaxes as she sits.

He turns to me. "Veronica, Veronica, let me see who's free for you."

"Oh, I don't need a haircut," I tell him.

He raises his eyebrows but says nothing.

I take the empty seat next to Carl's chair and spin it around to look out the window so I can watch the people in the parking lot. It's funny how many I don't know. In a town this small, you'd think I'd know all of them. Maybe that's my problem. Maybe Ramona is right and I stay cloistered away in my own small world.

Carl holds Nonnie by the arm. I can see just how thin her hair has become: downy like a baby's.

"Actually," I say. "Actually I've changed my mind. I do need a cut."

Carl grins and beckons over a woman with purple hair and a tattoo of Mary Poppins on her bicep. She looks at my long, limp hair as if she feels sorry for it.

"Cut it all off."

"How short?" She put her fingertips on my head and turns it from side to side.

"All of it."

She put her hands at my shoulders.

I shake my head. "I want it short-short."

"A pixie cut?"

"Yes."

"You're sure?"

"Yes. It's time for a change."

"Well, there's change and then there's change. And let me tell you that I am one hundred percent on board with this because this length"—she flicks the ends of my hair—"is doing nothing for you. But I've got to be sure because I can't tell you how many women come in here, maybe after a breakup?" She hesitates to give me time to fill her in, but I don't. "So I do what they say and then I've got this woman crying in my chair because she loved her hair and it's the guy she hates. And then she hates me."

"Do it," I say.

Nonnie says, "Really, Veronica?"

"Solidarity, Nonnie. Who knows, if you end up losing all your hair again, maybe I'll shave my head, too."

"Ghastly thought," she says, but she's smiling.

The Mary Poppins girl works quickly. She braids my hair, chops it off for Locks of Love, and then comes at me not with scissors but with an electric razor.

When we're done, we sit side by side and look at ourselves in the mirror. Nonnie looks younger: like a baby chick. I look older, and I fear it's in a soccer-mom sort of a way. The bruise is still there, a yellow echo of itself.

I reach up and feel the short hairs at the nape of my neck.

"I was about your age when I cut my hair," Nonnie says. "Right before I moved to New York I went and got my hair cut just like this. I wanted to look like Jean Seberg, the girl in *Breathless*."

She's told me this before: another sign of her dwindling mind, this repeating of stories. I still haven't looked up the actress.

"You look more like her than I ever did, Very," she says. "Though you're much taller, of course."

When we step outside, it's like my entire head is more alive. It's not just that I can feel more, though that is true, but I can hear more. I run my hand along the back of my prickly neck and get a chill. I feel more powerful, like the hair was weighing me down and now I am free to fly anywhere I choose. So where do I go?

v.

"We could go to the beach," Nonnie says, her hand trailing out the window.

My eyes shift to the clock. It's six thirty already.

"I remember going to the beach with my mother. We'd go once a summer. We'd drive to Maryland and stay one night in a motel. All my friends thought it was quite posh. We'd spend all day at the beach and we'd eat sandwiches that Mama had packed the day before so they were squished and soggy. I remember lying on my back in the sun. I had a blue bathing suit with white polka dots. Mama would get me a lollipop and I'd stare at the sky while I sucked, trying to see how long I could keep my eyes open against the bright sky." She's looking out the window at her hand, twisting her wrist.

"It's getting kind of late, Nonnie. I don't know if we have time for the beach today."

She murmurs something, but it's lost to the wind. Then she pulls her hand back inside and folds it with the other one on her lap.

"You never talk about Mom when she was a kid."

"What's to say? She was a fat baby who grew into a beautiful girl. She had friends. She had admirers. She hated me when I moved her here."

"Did you ever take her to the beach and have lollipops?"

She glances at me. "You know, I don't think we ever did."

We reach a fork that would lead us to our road, but instead I go left and ease onto the highway, jarring and shaking through third and fourth gear before hitting a steady pace in fifth. My eyes flit from the tachometer to the road to my hand on the gear shift. Dad taught me how to drive standard last summer, in his old Volvo. We went to one of the parking lots on campus, and he sat with his feet out the window, aviator sunglasses covering his eyes. "It's important that you can drive a stick, Very. It's important for every girl. You never want to get stuck someplace because you can't drive the escape vehicle." And so we lurched through the parking lot while Dad hummed "Casey Jones" by the Grateful Dead and occasionally offered advice, all of which could be boiled down to *ease up*. Ease up on the clutch. Ease up on the gas. Ease up on yourself. When I finally got the hang of it, I drove us out of the parking lot to the ice-cream place in the old train station.

Nonnie says, "Remember when we tried to go to Canada?"

"I do!" Finally someone else shares my memories. "We stayed in that awful motel."

"That's the type of place Mama and I used to stay."

My cheeks get hot, but Nonnie doesn't seem put off by my comment. Instead she says, "Your mother wanted to go anyway. Just leave us there and get on the ferry."

I glance at her and back at the road. "That doesn't make a lot of sense. What would she have done in Nova Scotia on her own?"

Nonnie looks at me as if she can't quite believe what I've asked. "I suppose you've never known the joy of traveling alone, of just setting out to see where you land. Talking to strangers. Never sure where you'll spend the night."

It sounds, as Nonnie herself would say, ghastly.

With a deep breath, I head into the traffic circle. And stall. I push the clutch in and out and I'm trying to move the gear-shift, but it just won't seem to go. My body begins to sweat with humiliation.

The car behind me honks, and Nonnie turns around and

actually shakes her fist in the air at the driver, which, for some reason, makes me laugh hysterically. Nonnie says, "Just ease it out."

Ease up.

I do, and soon we're rolling again, off of the highway and onto the long, twisting road that leads out toward the ocean. The speed limit is only thirty-five, so I keep it in third gear, even if the RPMs are up a little high. We bounce over the wooden bridge that crosses the salt marsh, and then the ocean is in view: dark and roiling under the pale blue sky. The scent of the sea comes in through our windows and we each take a deep, full breath.

I park in the lot with just a few other cars. The sun is start-ing to head down, but it's still bright and warm. Nonnie tucks her sweater around her more tightly, though, as we make our way to the concrete wall that separates the lot from the ocean.

I'm heading for the stairs down to the beach, but Nonnie stops and leans forward against the wall.

The wind is cool against my neck and I find myself touching my skin again, the hint of hair that remains.

Nonnie says, "The first time I saw the ocean, I was afraid. It looked like a live thing to me as a child. A monster. The way it churned and rolled and frothed." She holds one hand out in front of her as if reaching for the cold water. "People who know the water say you can never really trust it. Fishermen don't even bother to learn to swim. They know there's no use. Not out there."

I run my palms against the rough concrete. "Well, couldn't they hold themselves afloat at least until their friends could come back and get them?"

"Not with all their heavy gear on. In Ireland the wives knit a pattern into the sweater so they can be identified when they wash up onto the shore. I put that into a poem once. All about the knitting. I even learned to knit for it, though I was never any good, always getting my yarn tangled and dropping stitches."

Out at the edge of the water a man is throwing a tennis ball into the waves for his dog. The dog races out and brings it back, shaking and panting with excitement. Nothing could make that dog happier than to run into the freezing water and get the ball, drop it at his master's feet, and do it all over and over again.

"You're going to be okay," she tells me.

I look down at the concrete. Names are etched into the paint. *Roz and Billy 4eva, Aimee wuz here, Charlie, SBJ, Tokyo!* They wrote it to assert their thereness, to prove their existence. *I was here. I was here. I was here.* It won't take long for the sun, wind, and sea spray to wash them away, if there's not a fresh coat of paint put on first.

"When I'm gone, you're going to be okay."

"Nonnie—"

"It's not a question, Very. Not a hypothetical, someday down the road. You are going to be okay. That makes me feel better. Ramona and your mother . . ." She shakes her head.

"Ramona," I say, letting her name slip out between my lips like a curse.

"She's not like you," Nonnie says.

I roll my eyes. "I know. She's the creative one."

Nonnie puts her hand on top of mine. "I mean that she can't look at a problem head-on and just take it as it comes. Like those waves. She can't dive right into them like you do. She has to come at things sideways."

"You mean she's avoiding the whole situation."

"The pain . . . that is, if she looked at it straight—" Nonnie begins, but then seems to reconsider it. "Just give her a little time. A little space."

I turn to look at her and she's staring right at me with the most open expression I've ever seen on her face. Her eyes are begging me. I look away. "We should get you home."

I steal glances at her as I drive. Her eyes close. A few miles more and her mouth is open a touch. Her breath comes in wheezes that sound like a kitten just learning to breathe.

seven

i.

EVERY YEAR MY MOM hosts a cocktail party for the visiting artist, and every year Ramona and I are conscripted into service. This year it's no surprise that Ramona is nowhere to be found when we are preparing for the party. On my own I empty six cans of juice into a punch bowl and add peach slices and rum. I arrange a cheese platter. I place piles of cocktail napkins around the lower level of the house, each pile spun into a fan. I am Cinderella, except instead of being banished to the ashes from which I long to escape, I'll be expected to make small talk with my mom's colleagues. First, they will ask me what my college plans are. They've been asking me this since I started high school, and this should finally be the year that I have an answer for them. But I have none. MIT with Professor Singh. That would make Mr. Tompkins happy, and I'd be relatively close for Nonnie. Minnesota with Christian. Stanford is still pulling me. Then there's that school with the funny name in Southern California. Of course I could tell the people any one of these things and they would coo and tell me that I'm so lucky, a smart girl with the whole world in front of me, and I'll have to smile and say, "Gee, thanks."

Or they will ask me what I thought about the art, and I'll wish to be back on the college conversation.

All in all, Cinderella didn't realize how good she had it.

But this year I'm not sticking around. I've got my own party to attend. One without crudités. Or napkins.

My phone buzzes. It's Christian. **Want to go see a movie or something?**

My fingers hover above the screen of my phone, and then I type: **My mom's party is tonight. Remember?**

It's not a lie, exactly. It's the same excuse I used with Britta and Grace.

Mom is stretched out on the sofa with an empty glass resting on her stomach when I come into the sunken living room to check the levels of booze in the bar cart. She has a washcloth across her eyes.

"It's getting late," I say softly.

"Mmm."

"I think I've got it all set," I tell her. "Just checking the liquor in here."

"Mmm," she repeats. Then she blinks her eyes. "Nice haircut." She closes them again.

"Are you sure you're going to be okay?" I ask.

Finally she pulls the washcloth off of her eyes. "I'm just puffy, is all. Puffy and congested. This house . . ." She shakes her head as her voice trails off.

"You look fine," I say, though in fact, she does look a bit puffy.

"I do wish Nonnie had let me take the bottle caps and the rest of that mess off the garage."

"She likes them. What's the harm?"

She looks at me and it's like she's too exhausted to even try to explain. "Fix me a drink?"

I look at her disheveled hair and the wet ring mark the glass left on her dress. "You need to get dressed, Mom. Why don't you wait for your guests? I'll have that punch you like ready by then."

She sits up and runs her fingers through her hair. Her lips are pursed, like when Ramona and I got in trouble when we were little and she was deciding what our punishment ought to be. "Okay." She stands, and is heading toward her stairs, but looks back over her shoulder. "Dallas is going to be late."

"Everything okay?"

"Something came up at work. An article he needs to write. Or read. I can't remember. And then there's some advisee in crisis."

"Well, I'll help as much as I can before I have to go. I haven't seen Ramona, but—"

"Where are you going again?"

"Just a party thing."

"With Christian?"

"It's not really a go-with-someone kind of a party."

As if she's scented something, she straightens. "Will that boy be there? The butcher boy?"

"Dominic? Oh, probably."

"Is that why you cut your hair off?"

"No."

"Well then," is all she says. But a moment later she calls down the stairs in a singsongy voice: "The butcher, the baker, the candlestick maker."

ii.

The first guest to arrive is Olivia Knotts. She's always the first to arrive. It's like she's still trying to prove herself. "Veronica! Your hair looks stunning!" she exclaims, and puts one hand on each of my shoulders, then stares right at my face.

"Hello, Olivia."

She rearranges the features on her face into a slight frown. "I'm so sorry to hear about your grandmother."

So the word has spread out from the English department through the rest of the college. "Thank you," I reply.

She finally lets her hands drop from my shoulders. "She was such a talented woman."

"She still is."

Olivia Knotts, though, will not be put off from her speech. "As a female artist myself, I found such inspiration in her very being."

In her very being. I'll have to remember that and tell Nonnie.

The door is wide-open and I can see more cars driving up.

"Now, how are your college applications coming along?"

"I'm still working things out. I've been thinking about MIT, maybe. Or Stanford. Or I hear there are some good schools in Minnesota."

"Minnesota!" she declares. "But don't overlook good old Essex College. We have some amazing programs, you know. But then, I remember being seventeen, ready to see the world, to soar up and free like an eagle from its cage." She stares at our ceiling, and I can't help but look over my shoulder to see if perhaps there really is an eagle there. All I see is a dusty cobweb.

From the next car I see Melora Wilkins with the dean of the college. Everyone knows they are together, though the arrangement—intellectual, merely physical, emotional, some combination thereof—has never been entirely clear. Nonnie always insists that he has a wife and family back in Iowa, where he used to teach.

Melora has the calm demeanor and soothing voice of a massage therapist. Still, I like her. She and the dean are walking straight toward us when she suddenly stops, cocking her head. It only takes me a second to realize what they are looking at.

Mom floats down the final three stairs from her wing. "Why hello, Olivia, how are you?"

"Wonderful," Olivia replies. "This morning I was working in my studio and it was like the clay just flowed from my fingers."

Mom, though, is looking past Olivia, through the open

door, to Melora and the dean, who stare at our garage. "Crap. I knew I should have gotten that cleaned up."

"Excuse me?" Olivia asks.

"It's nothing, Olivia. I just need to step outside for a moment."

She sidesteps Olivia and heads for the door. Given a choice between discussing the work of visiting artist Marcus Schmidt with Olivia Knotts and going outside to see how my mom handles the whole sculpture-on-the-garage thing, I choose outside with my mom.

"Fascinating," I hear Melora say as we walk up. Most of the side of the garage is covered now with bottle caps, aluminum cans, and pieces of broken glass that seem to undulate in the early-evening light. There is a slight gradation in color, darker at the bottom, and lighter at the top, like looking at a sunset, only the colors are all wrong. The copper poles sway slightly in the breeze, clacking their flowers together. "This is really different work for you, Annaliese."

"Oh, I didn't do this." Mom can't bury the hint of disgust in her voice.

"Really? Who is the artist, then? Did you have it commissioned?"

"Commissioned? No, I—" She looks from them to me.

"Actually," I say, "it's a piece of street art, like Banksy or the Guerrilla Girls. We believe it's a tribute to my grandmother."

Mom smiles at me thankfully. "Yes. It just showed up."

"You have no idea who created it?"

"None," Mom says.

"I find it interesting," Melora says.

"I'd say that interesting is the kiss of death in an art review," the dean says.

She nudges him with her elbow. "I need to contemplate it. It's holding my interest. Ergo: interesting." She takes a step back. "On the one hand, I like the use of refuse materials in the creation of something quite lovely. It's imaginative and fresh. And the craftsmanship is amazing. It's like the bottle caps are growing out of the stucco like moss. Manmade materials used to create something natural."

Ramona swings down from the old oak tree and comes to watch the crowd that is gathering. She sucks on the ends of her hair.

A few more professors and a handful of students join the group. They move around the sculpture in an elaborate dance. A step forward, a cross to the side, a few steps back. One of the students crouches down. But no one touches it, giving it the respect of a museum piece, at least for the time being.

It makes me feel exposed, as if, rather than looking at the sculpture, they are staring at some disfigurement of our family. I back away and into the garage through a side door, then up the stairs to Nonnie's. She is waiting in her black pants, white T-shirt, and man's suit coat. "I thought you were never going to come," she says. "I can hear them down there, nattering away about the sculpture." She reaches out her hand to me.

"Are you sure you want to go down there?" I ask.

She nods. "There's a ghastly wheelchair down in the garage. Grab that scarf, the pashmina, and we'll try to make me look respectable."

I help her down the stairs and into the wheelchair and arrange the scarf around her. As I am wheeling her out of the garage, a small black convertible snakes up the driveway, temporarily shifting attention away from the sculpture. The man who gets out of the car wears loafers without socks, white pants, and a tight black T-shirt. He all but screams *European!* It is, of course, Marcus Schmidt, the German painter of squares.

Melora goes to meet him and takes him by the arm. "Look at this curious piece of art that's appeared on Annaliese's wall. They have no notion of who the artist is."

Marcus lifts his sunglasses from his eyes and nestles them into his thick hair. "The artist is irrelevant. Only the art matters."

"Do you mean that?" Ramona asks.

He turns to look at her. "Yes, of course. Artists die. Art lives."

"So the motivation doesn't matter?" I ask. "Whether it's a need to be heard or a lust for fame or screaming to be understood?"

"You can want all of those things, but the world doesn't care."

"The world doesn't care about much, does it?" Ramona asks.

"As it should be." Marcus smiles. "The artist can't control how the world will see his work, and he shouldn't try. That's what makes art a living and breathing thing, instead of a print you buy to match your living room curtains. All that matters is what winds up on the canvas, or, in this case, the garage. Does it say something? How does it function?"

"What do you think of it, Marcus?" Melora asks.

He doesn't speak for a moment. "Trash on the wall. Simplistic composition."

This from a man who paints squares of color.

"The technique is primitive. Like arts and crafts. The colors are not what they seem. I appreciate this work."

And then everyone knows what to think.

"It's like Baroque with bottle caps."

"The juxtaposition of the beautiful and the profane is compelling."

"It's like a pointillist painting, with each bottle cap the dot of a brush."

"The glass lends an air of danger to an otherwise calm scene."

I wonder if they can hear themselves. I wonder if they realize how ridiculous they sound.

At least one other person sees the comedy: beside me, Nonnie's laughter rattles low like a car with exhaust problems. When the laugh turns over into a cough, Marcus Schmidt turns his head and the mask of cool slips from his face. His eyes grow wide and he leans in toward her. "Imogene Woodruff?" he asks. He says her name in a languid, sexy way: Im-ah-jean, so it almost sounds like *imagine.*

Nonnie nods as she tries to get ahold of her cough. "I am," she finally manages to say.

He crouches down beside her. "I know you have no patience for your admirers—a stance I understand, and indeed, I can relate to this problem, the fawning, blah blah—" He waves his hand in the air. "And yet I must declare myself a great admirer of yours. I try to paint the way you write, spare and unflinching."

Melora takes a step closer to listen to the conversation. Behind her, I see my mother, her eyes shifting between the bottle caps on the house and Marcus at Nonnie's feet.

"Go on," Nonnie says. With the pashmina blanket over her lap and me at her side like a sentry, she looks like she is holding court.

"You dig in, turn the thing around, try to show a new side? I dig in, deeper and deeper until I show only the smallest piece, the truth of it. You come at a thing straight, but I must come with a less direct perspective, you see?"

Nonnie considers this. "You remind me of Kandinsky," she tells him.

"His focus on geometry?"

"No. His flop of hair and full lips."

This makes Marcus laugh. "If you met him, you were a baby."

Melora places a hand on Marcus's shoulder but speaks to Nonnie. "It's so wonderful to see you up and about. We missed you at the gallery opening."

"Oh, Very told me all about it."

Melora looks surprised, but Marcus stands and reaches out

a hand to me. When we shake, he wraps his other hand on top of mine. "Yes, yes. I remember you. You had long hair. This is better. Very, what an unusual name."

"It's short for Veronica," my mother says. She has put on her party face again, bright smile, dancing eyes. Marcus lets my hand drop as he turns to her. "Over there is my other daughter, Ramona. I'm not sure where her sudden strand of nihilism came from."

"Annaliese!" he says warmly. "What a lovely family you have. This lovely family of women. I shall paint this family someday, I am sure."

I wonder what color square I will be.

The sun is nearly down now, and so I ask Nonnie, "Do you want me to bring you inside before I go?"

"You're leaving!" Marcus says. "But the party is just starting."

"Veronica has another party to attend. She's quite the social butterfly, this one." Mom's face looks the same, but her voice is edgy.

"Just something with some school friends."

Marcus puts his hands on my shoulders, then kisses each cheek. He smells like cloves. "I will chauffeur your grandmother into the house. You need not worry, Very, she is safe with me."

"There was a day when I would have been rather unsafe with you," Nonnie says.

"It is I who am in danger, Imogene."

He spins the chair around with ease and continues chatting

with Nonnie and Melora as they go into the main part of the house. I walk past my mother into the garage. When I back Nonnie's car out into the driveway, Mom is still standing there, alone.

iii.

It's dark by the time I arrive at the party, but not pitch-dark. I have no clue what time these sorts of things normally start, and I'm relieved to see that there are already a number of other people here. It wouldn't do much to upend my image as a dot-your-i's-and-cross-your-t's keener if I showed up as early to the party as I typically do to class.

I park my car in the row behind the ice rink and then make my way up through a smattering of trees to a clearing, leaves and sticks cracking underfoot. There's a small bonfire letting off a thin line of acrid smoke, and, a few feet off, a keg. People are milling around chatting—it's all very casual, like a backyard barbecue. I don't know what I expected. Scenes of Dionysian debauchery? Naked people running through the woods? I tighten my sweatshirt, tied around my waist by its sleeves, and scan the group for Dominic. He's not here. Not by the fire, not by the keg, and not in the clumps of people sprinkled around the clearing. Wonderful. He totally played me. I'm not sure what his reasoning was, but it was nicely done.

Then again, maybe he's just not here yet. He seems the

fashionably late type. So, I search for someone I know. Of course I know all of them: our school has only about five hundred students, and almost all of us have been here since kindergarten. But I'm looking for someone I consider an acquaintance. Someone respectable. Sitting on a rock by a fire is Brooks Weston, the flames making his blond hair seem orange. He's talking to Sadie Sayrebrook, a junior from my English and chem classes. With a deep breath to steady myself, I make my way over to the rock and say, "Hello."

"Oh, hey, Very," Brooks says, smiling warmly. "I didn't recognize you at first—"

"Your hair, oh my God, it's so cute!" Sadie reaches up and runs her hand through my hair.

"Thanks," I tell her.

"It's so cool that you came," Brooks tells me.

"Thanks," I say again. "I figured I would check it out."

"So what do you think of chem?" Sadie asks.

That's what people talk about at these kinds of parties? I mean, I don't know what I expected the topics of conversation to be, but certainly not school. I wrinkle my nose. "It's not exactly my strong suit, but I think it's a good class."

Sadie nods. "Yeah. Mr. Tompkins is a good teacher. That helps."

"Yeah," I agree lamely. "Plus I've got Christian to help me, which is like a lifesaver."

"Where is he anyway?" Sadie asks.

"Oh." I cough as if the smoke from the fire has entered my

lungs. "He has something else to do tonight. He's hoping he can stop by later."

"Cool," Sadie says.

"You don't have a drink," Brooks says. "Let me get you a beer."

"I'm not much of a drinker," I say before I even think about it. Stupid. I should just get a beer and hold on to it. Everyone else has a cup.

"That's cool," he says.

"All right," Sadie says, leaning in toward us, "I'm sure you are both sick of this question, but I just have to know where you are applying."

"You and half the world," Brooks says.

"It's the elephant at the zoo," I say.

Brooks raises his eyebrow, then turns his attention back to Sadie.

"I'm applying to Harvard—" Brooks begins.

"Of course," Sadie interrupts.

He ignores her and continues, "Harvard, Princeton, Yale, Dartmouth, and Cornell for my Ivies. And then some small schools, I haven't decided exactly which yet, but probably Colby. I went up to visit, and it was so chill. And then I guess I still need to figure out my safety school."

I try to tuck these names away in my head. Britta wants to know where he's applying. She has her heart set on Brown, and will be happy to hear he's not applying there, too, but I know she was also thinking about Princeton. She's convinced no school will accept both of them.

"What about you, Very? Still heading to Stanford?"

Last year a Stanford rep had come to visit our school, and Brooks and I had been the only juniors to attend. I'd been over-eager, showing up with my application already completed. I roll an acorn under my foot. All of that had been before Nonnie got sick. "It's still on my list, but I don't know. Mr. Tompkins is really pushing MIT, but I'm wondering if I want something smaller, like Carleton or, um—" I search my brain for the name of the math-and-science school in California that Christian had mentioned. "Harvey Mudd!"

"Nice," Brooks says, and I realize I could've rattled off a list of top schools from the *U.S. News and World Report* rankings and their response would've been the same.

"Of course I can't rule out good old Essex College," I say.

Sadie giggles, while Brooks chuckles and shakes his head.

"What?" I ask.

"You're not serious, are you?"

"I'm taking that math class there now, and it's pretty good."

Brooks stares into his beer. "Well, I guess everyone has to make their own choices."

"I guess so," I agree.

The bonfire's flames are growing tall and lean, reaching up into the night sky. The smoke blows away from us, back in the direction of the parking lot. Like something out of a romance novel, Dominic emerges from the cloud of smoke. When he sees me, his grin spreads across his face—crooked. He stops before he gets to me, which means I have to go to him. "Excuse me," I say to Sadie and Brooks. I wait a moment before I turn and walk over to Dominic. I know they're watching me. I'm sure of it. And if they are watching me, then they are curious, but for once I don't care. The thrill of it—of not caring, of belying people's expectations—courses through my body.

"You came," he says.

"I said I would."

"Good to know you're a woman of your word." He reaches out and traces the side of my face where the yellowing bruise lingers. "I like the haircut," he tells me. He looks down at my empty hand. "No beer?"

"I just got here."

"Cool." He turns, takes my hand like it's something we've done every day of our lives, and leads me over to the keg. Adam Millstein is sitting next to it, holding a stack of red plastic cups. "It's on me," Dominic says, and hands him ten dollars.

Adam takes it and begins pumping out two cups of beer for us. "Oh crap, Very, I hope hitting your head didn't knock something loose up there."

"What do you mean?"

"I've never seen you at a party before."

"Don't worry, Adam," Dominic replies for me. "You're off the hook. The corruption of Very Sayles-Woodruff is all on me."

I slip my hand from his. "This isn't corruption."

"So this Very was there all along?"

"This Very is the same Very. It's just Very with a beer."

Adam laughs and hands me my cup.

Dominic and I step away from the keg and the fire, moving closer to the edge of the clearing. "Seriously, I wasn't sure you'd come. This doesn't seem like your scene." He's got one hand around the beer, the other in the pocket of his coat—not black leather as I would have guessed, but a wool flannel thing that looks like it belongs to a grandpa.

"I'm not sure why you think you know what my scene is." I take a drink from my beer, which is warm and flavorless. My dad drinks dark, heavy beers that he lets us take sips from, and this is nothing like those.

Dominic drinks deeply from his cup. I watch his throat work as he swallows; his neck is pale and thin and I have an urge to touch his Adam's apple. I drink again, a bigger gulp this time, trying to keep up with him.

"Anyway, this doesn't seem anywhere near as exciting as you made it out to be," I tell him.

"Parties never are."

"So why did you want me to come?" I ask.

He looks over my shoulder toward the bonfire, then back at me, right into my eyes. "I wanted to see if you would. If I asked you."

I can't hold his stare. I look down at the ground, at a patch of poisonous red berries. "Give me your cup," he says.

"Why? I'm not done yet."

"You need to be topped off." He takes my cup and returns to the keg. I watch him as he walks, this loping, graceful stride that somehow seems to contain the same smirk of his lips. Adam grins at something he says and I redden, sure they are talking about me.

Dominic returns and says, "Come on, let's go," as he starts off deeper into the woods. I follow him. I don't even hesitate—just start climbing up the gentle slope through the trees. The smell of the bonfire gives way to the overwhelming scent of pine. My foot slips on some needles, and I stumble forward, spilling some of my beer. "You okay?" he asks, reaching back to take my hand again. His palm is warm as he leads me still farther onward. The voices down by the bonfire fade; I can hear, ahead of us, occasional snatches of conversations and laughter. At that moment, the whole night—the disembodied voices, my hand in Dominic's, the warm end-of-summer night air—is all so beautiful and serene, it's like a dream.

"My parents used to bring us here when we were little," he says. "And my sister and I would come up into the woods to play. Cops-and-robbers type of stuff. Detectives and spies. She would follow me around and write down my nefarious activities."

"That's sweet," I say. "And oddly prescient."

"I blame her for all of my wayward ways."

"Which is why I wait for my sister every day. Not that it's doing any good. She spends half the time in her own world, and the other half being a pain in the ass—hanging out in trees and avoiding my grandmother."

He stops walking and looks at me with curiosity.

"She's sick," I tell him.

"I'd heard that."

I gaze down the hill back toward the party. "It's bad. Sometimes it feels like she's already slipping away. Like I'm already starting to grieve for her." I don't tell him the whole truth: that sometimes I wish it were all over. "I'm trying to hold on to my memories, but those are going away, too. It only makes it worse when we have to do things like discuss her poetry in class."

"Well, Hunter's a jerk. But her poems are a part of her."

I turn back to see his face. His smile is gone, and he leans in toward me.

"That's just her public persona. What she and I are like together, that's different. That's what's real," I tell him. I know my grandmother. I've lived with her all my life, breathed her air—you don't know anyone better than that. I know what parts of her are real and which are the facade.

He nods and says, "I get it."

I lift my eyes. "Have you had someone in your family die?"

"Not exactly. My mom, she—she's gone, I guess is the best way to put it."

"She left?"

"It was rough. I was seven when it became clear that she wasn't going to be in the picture, and I didn't understand how she could leave me and Lucy—that's my sister."

"That's because it doesn't make any sense. You don't just leave your children." My words are small, nothing compared to this statement: his mother left.

Our bodies are tilting in toward each other, like we have no choice, gravitational pull.

"I don't normally talk about this," he says, pulling back.

"I'm sorry."

"No, that's not what I meant. People don't normally take an interest. And it's not like my dad is around to talk about it."

"He's gone, too?"

"He travels. He's in Cincinnati tonight, I think."

"You think?"

"He's on the road a lot. He crews for bands and stuff. Right now he's on a tour with Bob Dylan. He wanted to be a musician."

"He must love being around all that, then."

"Not really. It just reminds him that he never made it."

"So you're on your own?"

"Most of the time. Lucy's going to school down in Georgia."

I lean toward him. "But, I mean, don't you get lonely?"

"Sometimes. I'm used to it, though." He pauses. "You can't tell anyone. Technically I'm still a minor, and the state frowns on this sort of an arrangement."

"Sure," I say quickly. "I mean, of course."

"It's not so bad. Being alone, I mean. I get to take care of myself and do what I want. Nobody bugs me, and so I can—like today I was just reading all afternoon, and it was nice, you know?"

"A man of leisure." It comes out more flippant than I mean it to, and he looks away.

"Something like that."

I look down at the bed of pine needles on the ground. A stray maple leaf sticks straight up and quivers there.

"You want to know why I invited you?"

I nod.

"I saw you in that gallery staring at that photograph. It was like you were mesmerized, and I couldn't figure out what you were seeing there. I realized I'd been around you forever, and I didn't know one thing about you. I mean, our dots were right next to each other on the carpet in kindergarten."

"They were not. I sat next to Grace until—" But as I say it, I realize he is right. Grace sat on my left, until Mrs. Hall got so tired of us poking and giggling and playing with each other's hair that she swapped Grace with this other girl—Lauren, I think, who ended up moving to Texas. But on my right was the quiet boy with dark hair and green eyes who always smelled like the apples he had in his lunch box every day. Dominic. "You liked it when she read to us. You would close your eyes, but you weren't sleeping."

He smiles, slow and easy and real. "See. You didn't even remember it was me. So I decided I would try to get to know you."

"Like a project."

"Like a social experiment, I guess."

I take a step back. "I don't want to be anyone's experiment."

He steps closer. "That came out wrong. I say stupid things when I'm nervous. I mean, I just wondered if two people that everyone thinks are totally different—I just wondered what would happen, if we were really so far apart." He takes my hand again. His palm is warmer now, and a little damp. He blinks and I notice a bit of crust right at his tear duct. I consider brushing it away.

The air between us is charged, like before an electrical storm. My heart beats faster. He steps closer still. Closer and closer and closer again. There are no more voices. The only thing I can hear is his breath, coming faster and faster. I know what is going to happen next. There's nothing else quite like that feeling: heart beating, time stretched out, mouth buzzing. I lean in to him, and he leans in to me until our lips press together.

The weight of my body seems to leave me. I place my hand on his shoulder, pulling him closer so our bodies are right next to each other, pressing hard. Our teeth clack together and I giggle, but we're still kissing. He gently moves his tongue across my lips. I open my mouth a little wider. Then, I rock away, just enough to tilt back my head and sigh. The world won't come into focus. His lips travel down my neck. This is nothing like kissing Christian. This is the way my mother wants me to be kissed. I step away abruptly. "I'm sorry," I say quickly. "I'm sorry, I have a, a—"

"A boyfriend? I know; we've been over that."

I shake my head. "This isn't like me. This isn't . . . I don't . . ." The words won't come, and so I turn and start down the hill.

"You sure about that, Very?" he yells after me.

iv.

A kiss. Lips on lips. Such a simple act, but it spins me loose. I barely even finished my beer, but driving home I can't focus on the road. I find myself drifting right, then left. *This is what it means to change?*

My teacher brought a caterpillar in to class in first grade. We watched it build its chrysalis, then waited, waited, waited for the beautiful butterfly to emerge, gorgeous gossamer wings spread wide. Finally one day it oozed out. Its orange wings were crinkled and slimy-looking. I remember Grace saying, "Ew. What a disappointment." I should have paid more attention. I should have known there was no such thing as metamorphosis.

Our driveway is still full of cars, and I snake up along beside them. Subaru with rusting bumpers, an ancient Mercedes converted to run on biodiesel, tiny cars lined up on the edge of the driveway like children waiting to go to recess. I'm just able to pull Nonnie's convertible into the garage, then walk around back so I can get into the kitchen that way without having to go through the party.

The kitchen is full of festive detritus: plates with half-eaten appetizers, a stack of plastic cups, a purse, and two sports coats. Voices filter in, too.

On the counter sits a huge bag of lemons, and half a bag of limes. Mom always orders too much of things like this, and not enough actual food. They're beautiful sitting there, but also sad. I can already picture them molding, and the sour-sweet-sickly smell that will permeate the kitchen until I take them and throw them into the woods. A waste. So I decide to do something with them. I know we have a special tool somewhere that peels off perfect strips of the rind. The rind curls like a spring, and you can drop it into a drink. But I can't find it in our kitchen, which is more for show than for use. I look in the drawer where we keep all those sorts of random tools—melon ballers, citrus reamers—no luck. Shoving it closed, I move on to the next drawer. This one has another disconnected assortment. There's string for trussing a turkey, wooden skewers, and knives for spreading dips. I rustle around in it, and then yank my finger back. Shoving my finger into my mouth, I taste blood. I pull it out and see a small cut, just a bit thicker than a paper cut.

"Damn it," I mutter, and slam the drawer closed. "Screw it."

Nonnie taught me how to make the twists without the tool. She said it was a necessary skill since fruit twists were one of the ways you could tell if you were in a classy joint. "It's not that I mind a dive bar. In fact, I'd actually prefer it. But if they're going to charge me more than the cost of one of my books for a cocktail, it better be the real deal with all the frills."

I can almost see her, leaning back against the counter, holding a pencil as if it's a cigarette (this was after she quit, too late as it turned out). As she gives me the directions in my mind, I follow them. "Cut those pointy nubs off the ends of the lemon. Then cut it in half." As I slice the lemon in two, its juice seeps into my fresh cut and I wince. But I keep going. It feels like a penance. *I'm sorry I kissed Dominic Meyers, Christian. But if it makes you feel better, I cut myself and poured lemon juice in the wound.* He'd probably just kiss it and tell me that it would be all right. That's how nice he is.

I use a spoon to scoop out the lemon pulp, and set it aside in a bowl. *Make sure to get all of it out, and some of the white stuff, too.* More and more juice gets into the cut. I think the pain will go away, but each fresh drop brings a new spike.

I'd been in those woods before, maybe ten or eleven years ago. The town did this fairy-house event with girls in gauzy dresses and wings and a maypole dance. Mom and Nonnie brought us. We trekked up into the woods with scads of other kids and found a quiet spot to build our own fairy house. The rules were simple: use only items you find in the woods, no plastic. The organizers had gathered buckets of shells and sea glass from the ocean.

I built the structure, crisscrossing sticks and stacking rocks. Ramona furnished the place with a mussel-shell chaise lounge and a dining set of a stone and pebbles. "We'll leave them some peppermint," she said, placing a leaf on the table. "So when they kiss they won't have bad breath." She draped leaves over my structure and fanned pine needles over the doorway for privacy. "Look," she said, as we surveyed the work. "The pine needles, they've got a bit of a gap. There's a fairy there already." She dropped to her belly and peered in the gap. "Hello, little fairy. Hello, little, little, little one." Mom told us ours was the loveliest and all the fairies would live there. She looked with pity at all the other houses we passed.

Two weeks later we returned. The wind or an animal or an angry middle schooler had romped through the path. Houses tucked in on themselves, shells crushed to shards along the way. Our house fared no better. It was only sticks and leaves, after all. One whole wall had slid off, exposing the interior. The mussel-shell chaise was missing, and the pebbles were spread around. The only thing still in its place was the peppermint leaf, brown but untouched by fairy lips. I blinked back tears. I had wanted so much to believe. Ramona fell to her knees. "Don't you like your peppermint, little fairy? If you don't eat your greens, you won't get any dessert!"

"There's nothing there, Ramona," I told her.

"Of course there is." She laughed. "It's Petaluna. She's being stubborn about her supper."

"There's *nothing* there," I repeated.

Ramona turned to the house. "She *is* a child, but she's a strange child. That's why she can't see you."

The rage built in my small body and my foot shot out, destroying what was left of the fairy house. Ramona stared. I expected her to weep and wail. Instead she put her face into the wreckage. "Petaluna? Petaluna? Ah, there you are!"

Nonnie led me back to the car.

"There are no fairies. Right, Nonnie?"

"Of course there aren't," she said, extracting a cigarette from her silver case. "But in this world we see what we need to." She sucked in hard as she lit the cigarette. Then she turned and reached in through the open window to dig in her oversize bag, pulling out one of her steno books.

I had wanted to tell this to Dominic, even the part where I crushed the fairy house. Now I'm glad I didn't. I can't be passing around memories like dealing a deck of cards.

My phone shakes and rattles on the counter. I wipe my hands on my jeans and check the text from Grace: **Please continue with your field report on the Essex College Male.**

I text back: **Observing from secure vantage point. Little to report.**

It feels like a lie.

It is a lie. This night is full of them, like stars popping out in the clear, black sky.

I slice the lemon peel into thin strips and then reopen the random drawer, where whatever cut me still lurks, and grab one of the skewers. I roll the lemon around the skewer into perfect spirals.

One down, about two dozen to go.

My hands burn.

At first the job requires just enough concentration to keep my mind occupied, but as I work through the lemons, it becomes a habit, and then my mind is free to wander. I replay the kiss. I replay how we got there, trying to assign blame.

I lift my fingers to my lips and taste lemon instead of him.

Christian's kisses are softer. His lips are loose. It's like he's afraid he's going to hurt me. I just assumed that's the way it was.

I try to picture how his face will look when I tell him. If I tell him. No, I have to tell him. And when I do, will he cry? I wonder. Get angry? I have never seen him angry.

Ramona breezes in from the sliding door to the outside. She picks up one of the lemon rinds, spins it around in her fingers, then tucks the end into her mouth. "Bitter," she says.

I nod.

"Do we really need this many lemon twists?" she asks.

I don't protest her use of the word *we*.

"Can you bring them out to the party?" I ask.

"Your hands are all pink."

"I guess from the juice."

She lifts herself up onto the counter beside me, even though it's splattered with lemon juice. "Do you care what Marcus Schmidt thinks about the sculpture?" she asks.

I laugh. More accurately, I guffaw. "No." What Marcus Schmidt thinks about anything is about as far as you can get from what I care about.

"Me, either. What about you, though? Do you like the sculpture?"

"I don't know, Ramona. I'm not much for interpreting art."

"I didn't ask you to interpret it. I asked you if you liked it."

Our parents always say that whether you like the art is irrelevant. That's the lowest form of interaction. "I like the way the sun hits it in the afternoon. I think that's pretty."

"I think so, too." She nods. "Do you think Mom's still going to take it down?"

"No. Not after the reaction tonight. The only way she'll take it down is if they want to move it into the gallery."

"You don't think they'd really do that, do you?"

"No."

"Good."

She chews thoughtfully on her lemon rind, staring at me. "You weren't at that party very long."

"It was kind of lame."

"But you knew that going in, didn't you? What happened?"

I shake my head. "You can't tell anyone. Anyone."

"Who's to tell?" she asks, the lemon rind sticking out from her lips like a spiraled cigarette.

"I kissed Dominic Meyers."

She nods and chews. "That's a good reason to leave a party."

"That's all you're going to say?"

"What else can I say?"

She's right, of course. "I wasn't telling you just to tell you. What should I do? I don't have to tell Christian that I kissed Dominic, do I? It will hurt him too much to tell him. It's my mistake, not his."

"I don't know the answer to that question, but protecting someone as a reason to keep a secret doesn't make sense to me."

"Why not?"

"It protects the teller as much the person told, so you can never be sure if you're doing it for the other person, or just to protect yourself."

"I guess. But I can't just give up Christian for this thing with Dominic. Because this thing is nothing. It's just like, like a magnesium explosion." On the first day of chemistry class, as soon as we were all settled in our seats, Mr. Tompkins had lit off a tiny amount of magnesium powder. The flame was bright white, and hot, and went out nearly as quickly as it had started. "Christian and I have a slow burn. That's worth keeping."

"I don't really want to hear about you exploding or burning."

"Can you please just bring these out to the party?" I ask.

She doesn't move at first, but then she pushes herself off of the counter and grabs the small bowl of lemon curls. "In the grand scheme of things, there are worse things you could have done."

As she pushes the door open, I hear the din of the party rise and fall. I have a sudden urge to call her back, like she's walking into a trap. It's ridiculous. Instead I move on to the limes. The first one I choose is small and perfectly round, smooth in my hand. I once heard that if you looked at the earth from far, far away, it would be smoother than a marble. Smoother, by far, than this lime. I want to draw some perspective from the comparison, but all it does is make me feel small.

v.

My father is in the kitchen the next morning, taking cupcakes out of plastic containers and smoothing out the frosting so they look homemade. He used to do this when Ramona and I had to bring cupcakes in for classroom parties. He'd decorate them with sprinkles for our birthdays, and we'd tell our teachers and friends that he had made them himself.

"Cool do," he says.

I rub my hand over my hair, which is spiking out in all directions. "What are those for?" I ask as I fill a glass with water at the sink. My mouth is parched.

"Advisee lunch," he replies.

I gulp some more water. "Can I have one?" I ask.

"For breakfast?"

"Why not?"

He grins. "Are you going to love it like it's the best cupcake you've ever had in your life?"

"I can pretend I do."

"Okay, then."

I take one of the ones he hasn't smoothed out yet and sink my teeth in. Like most grocery store cupcakes, the frosting is too sweet and stings my gums. It probably turned my mouth blue, too, staining my lips like a puritanical punishment. "Any cool new advisees this year?" I ask, more to distract myself than out of genuine curiosity.

"One's from Mongolia. A comparative lit major. I wonder what Mongolian literature is like. I wonder what Mongolian *music* is like. I'll have to see if I can download some."

I know that not every professor is like my dad. Nonnie's excused from having advisees; even before she got sick she only took them on in the rarest of circumstances. Mom meets with hers one-on-one once a semester and invites them to art-department functions. Dad, though, takes a real interest. He knows where they come from, knows their strengths and weaknesses. He sends them emails on their birthdays. He makes room for them in his overcrowded classes, even if they aren't music majors.

"You're a good adviser," I say. "I hope when I go to college, I get one just like you. But maybe he can really make his own cupcakes."

"Sure," he laughs. "But, you know, giving your advisees cupcakes doesn't help with tenure review, and you can't put it on your curriculum vitae for the old job search, can you?" He takes another cupcake from the plastic container. He licks the knife before he begins spreading.

"Ew, Dad, that's gross."

"Our little secret," he says with a wink.

"Listen," I begin, and then I use the oldest trick in the book. I just go for it with gusto and hope that my dad lets it slide. "I have this friend—Grace, actually. There's this guy who might be interested in her, she can't quite tell if he's flirting with her, or just like, I don't know, messing with her."

"Messing with her how?" He sounds concerned. He really likes Grace. "Is he making her uncomfortable?"

"No," I say quickly. "No, it's more like she's having trouble understanding his intentions. One day he's funny. Another day he's aloof. Or he's trying to prove how smart he is. Plus he has a thing for—" I cough. I'm not exactly sure how to translate Dominic's interest in poetry to Grace. "He has a thing for Asian girls, so she's not sure if he's interested in her for her, or because she's Asian. If he's interested in her at all."

"That's tricky." He puts the knife down on the counter,

leans back, and crosses his arms over his chest.

"It's a bit more complicated than that."

"How so?"

"Well, they were at a party and they kissed."

"Like lips brushing or a take-your-breath-away kind of a kiss?"

"Somewhere in between," I lie.

This seems to satisfy him. "Here's the thing about teenage boys, Very. They are clueless. They think they know everything—an attribute that only gets worse when they get to college—but they are also painfully aware that there is one thing about which they know nothing. And that is girls. So there are a few routes they follow. Some bumble, some stumble into suaveness that surprises even them, and some try to imitate the characters they see in movies and books and try to be cool—which might be why he's aloof sometimes. Or they try to make these grand gestures that, sadly for them, often fall flat. I mean, *Say Anything* is one of my favorite movies—fantastic soundtrack—but if a boy showed up with a boom box outside of your or Ramona's window, well, I'd be calling the cops. You see?"

"Sort of."

A grand gesture: like graffitied song lyrics.

"I'm guessing this guy falls into group number three. He wanted to do something big and unforgettable, so he just grabbed her and kissed her. No big deal if she's into him. If she's into him, then it's the most amazing thing and he's the most amazing guy. But if she's not into him—well, then it's awkward."

Or a grand gesture like a bottle cap sculpture. No. The

bottle caps are for Nonnie. Unless they are for both of us.

"What if she's not sure?"

"Well then she'd better figure it out before this guy's heart breaks."

He squats down and starts rooting around in a drawer for something to carry the cupcakes. "If someone invented Tupperware that absolutely would not lose its top, they would be a millionaire." He sticks his arm into the drawer as far as it will go. "I mean, honestly, it wouldn't be that hard. Magnets maybe. Or maybe flip tops so they'd always be connected."

"You're onto something there," I said. "Forget music, become an inventor."

"If only. But the heart wants what it wants, and my heart wants to study music. Oh hey, that reminds me, do you think kids would read a book called *A Hip-Hop History of the United States*? I'm thinking of writing a book aimed at high school students that shows how hip-hop reflects politics and society in US culture. It would be great for high schools, right? I mean, teachers are always talking about how they need to have new ways to connect kids to the material. Do you think your teachers would use something like that?"

The social studies faculty at my school has an average age of approximately sixty-seven. So the thought of any of them using hip-hop in the classroom seems far-fetched. Dad senses my hesitation and looks down at his cupcakes.

"Maybe," I say. "I think it's a great idea. I would totally read that book."

But I'm thinking about what he said, setting it up like a mathematical equation in my head:

If she likes him, then all is fine. If she doesn't like him, then there is a problem. If, then . . . if, then. But she is me and I don't know how I feel about the ifs.

Let V = she and D = he.

If V likes D, then +

If V likes D, then –

There are other conditions to consider as well. How will the outcome be affected if he thought I knew about his grand gestures? And what if he really is making the bottle cap sculpture?

Another complication: What if I'm coming at this backward? What if it was Nonnie who first drew him to me? He said it was me staring at the picture, but what if his interest in poetry made him want access to Nonnie, and the best way to do that is through me?

I don't want it to be for Nonnie.

Of course there was another piece—a bigger, larger piece—if V likes D, what does that do to C?

Thinking about it like a mathematician does make sense in one way: my problems are not a system of equations. I do not need to solve for C to determine D, or vice versa. In fact, it seems wiser to keep them separate. The problem, I know, is that there are two equations at all.

Dad nods and begins arranging the cupcakes in the Tupperware he found. "Okay. Done and done."

"Thanks for sharing with me," I tell him.

"Sure thing, jelly bean." He closes the cupcake carrier and starts out of the kitchen with it. Then he stops. "Tell Grace she'll be okay. And he will, too. But as for you, I'm thinking a women's college might be the best choice. I hear Wellesley is good."

"I hear they bus in boys from MIT," I say, using my finger to swipe some frosting off the cupcake. "Have fun at your lunch."

He grins over his shoulder. "Oh, don't you worry about me."

The door shuts behind him. As it swings back and forth, I get a freeze-frame view of him, cupcake box under his arm, keys in the other hand.

In math, it takes at least three terms to determine a pattern. You have one and four and nine, and you think, *Squares!* That's math, though, and this is life. Kissing Dominic once is enough to prove me unfaithful. I have to break up with Christian.

Dominic isn't the reason: he is the catalyst, the thing that finally allows a necessary change to happen. Like you could have two elements just sitting there totally stable, and then the catalyst came in and bam! Explosion! I am pretty sure, too, that the catalyst usually gets completely destroyed in the reaction, which maybe was the best thing that could happen. Kissing Dominic made me realize things were over with Christian, but I need to forget all about that kiss. It's best to be on my own.

Now I just have to set the chemical reaction in motion.

eight

i.

THE COUGHING IS LOUDER than usual. More insistent. I can picture her inside the room. Hunched over. Then a moan. A gasp.

I hesitate.

This is it. This is it, this is it, this is it.

ii.

Up the stairs two at a time. I throw open the door without knocking. She will yell. She will yell and make some remark about how just because she's old and dying doesn't mean she's given up her right to privacy. All this goes through my mind as the door swings open on slick, silver hinges. Hope, that thing with feathers—*I understand it now*—still clings to the branch.

But no. She is not churlish. There is no reprimand.

She is slumped in her armchair, bent at an odd angle, her face white, glassy eyes circled in black. Sweat on her upper lip. A drop of red-brown (blood? mucus?) on the collar of her white, white shirt. Like one of Marcus Schmidt's paintings in miniature.

"Very," she whispers. "Very, it isn't good."

"Mom!" I yell. "Dad!"

I don't bother to yell for Ramona.

iii.

Ambulance chaser. That's me. Careening through traffic in Nonnie's blue Rapier right behind the blue and red flashes of the ambulance. The sun is orange-red as it lifts itself into the sky. The ambulance pulls around the back of the hospital while I find a parking spot. I choose one right by a streetlight, still lit. It makes the whole car glow white. I freeze. How can I get out of this car and face the possibilities?

iv.

"There's so much I haven't told you, Very. So much you need to know. About life. About my life."

I'm lying in the second bed in the hospital room, on my side, facing her. "So tell me."

They had to drain fluid from her lungs. *Pleural effusion*, that's what it's called when fluid fills your lungs so it's like you're drowning out of water.

When Dad finally met Mom and me at the hospital—held up in some meeting or phone conference or something—he told me there was nothing I could do for her, but I stayed here to watch her sleep, watch her breathe.

She closes her eyes and I can see every blue vein on her eyelids. "My father used to take me fishing off Snapper Bridge on Carolina Creek. We'd catch trout mostly—never snapper—and we'd bring them home and Mama would cook them in the frying pan with the heads and everything still on. My brother Rufus liked to eat the eyes just to make me squirm."

When she says "Mama" a bit of the southern accent comes back and it sounds like "Mawma."

"Did you practice?" I ask, interrupting her story. "Did you rehearse to get rid of your accent?"

"Yes. I could have kept it," she says. "But northern folks like their southerners to be sweet as sugar—refined southern belles. Not Appalachia. I'm no belle."

She coughs and I get out of bed to hold the straw from her ice water to her lips.

"I lost it quick. Soon as I realized what their game was, I lost that accent, buried it deep." As she speaks, it flits back up to the surface. "They were proud of themselves. Arthur Miller and all the rest of them. They patted themselves on the back for finding this diamond in the rough. A chambermaid. A *southern* chambermaid. And she could write. They pranced me around like a show dog. Like I was their big discovery. Their treasure. Their project. I was Pygmalion's Galatea to them."

She coughs again and I squint, checking the chest of her hospital gown for blood. Dad went back to campus, saying he had an appointment with an advisee that he couldn't miss, and Mom went down to the cafeteria for some coffee and a snack, so it's just me up here. As I crawl back into my bed, I eye the call button, ready to press it and yell if she slips back under.

"Well, *I* was the one who got on the bus. *I* was the one who scrubbed their toilets. And *I'm* the one who wrote the words. And if they needed that story to make sense of it all, well, sure, I would let them have it. You've gotta give people their stories, Very. You know that." She looks at me through heavy-lidded eyes. "People have their story of you, don't they, dear? And you play that part just fine."

"What if I'm sick of this story?"

"You write a new one."

Another cough. Another sip of water. Her eyes are still closed, so maybe she's falling asleep. She coughs again and then says, "The hardest thing about writing a poem is the beginning. In your head it's whole and lovely and perfect. Shakespeare would weep. It's when you sit down to write it that the words get jumbled and you have to rein them in, put them in line. It's exhausting work."

"Are you trying to talk to me in metaphor, Nonnie? Because

I don't understand it."

"Well you'd better start because I'm not going to be around much longer to explain it to you."

"Nonnie, don't—"

"Did I ever tell you about Andy Warhol?"

I nod. "The painting of your poem. The woman who shot him."

"Valerie Solanas. Pretty in her way. He took me to Studio 54. You should have seen it. The clothes, the music, the drugs. It was like everyone heard the stories, and the stories grew, so the reality grew to meet them. I had brown patent-leather platform heels in a tortoiseshell pattern and a gold minidress. People hardly recognized me all glammed up like that. But there's a picture. He's walking a few steps ahead of me with his hand shielding his face. I'm looking right at the camera like a deer in the headlights. I hate that picture."

I'd like to see it sometime, but I don't tell her.

Nonnie coughs again. And then again. "My mother saw the picture. It was in *Life* magazine. She cut it out and framed it. She hung it on the wall right between my confirmation picture and a crucifix. She never saw how funny that was."

I press a button on the side of my bed and it lifts the whole thing up so now I'm looking down at her. The light is better on her this way, more forgiving. It softens out her wrinkles and makes her eyes shine like they used to.

"I've had nine cats. Nine. That's more cats than lovers, Very. Never have more cats than lovers."

Since I've never had a cat, it seems I'm ahead in that game.

A tinkling of bells rings. "What's that?" I ask.

"A baby was just born. Every damn time a baby is born they ring those bells. This is the third time they've rung since I've been in here. Why are all these people having babies?"

"That's what people do."

"They shouldn't," she says dismissively. As if she herself hadn't done it. As if she herself wished she hadn't.

Someone opens Nonnie's door, and then closes it again just as quickly. A mistake.

"I thought about being a recluse, Very. I thought I should just leave my work and hide in the woods."

"You just didn't go far enough north."

"You'd think anywhere in New Hampshire I could be a hermit. What would have been perfect is if I could've inherited Salinger's place. We could've called it the Hermitage. You write. You stop writing. You go there. People whisper and wonder, and when you die, it's all over the news."

"You'll be all over the news."

"What matters is being remembered."

I'll remember you, Nonnie.

I don't say it, though. Because I know when it comes to Nonnie and her legacy, I am not the *New Yorker* or a museum in her honor. I am not enough.

"It's my fault. I should have just gotten up and gone. Could I have been a hermit in Mexico? Puerto Rico? I would have liked that better, Very. It's my fault."

"It's not your fault."

"In Puerto Rico, I wouldn't need a passport or a visa or anything, right?"

"I'll bust you out, we'll go together."

"It's not your fault," she says back to me. She looks up at the blank television. She is as still as slack tide. Then she raises up the back of her bed with a robotic groan. "You have to leave."

"What?"

"It's Sunday. The weekend. Surely you must have something better to do today."

There are things I could be doing. Homework, of course. Starting my college applications. It's still warm enough to meet Britta for some tennis. I could be sitting with Christian in his basement rec room, watching a movie or something else like sex or the breakup that this rush to the hospital has forestalled. He texted me last night, over and over, more and more insistent:

Hey!

What're you up to?

How was your mom's party? Lame?

Are you sleeping?

Are you there?

Hellloooo?

Is something wrong???

Then he actually tried to call me, but I just let it go to voice mail. You aren't supposed to talk on your phone in the hospital, and anyway, what could I possibly say to him?

I do text Britta and Grace so they know where I am.

"I don't have one single solitary thing to do other than this," I tell Nonnie.

"I can't tell you how much that depresses me."

I curl myself into a ball on the bed. I've been hoping they would just let me stay here all night with her. I don't mind the beeps of the machines, the nurses going in and out. "I just want to be here in case anything happens."

Nonnie lifts her arm up and lets it fall onto the pillow. "I won't let anything happen without you. No sudden recoveries. No horrible descents."

"Nonnie—"

"You should spend time with that boy."

"Christian?" Now she's grasping. She never wants me to spend time with Christian.

"No. The other one."

"What other one?"

She raises her eyebrows. "Didn't you know that there's a vent that goes right from the kitchen to my room? I can't believe your father fell for that *my friend* story."

I redden. As soon as she mentions him, it's like I'm in that moonlit forest with him again, the scent of smoke drifting up and around us.

I wonder what else she's heard. Conversations about her health, about her life.

"Leave," she says, more firmly now, and I can't tell if she wants me to go because she's worried about me, or because she wants to be alone.

"You just said you had so much to tell me."

She turns her head away. "I'm tired, Very."

"Okay," I say. "But don't count this as a victory. I'm not going to do anything fun. I'm going to go to the library and study."

"That seems a waste of a Sunday to me."

"I'll be back later tonight," I tell her.

She picks up the remote that's attached to her bed by a cable, clicks on the television, and flips to the home shopping channel. "I'll be here," she says without looking up. "Unless I'm not."

Sometimes I can't handle Nonnie's sense of humor. Still, I kiss her gently on the forehead on my way out of her room. Her breath crackles through her lips. They are countable now, those breaths, falling away toward zero.

v.

It seems strange that awful things can happen and yet the sun still comes up. But it does. In fact, it's a beautiful afternoon outside, the sky a Technicolor blue, so when I get home I walk around the house to the lawn, which slants down toward a wall of trees. I slide through a break between two pines and onto our short, crooked dock that juts out into the bay. Sitting, I let my feet hang down, so close to the water I can feel its cool.

I pick up a rock and skip it one, two, three times before it sinks. I look out at the ripple line in the water where the current changes from slight to severe. If I lean way forward I can follow the coast as the bay expands, and maybe see the bridge over the bay into Portsmouth, where it opens up to the Atlantic Ocean.

I dip my toe into the water, too cold for swimming, though when we were kids it hadn't bothered us. The current around the bridge is one of the strongest in the world. At our beach, the strength's just a shadow. You have to swim out about twenty yards to get where it's really strong. I've felt it only once. I waded out to where the water was almost neck deep. It tugged at my foot. Incessant. I knew that if I took just one step, one stroke more, it would suck me under. I thought, though, that I could go back. Just turn around and swim back, as simply as I had come. But the water was an invisible force field, holding me there. I began to panic. Dad dove in and swam to me in quick strokes, his head out of the water, eyes on me. He pulled me back out of the spiral by my wrist, tugging so hard my shoulder popped.

Normally it was Nonnie who walked us down to the water. She sat under her tree and took her thin silver cigarette case from her suit jacket pocket, engraved with her initials, IRW, and pulled one skinny cigarette out and lit it. When she finally quit, she claimed it was because the government kept raising the cigarette tax. "They get enough of my money to fight their tin soldier wars."

The cigarette case is cool to the touch when I take it out of my bag. This would please her, I know: that I took the case from her dresser drawer without asking. Others would lay claim to it, of course. My mother first of all. Or the college, maybe, to keep with other memorabilia. Perhaps even Ramona. But I took it, slipped it into my bag before anyone could notice. If they remember it at all, they'll think it has been lost.

I run my fingers over the engraved initials, thin as the whorls of fingerprints.

IRW

Imogene Rosemary Woodruff.

Nonnie.

I flip open the case. Inside is one old cigarette. "I might be shipwrecked, Very. Or maybe I'll be at one of the great dive bars in New York, and some young man will ask me for a cigarette. You have to be prepared."

There is nothing left for her to prepare for. So I take out the just-in-case cigarette and hold it to my lips. It is warm, soft, like a straw filled with sand. I have a pack of matches in my bag, too, from a restaurant in town. It takes a couple of tries to light the match. The smell of sulfur fills the air. Then I hold the match to the end of the cigarette and suck in. The cigarette catches, and my mouth and lungs fill with smoke. Predictably, I start to cough. I can hear her laughing, and she whispers in my ear: *You'll get the hang of it, Very.*

I wonder if Dominic ever smokes, and decide he doesn't. Not cigarettes anyway. He hadn't tasted like tobacco smoke. He tasted like something warm and soft and just a little sweet.

Christian would never smoke. Ever. And that rigidity is probably why Nonnie dislikes him. I needed that steadiness once, back at the start when Nonnie was first getting sick and the possibility of a happy ending still existed.

I look back over my shoulder, to the tall tree under which Nonnie always sat. If I blink quickly, it's like I can still see her there in her tapered black capri pants and white T-shirt. She holds her hand up to shield her eyes from the sun, and slowly, slowly exhales.

nine

i.

GRACE HAS MUFFINS FOR me in homeroom. "I made them when I heard Nonnie was in the hospital. They have, like, chia seeds and quinoa flour. We just need to save one for Britta to balance out all the coffee and crap she puts into her system. Do you know what's in those lattes she drinks?"

"My mom and I ate a whole box of Twinkies last night." We sat on the sofa together eating one after another while my dad worked in his office. We could hear his heavy fingers pounding on the keyboard. Finally Mom stood up and said, "She's not going to die. Not this week."

I take one of the muffins and bite into it. It actually tastes pretty good. Soft and gooey.

Josh slides into the seat on the other side of Grace and helps himself to a muffin.

"These are mourning muffins," she tells him.

"I'm not mourning. Not yet," I say.

"I didn't mean that. I meant, like, banish sadness."

"Sadness banished," Josh says. "Hey, Very, I heard you went—"

"Josh, she doesn't want to talk about the hospital, okay?"

"You went to the hospital? Are you sick? Did you drink too much at that party?"

My muffin is crumbling in my fingers.

"What are you even talking about?" Grace asks. "Very doesn't drink at her mom's—well, Very doesn't drink, period. And anyway, it was her grandmother who was in the hospital."

"Oh." Josh looks at me, at the muffins, then at Grace, and I can see him making calculations. He heard I was at the party in the woods, which means he probably heard I was with Dominic. My money is on Sadie being the one who told him. Who told everyone. Everyone, of course, being a set that includes Christian as one of its elements.

Mr. Tompkins grabs a folder from his desk before he comes over to us, pushing his hair out of his eyes.

"Mr. Tompkins, would you like a very healthy muffin? It should help to replenish your muscles after your long hike with, who did you say you were going with again?"

"I'm not sure I did say, Grace, but it was with some buddies in my hiking club. We knocked off another four-thousand-footer, so only three more to go. I should have it done this year."

I imagine him on top of a mountain, the air so fresh and clear. You could see for miles and miles, and the world below and all its problems would seem so little when you were four thousand feet high, wouldn't they?

"Listen, Very. We should probably think about rehearsing our presentation. I've got my slides all ready. All I need you to do is walk through your slides and then read your narrative."

"Sure, of course."

"Maybe today after school?"

"Today?" I ask.

"We don't have math team, so I thought it would be good."

"It's just that—" My voice cracks.

"Very's grandmother went into the hospital this weekend."

"Oh, Very, I'm so sorry. I had no idea. Usually parents—"

"Usually parents what?"

"Well, it's just the type of thing we like to know as teachers, so we can be accommodating, and a lot of times parents will call in, but I know this is taking a toll on them, too. So don't worry about it."

"Okay."

"And listen, if something comes up, and you think you're going to have to reschedule with Professor Singh, just let me know. I'll take care of it, okay?" He says this, but his face is pinched tightly and I know it would actually be an imposition to try to reschedule with this big-deal professor.

"Okay."

"She's only here for the day, so."

"Okay," I say again. *Okay, okay, okay.* Such a hollow little word. He looks like he's about to say something else, but the bell rings, and I'm off to English class. I navigate away from where I think Christian will be, but of course there's no avoiding Dominic. He's already in the classroom, so I head straight for Ms. Staples. "I just thought you'd want to know that my grandmother isn't doing so well. She went into the hospital last night, but we're hoping she'll be out tomorrow."

"I'm so sorry, Very. Do you need some more time with the response to Dickinson?"

"No. I've got it. I wrote about the hope one—the thing with feathers and all that. I just thought you should know, since you like her poetry and everything."

"I do like her poetry, but I'm more concerned about you."

"I'm fine," I tell her.

"Well, have a seat and take it easy."

Dominic is watching me as I sit down next to Britta. She takes my hand and gives it a squeeze. Dominic raises his eyebrows and mouths the word, "Okay?"

I shake my head.

No I am not okay.

No I don't need your help.

No, kissing you was a terrible idea.

My mind is everywhere but on the poems. On Dominic, who keeps staring at me the whole time—a careful observer. On Christian, and the magical thinking he must be using to explain away the rumors. And Nonnie, of course. Always back to Nonnie.

Dominic waits for me after class. He sidles right up next

to me as we make our way out the door of English class. "Hey, Very."

I look over my shoulder, back into the classroom, where Britta is talking to Ms. Staples about the poem we were just discussing, something by Adrienne Rich.

"Very," he says again.

I wonder if I can just keep walking and pretend I don't hear him, but he is so close I can feel him, so I say, "Hey."

Heads actually swivel to see us. At least that's how it seems to me. I'm looking at the black and white tiles of the hallway floor.

"I want to thank you for listening Sat—"

"It's no big deal," I say quickly. I check back over my shoulder. Britta is still talking to Ms. Staples. "I need to wait for Britta. You should go on to your next class."

He grins at that. "English is pretty much the only class I'm on time for."

"Why?"

"Why what?"

"Why do you think it's so cool to just saunter in late? Like nothing really matters to you? Like you're just so cool you can't even be bothered?" I clamp my mouth shut. People are definitely watching us now.

"Things matter to me."

"Okay, sure. Whatever. You're welcome."

"I don't normally get to talk about my family with anyone."

"Well, I am a peer counselor. That's what we're here for."

He stops then, midstep. "Right, Very. Of course. Keep up the good work."

I keep walking without looking back or waiting for Britta. It's not something I'm proud of. It's just that all those eyes were on us and the weight of expectations and gleeful gossip was too much on top of thinking about Nonnie. I'll tell him all of this after school. We'll meet at the wall while I wait for Ramona and I will tell him this. There will be fewer people around and we can really talk. I'll explain that he's a nice guy and most people have him all wrong, which is too bad, but that now, this moment, is a monumentally bad time for me to have a complicated relationship. Also that he needs to stop gluing shit to our house.

ii.

Dominic doesn't show up.

I wait for him and I wait for Ramona, and neither one of them emerges from the school. Waves and waves of students come out, but not them.

If they had come, either one of them, perhaps what happened next would be different.

I drive Nonnie's car to Christian's house with the windows down and the radio off. I need quiet to prepare myself. Nonnie going into the hospital delayed the inevitable. I plan out what I'm going to say. My first instinct is to be frank: *Listen, you're a great guy, but this just isn't working out. We can still be friends, if you want.*

Next I could say that it's not him, it's me, and wrap it up with an "I need my space" to give him one humdinger of a breakup cliché. No. Try again.

I've been doing a lot of thinking lately, and this is going to be a big year for both of us. We've got college applications to do, and decisions to make. You have hockey, and I have Nonnie.

No. Leave Nonnie out of this.

I just don't think I have the energy to devote to our relationship right now.

The problem is that he's likely to tell me it's okay, and he'll just take whatever I can give him.

You've been wonderful to me, but I just don't think I feel as strongly about you as I should. It's not fair to either of us that we stay in this relationship. You deserve someone who can really, really love you.

Perfect. How can he protest the fact that I don't love him?

I coast up Christian's short driveway. He's sitting on a bench in his side yard. His hockey stick is clasped between his knees, and he's wrapping the head of it with white tape. He concentrates, his head nods sharply with each go-round of the roll. When he finishes, he leans forward and uses his teeth to tear it. The roughness of the move startles me. He lifts his head, and a smile spreads across his face. "Very, hey!"

As I shut the car door behind me and walk to him he stands up, flipping his stick over so he's holding it by the handle. The words are waiting there on the tip of my tongue, ready to spill out. Before I can do it, though, he leans forward and kisses my cheek, and he smells salty with sweat: real and familiar.

"I like when you come to visit me unexpectedly," he says. "It's a good surprise. Especially lately."

"Well, you know, I don't have too much homework tonight, so I thought I might just swing by." Swing by? I am not a swing-byer and Christian knows that, but he doesn't even blink.

He holds up his hockey stick. "What do you think?"

"Um, very sticklike?"

"It's new. They were having a sale at Philbrick's and my dad picked it up for me. It's nice. Trust me."

"Okay, good. I like it. It's swell." I follow him into his garage, willing my lips to move. He puts the stick into a stand with several others and grabs a different one.

"Help me practice?" he asks.

"All right."

I mean, why not? It's not like there's any other reason I came to his house this afternoon.

He takes another stick down, this one with a bigger flat part, and hands it to me. "Is this like the lady stick?" I ask. "Why does the lady stick have a bigger head? I mean, the puck isn't any bigger. It's not like softball."

"Slow down there, Gloria Steinem. It's a goalie stick."

"I'm not playing goal."

We are crossing his driveway to a small hockey goal.

"I just need you to feed the ball to me, and I'll work on

hitting it in. I thought the bigger stick might be easier for you since you don't play. But we can get a regular stick if you want."

"No, this is fine."

"Lady stick," he laughs. When he laughs his whole face crinkles up like paper crumpling. Next to the net is a bucket of tennis balls. "Just push them to me and I'll slap them in. Hopefully."

I slide the bucket over and take out one of the balls. As instructed, I push it toward him. He holds his stick with one hand at the top and one hand much farther down, and the muscles on his forearm flex as he whacks it straight into the goal. "Score!" I call out.

"A little faster," he replies.

So I push the next one a little faster, and the next one even faster. We go through the whole bucket, and then gather them up. As I resituate myself for another round, he grips and regrips the shaft of the hockey stick over and over again. I clear my throat. And suddenly it seems remarkably easy. I'll just say the words and it will be over and we'll both go about our business. "Everything okay?" he asks.

"Yeah," I say. "Hand cramp."

Not so easy after all.

"Part of the game," he replies.

I pick up a ball and put it on the ground. The voice keeps going around in my head. *Break up with him. Break up with him.*

I hit the ball hard toward him, it goes way off course, and he has to jump for it. It pings off the pole of the net. "Sorry."

"No worries."

No worries.

I line up another ball and slap it. He controls it and knocks it into the net. I shoot another and another.

"Crap," he mutters.

"Am I doing it wrong?"

"What? No. You're doing fine. *I'm* doing it wrong."

"It looks good to me."

He frowns. He never frowns around me. "I'm trying to get the corners. In the corners the goalie's chance of getting it are much slimmer." He shakes his head. "It should be simple physics."

"Vectors."

"Exactly. But it doesn't go where it's supposed to."

"Not the ideal conditions," I reply. "Too many variables."

He tugs at a loose bit of grip tape. "Have you ever seen Bobby Orr skate?"

Bobby Orr. Bobby Orr. The name is familiar, but nothing is sticking. "No, I don't think so. Does he play for Dover?"

"No. The Bruins. In the 1960s and '70s. The way he would skate, leaning so far to one side or the other, his ankles were practically on the ground. And he could shift his speed on a dime. Fast, slow, fast, really fast. Passing, too. He could always get just the right speed, just the right place on the ice. It's all friction. He was a smart hockey player. He could see the game steps and steps ahead. But if you asked him to explain how the puck moved on the ice, the spin and the friction, all of that? No way. Me, I could do a whole presentation on the forces involved, but, well—" He doesn't finish his thought but starts picking up the errant tennis balls. I know he tutors half the hockey team, guys who can't understand trigonometry to save their lives but can hit a slap shot every time.

The guilt in my stomach grows. How can I break up with someone when he's just confessed that he wants something so small as to be a decent hockey player?

He pauses, ball in hand. "Are you doing okay?"

I nod. "Yeah."

"I don't ask too often because you don't seem to want to talk about it. About your grandmother, how sick she is. But if you wanted to talk about it—"

"She's okay," I lie. I never told him she went into the hospital, and he doesn't seem to have heard it from anyone else. Maybe they all assumed that I told him, maybe that he was even at the hospital with me, because they have no idea that anything is wrong between us.

"—that's what I'm here for."

"I'm okay," I say, another lie.

"Well, any time, Very. If you're upset, or if there was something you wanted to say, about anything, I'd hope you'd come to me."

"I know. I mean, I would. But actually," I say. "Actually, there's something I need to tell you."

Christian reaches over and brushes some fuzz off my

T-shirt. I don't know what it is about the tenderness of that gesture, but I start to cry. I wipe roughly at my eyes.

"Oh, hey, hey, shhh, stop crying. It's going to be okay. Don't cry. Don't cry." He rubs his hand on my back.

Which just makes me blurt out, "I want to break up with you."

He pulls his hand away from my back and blinks his eyes rapidly. "What?"

It wasn't a *What did you say?* It was a *What the hell are you talking about?*

I wipe my eyes again and try to go back to the script. "It's just that, well, it's just that I've been doing a lot of, you know, thinking." I can't look at him as his face collapses in on itself. I want to reach out and stroke his cheek. I can stop this. I know I can stop this, keep him from hurting, but I have to go on. "About our relationship and love, and I think that the way I feel about you, it's not . . ." I shake my head. He's started to cry, too, and it makes me lose my train of thought. I breathe in deeply. "I don't feel as strongly, it's not fair, and I just think you'd be better off with someone else."

"Who?" he asks. I hadn't expected him to ask this, and it hits me like an out-of-unit question on a test.

"I don't know. Someone."

"But I don't want to be with someone else, I want to be with you." His voice is choppy, and red splotches have appeared on his cheeks. He doesn't even seem embarrassed that he's crying.

"I know, but it's not fair to you if I don't love you like I should."

"What does that even mean?"

What did it mean? "It just doesn't feel right."

"Since when?"

Since ever. But I can't tell him that. "I don't know. Listen, Christian, I didn't mean for this to go this way." As he gets more upset, calm returns to me. "Really. I've given it a lot of thought, though, and I know this is the right choice."

"Do *you* want to be with someone else?" A question I probably should have anticipated, but I can't make any words come out. I know who he's talking about; he doesn't need to say it. And my silence is all he needs. "I see." He doesn't accuse me. He just looks away, disgusted. He knows. Of course he knows.

"This is about you and me," I finally manage to say.

"Sure it is." He stands up. "See you around, Very."

I watch him walk across the driveway and around to the back of his house. Vomiting seems imminent. I didn't know it could hurt so much to hurt someone else.

iii.

Ramona's feet hang from the old oak tree. She swings down from the tree right into my path. "Have you been crying?"

It would be foolish to lie, so I say nothing. She trots after me as I head toward the house.

"Where have you been?"

"Breaking up with Christian."

Something—some emotion, surprise or dismay or maybe even anger—flutters across her face and then is gone. "Was Christian upset?" she asks, her voice even.

"Yeah," I say. "I don't think he expected it."

She nods. A breeze comes up the hill and makes a whistling sound as it passes through the sculpture of bottle caps and pipes on the house. "Because you're fooling around with Dominic?"

"I'm not fooling around with Dominic. I kissed him once."

She bends over and picks up a small pebble from the ground and rolls it between her fingers.

"Sometimes I think he's the one making the sculpture at our house," I tell her.

"Dominic?"

"Yeah," I reply.

"You really think so?"

"I don't know. Maybe." I look down at a small pile of acorns, then shake my head. "No. Forget I said anything."

"Okay."

She isn't listening to me anymore, though. She's already pushing the door open and going into the house, where we find Mom sprawled out on the couch in the sunken living room, a glass of gin perched on her chest, while she reads through one of Dad's *Rolling Stone* magazines.

"Very and Christian broke up," Ramona announces on her way to the stairs, not even stopping to say hello.

Mom sits up quickly, almost spilling her drink. "Oh, baby, come here," she says, patting the seat beside her. I drop my backpack by the door and cross the room to the sofa, sitting a few inches away from her. She lunges toward me and pulls me close. "It's okay to cry, Very. Don't be ashamed." I'm smushed up against her chest, and every time she breathes, I smell the gin. Her body is oppressive. Finally she lets me go, but there's no relief, because she just stares at me with the saddest expression on her face.

"It's okay. I broke up with him."

Mom sips from her glass, and then stares at the ice cubes as she twists her wrist to clink them together. "Did Christian do something to you?"

"No," I say.

"Is it because of the boy? The butcher boy? The one with the grand gesture?"

So Dad hadn't been fooled after all, and Mom had figured out that I'd been talking about Dominic. "It's not because of Dominic. It just wasn't working out. I didn't really love him."

This makes her smile, and I'm afraid she's going to say something like, "Of course you don't love him, you're only seventeen," but she doesn't. She reaches out and runs her fingers through my short hair. "You're going to be all right."

"I know."

"Before I met your father—before we moved to Essex—I dated another man. A boy, really. We were still in high school, after all. He was everything I thought I wanted. It was in New York. He was sophisticated—the son of a stockbroker and a lawyer and his family were huge patrons of the arts. He brought me to concerts at Lincoln Center. We'd stroll through the galleries at the Met. We could spend hours in Central Park."

Ramona lingers at the top of the three stairs that lead down to the living room. "That sounds like when you and Dad met," she says.

Mom blinks her eyes, and then moves closer to me. "I'm sorry. You're the one who had your heart broken, and here I am talking about me."

"I didn't have my heart broken."

"I'm sure you're in pain. It's okay to admit it."

"Fine. I'm in pain. I also have a huge problem set that I need to do for chemistry."

"That can wait."

I shake my head. Before I go, I ask, "Have you heard from Nonnie?"

She looks away, toward the old stereo and the bar cart. "I went in this morning. She was sleeping. Her doctors say she should be able to come home tomorrow or the next day. You sure you don't want to talk about Christian?"

"Not right now."

"Okay," she says, nodding her head and trying to put on a concerned-mom face. "Okay, I understand. But when you do want to talk about it, I'm here."

"I know." I stand up, and as I do, she grabs my hand.

"I mean it, Very. Any time."

"I know."

Her eyes are shiny. They implore me, but I can't tell what

she wants from me. So I disengage my fingers and head toward my dad's office. I want to be the one to tell him, at least, and not have Ramona gleefully report the news to him. But when I push open the door, he isn't there. Just some dry cleaning hanging from the chair looking almost like a real person.

iv.

I do have a giant chemistry assignment, more on specific heat capacity, but I've stared at the formulas for fifteen minutes, and everything is swimming. So I get in the Rapier and drive to the hospital. I have the top down, and the air washes over my shorn head.

Nonnie's in her room, her bed tilted upward, the television on with no volume. "Veronica," she says.

"Tell me more," I beg. "Tell me more about who you were before you were Imogene Woodruff."

"You mean when I was Genie Wood-ruff." She divorces the *D* from the *R*, breaking the syllables in a way that seems much less refined.

"Yes. And how you changed. How you became her. It's not so simple as writing your own story."

"But it is, Very. You just tell people who you are, and they'll believe you as long as you make the right choices—provide the supporting evidence. The problem, the danger, is thinking you can control a story once it's out there, once you step away from the truth." She holds her fingers in front of her mouth and coughs, just a little one, but still she winces. "Did I ever tell you about my *Vanity Fair* article?"

"With the monkey." I smile, thinking of the picture in her room and the stories she had told me.

"I thought, 'This is it. I've arrived. Serious work in a serious magazine.' They sent me on this African safari, and I just had to write an article about my experiences. First-person travel narrative. Easy peasy. Then I get there and suddenly there's a new clause to the contract: a pictorial. A fashion shoot. They dressed me up in that safari getup, with the blouse unbuttoned, made me stand next to that old car. The monkey had the right idea never holding still. The monkey had more gumption than me. I wanted that byline. So I looked right at that camera and let the man shoot away."

She fumbles for the oversize plastic water cup that they've left for her. I grab it and hold the straw to her lips. "I'm sorry. You need your rest."

"No." She shakes her head. "No. You asked about Genie. I can tell you about her. What do you want to know?"

"You said you were just like me then."

She glances up at the silent television, where a cat is looking embarrassed about its litter box. "I suppose I was, Very, though not as sure of myself." She holds the water cup in two hands. "We weren't the bare-feet-in-the-dirt kind of poor, but everyone had to pitch in. We had chickens, Very. Chickens. Right in the yard. Shitting on everything. Pecking at grubs. And us running around and playing in that same yard. We're lucky we never got tetanus."

"I don't think tetanus comes from chickens."

"Salmonella, then. The point is—" Her thought is interrupted by a rough cough that seems to heave itself up and out of her chest. "The point is I was healthier when I was living in filth, chicken shit, and poverty."

I can't tell her that she would have gotten cancer no matter what. Or maybe she wouldn't have. Maybe she should have stayed on the farm, married some nice farm boy, never published a word. Maybe *she* should have gone to Minnesota. Who's to say she wouldn't have been happier?

"So what's this all about?" she asks.

"I just don't know—I just don't know who I am anymore. It's like there are all these different versions of me, different faces on a cube. But they're divided into pieces, and I can't get them back together because I don't know who I want to be."

"Well, good." She leans back into her pillows and closes her eyes. I don't say anything else and neither does she. Eventually her breathing slows, though I can still hear the ragged wheezing. Her eyes move under her eyelids. I sit beside her and watch her lungs raise her chest up and down, up and down. It begins to feel like a ritual, like superstition, like if I stop watching, they will stop moving. This is when I know it's time to leave.

As required, I turned off my cell phone when I went into the hospital. Passing through the sliding front doors on my way out, I click it back on. I have three voice-mail messages and eleven texts. They are all from Grace and Britta.

I go to turn my phone back off, but I'm not quick enough. The phone rings and I hit the answer button without meaning to. It's Grace, but Britta is with her, on speakerphone. I sit in the median of the hospital parking lot on a green bench, which is surrounded by cigarette butts.

"Is it true?" Britta asks. Her voice, edgy at the best of times, crackles through my tiny speaker.

"Which part?"

"Which part of what? The Christian part, of course."

"Yes."

An ambulance careens into the parking lot toward the side entrance for the emergency room.

"Where are you?" Grace demands.

"At the hospital. Nonnie is not doing so well. She's still here."

"Oh." I'm not sure which of them says it. Maybe it's both of them, the air dribbling out of their indignant balloons.

"I'm sorry," Britta says.

"Yeah," Grace agrees. "Sorry."

"Me, too." I know I'm being purposefully unclear about what I'm sorry about.

Britta coughs. She called for a reason, and she's not going to let it go so easily. "The thing of it is, it's like we are breaking up with Christian, too. And I don't want to break up with Christian."

I swing my feet to clear a space from cigarette butts. It's the workers who smoke them—the orderlies and nurses and even the doctors, out here sucking the nasty air as if flaunting their good health to their patients. They do it surreptitiously, don't make eye contact when you walk by, but I know they feel the secret thrill of being so alive you can take it for granted.

"I don't think Christian wants to break up with you, either."

"I know," Britta concurs. "And it's not like I didn't expect it to happen someday."

"Mommy was bound to leave Daddy eventually," Grace says.

"It's just that I would have liked a warning," Britta says.

"How did you know we would break up?"

There is silence on their end. An orderly comes across the parking lot, hesitates, then seems to say, *Screw it*, and stands by the far edge of the bench as he lights his skinny cigarette.

Britta clears her throat, but it is Grace who speaks: "We didn't think it seemed like you were super into him, but we thought that maybe that's just the way you are."

Subtext: *We knew you didn't love him, but we thought maybe you were incapable of love.*

"I guess that is just the way I am."

"Very, I—" Grace begins.

"Listen, I have to go. I've been here for hours. I haven't even started my chemistry problem set."

"Okay, but if you need anything, we're here," Britta says.

"One hundred percent."

"We love you."

"Love you, too," I say, and hang up the phone before turning it off for real.

I run both hands through my hair and glance over at the orderly. He has long hair pulled into a ponytail at the nape of his neck, and stubble sprouting in uneven patches. He holds out his pack to me. "Need one?"

"My grandmother is inside dying of lung cancer."

He knocks the pack. "Take two, then."

I laugh. I laugh and laugh until there are tears streaming down my face and I don't know if I'm still laughing or crying, but my body is shaking. I am making the most inhuman sound: a guttural sob that sounds like it's from some pre-evolutionary part of my body, some part we don't even need anymore. I wipe my eyes. The orderly is still holding out the pack of cigarettes toward me.

"I'll pass," I tell him.

"Smart girl."

"That's my name, don't wear it out."

His smile falters, but he has it back on in a second. Surely he's dealt with grieving family members before. Surely he knows the best way to deal with us is calmly, slowly, like we are rabid animals. His voice is low when he speaks. "The truth of it is, it's awful, and you want it to be over, for them and for you, and then it is over, and it's a thousand times worse."

I reach out my hand and take one skinny cigarette from his pack; I do have to replace the one I smoked from Nonnie's cigarette case. "I guess I'll just save this for later, then. In case of emergency."

"You do that," he tells me.

"Thanks," I say. "For telling the truth."

"Don't tell no one on the inside. I could lose my job for telling the truth."

"My lips are sealed."

I give him a half wave, half salute as I cross the parking lot and then get into Nonnie's Rapier, where I take the cigarette and put it in Nonnie's case. Then I slip into reverse, back out of my spot, and head home—what's left of home without Nonnie.

Outside our house, I open my car door and step out into the cool night air. The seasons are finally starting to behave and it feels like fall. A tinkling sound makes me turn my head toward the bay. There's something about the water down behind our house that bends sound. Voices come trailing up, words spinning around like mist. I used to sit by my window listening to them, imagining the speakers and the lives they led. I wanted them to come for me. I wanted them to wind up the hill, across our lawn, around the house, and then to throw pebbles up at my window and ask me to come down, to come with them on whatever wonderful adventure awaited.

I hear the voices again tonight.

The moon is full and shines in slats on our driveway. The light hits the bottle caps—have they grown in number?—and they seem to dance on the side of the house like water shimmering in midday sun.

There's another square of light on the driveway, more yellow, and when I look up to the house, I see that the light is still on in my mom's studio. She's up there moving around in an almost choreographed way: twist the hair, cross the room, hand to cheek, cross back in the other direction. She seems to be circling something, regarding it, but of course I can't see what it is.

Even from this distance, you can tell she is beautiful by the curves of her body and her posture. I straighten my own back.

She stops short and raises both hands to her head and leaves them there, as if she's posing. Her elbows jut out to the side the way Ramona and I would pose for pictures when we were younger. We called it the supermodel pose, although honestly I've never seen a photo of a supermodel standing with her hands behind her head as if she were resting on them, hip jutted out to the side.

Mom's pose doesn't look silly. She looks like she might suddenly yank her hair out at the roots. I begin to worry. If you have a stroke, I wonder, could you freeze like that, in that eerie pose? Or a seizure, maybe. People think they leave you thrashing on the floor, but more often than not, the victim seems to be staring into space.

As if Mom can sense my worry, she drops her arms to the side, pivots, and walks straight toward the window. My heart speeds up in panic. She'll know I've been watching her. She comes right up to the window and puts one hand on the sill, her forehead on the glass. The moonlight makes her ghostly. There's no sense hiding, so I raise my hand in a small wave.

Mom doesn't react at all.

v.

Mom tries to sneak into my room late at night, but the door squeaks and her ice cubes clink as she walks over to the side of my bed and sits on the edge. When I was young, this was how she used to wake me up in the morning. She sat beside me and rubbed my back and maybe hummed a little song. Sometimes I'd pretend I was still sleeping just because I liked it so much.

"You've been avoiding me," she says.

"I'm sorry," I mumble, and hope that will be enough.

She scoots farther onto the bed, and I slide over to make room for her. Her knees are drawn up to her chest and she balances her drink on them. I wondered if she's been up all this time drinking. "I understand what you're going through, I think. It means so much, but it means so little, you know?"

"Mm-hmm." My eyes are dragging down, desperate to close.

"Why don't you tell me about it?"

"It's not important," I say.

"Sure it is." She pushes some hair out of my face, her fingers cool and damp from the condensation on her glass.

I squint at the clock. It's 2:27. She isn't going to go anywhere until I talk to her. I can feel it in the way she tucks her body against mine. I don't know where to start, so I just say, "I kissed a guy that wasn't Christian."

"And you said there was nothing to tell. There's a story there, I'm sure."

I'd been expecting her to be trembling with excitement,

leaning forward, cheeks flushed. *Finally! Finally her daughter was acting the way she was supposed to.* But her face is soft. She holds her drink in both hands and studies my face so carefully, I bury it in my pillow.

"You wouldn't have kissed the butcher boy if everything was good with Christian."

I rub my fists into my eyes. "I just didn't think it was right. There was nothing there. It wasn't right."

She takes a sip and extends her legs out in front of her. "The hardest thing is thinking about all the time you spent trying to make it work when you could have been doing something else, pursuing other dreams. I mean, all that time you spent watching hockey games. You don't even like hockey."

I have never been to a hockey game: our six months together missed hockey season.

"So there you were freezing and watching him on the ice when you could have been, I don't know, solving some amazing math problem. I'd hate to see that dream lost to you." She takes a long drink, and then another, and when she begins to speak again I realize she has been pausing while she decides whether to tell me the next bit of information. "I was going to go to Pratt. I was all set to go when I met him. Your father. And then I decided to just study art here at Essex."

This is not the fairy tale I'd always been told. "But you were already done with college when you met him."

"I took his music class over the summer. He was teaching summer classes then, to make extra money. I was only seventeen, you know, young for my grade." She kind of giggles, kind of sighs. "I walked into that lecture hall, and it was like something out of a movie. Everyone else just faded away, and there was a clear line between us. What choice did I have?"

"You started dating Dad when you were seventeen?" I left out the second half: and he was twenty-seven.

"Instead of Brooklyn, I got this tiny town, and instead of galleries in SoHo, I've got the Essex grind. Don't get me wrong, I love your father. I'm just saying that the choices we make, they ripple out into places we never expected them to."

It never occurred to me that Mom might be disappointed in her life. "Your art is really, really good."

She laughs. "No, it isn't. Not the stuff you've seen. My new stuff . . ." Her voice fades out. "Maybe that. Anyway, that's not the point. The point is that instead of studying art in New York City, I was watching the proverbial hockey game. So I know how you feel, Very. Even though it was your decision, I know how disappointing this is."

Outside, an owl hoots a mournful cry.

"But this is the time in your life when you are supposed to make those mistakes. I don't mean that condescendingly. God, it used to drive me crazy when my mother would tell me that I was wasting my youth. But she was right, you know. She wasn't right about a lot, but she was right about this. And I am so glad—I am so proud of you—that you aren't making the same mistake as me. That you aren't letting yourself get swept up in your first romance, that you have some perspective."

Her words are gentle and tumble over me, and I have a hard time holding on to them. "It's okay, Mom," I say.

"This is the time for figuring things out. Figuring out how to be in a relationship, what makes a good one. How to end it. You're doing it right, Very. Don't let anyone tell you otherwise."

Perhaps Dominic is something else I'm supposed to experience. My bad-boy phase. But I know it's more complicated than that. Not that he isn't really bad, or is a bad boy with a heart of gold or whatever. I don't know. Maybe it always seems like more when you're the one living it.

"You are supposed to live through these things now, not hold on and stick with it for the rest of your life. Christian is a nice guy, but if you had told me that he was it for you, that you were going to get married, or even just that you were going to go to college together, I would have sat you down and tried to talk you out of it. Not that it would have done any good. My mother's talks just made me want your father more."

She puts her drink down on my bedside table and curls up beside me. "You ought to get some rest," she says. "I'll just wait here with you until you fall asleep, okay?"

"Mom?" I ask.

"Mmm?"

"You were telling me earlier about a boy you dated before Dad. In New York."

She does not say anything for several minutes. "Ancient history," she finally says, but that pause tells me the truth: she regretted leaving him. Who knows if her life would have been any better if she'd never come to Essex, never had to leave that boy. I know she doesn't miss him, not really. She regrets the potential he represents, the road not taken.

I feel her breath as I try to sleep. I listen to it get slower and slower as she succumbs. It is later—how much later, I'm not sure, but it seems like forever—that I fall asleep myself.

When my alarm goes off in the morning, she is still there. She moans and rolls over. I turn the alarm off, slip out of bed, and cover her with a bedspread, tucking it around her shoulders.

ten

i.

IT'S BEEN TWO DAYS since I broke up with Christian. Three days since Nonnie went to the hospital. Four days since I kissed Dominic.

Ramona greets me in the morning wearing wide-legged pants with an untucked button-down shirt and tie. She's twisted her long hair into a bun.

"Drag day?" I ask.

"Women can wear ties. Not very enlightened of you, Very."

I had hoped that maybe Nonnie getting sick would snap Ramona out of her attitude, but no such luck. She didn't come to the hospital for a visit, not even a quick one like Dad, who managed to pop in to the hospital for a few minutes each day. Instead, evidently, she was at home reworking her look from hippie chick to Annie Hall. She picks up a pencil from the kitchen counter and tucks it into her bun. When she opens the refrigerator I say, "The food's all gone. Mom said it spoiled." Still she looks for a moment longer before conceding that there is in fact nothing to eat in the refrigerator. I'll have to go to the grocery store after school. Maybe I'll go to the bigger one in Dover so I don't run into Dominic.

We head into the garage, but then she reaches for the door to the outside. "I don't want to take Nonnie's car."

"She gave it to me. It's mine now."

She removes the pencil from her hair and bites it between her front teeth. We stare at each other like that for a moment, not saying anything. And the truth is I have no idea what direction this conversation could go. Will she be jealous? Will she talk about Nonnie? After twirling it in her fingers, she slips the pencil into her pocket.

"Are you trying to become her?" she asks.

"No."

"Because you can't, you know," she says, as if I hadn't answered. "You can't just cut your hair and drive her car and poof, you're Imogene Woodruff."

"Obviously."

"I don't even know why you'd want to."

"Stop it, Ramona."

"She wasn't perfect. It doesn't do anybody any good to pretend that she was."

"She *isn't* perfect. *Isn't*." I squeeze my hands into fists until my fingers turn white. "Not that you'd know. She could be dead already for all you care. What were you doing when she was in the hospital? Shopping at Goodwill for your next transformation?"

"No. Not for that."

"Don't bother being cryptic. I don't care. I don't care what you do anymore, Ramona. You're so set on being weird, being the supercool or deep or whatever version of yourself, that you aren't even you anymore, and I don't care because I actually love Nonnie and it matters to me whether she lives or dies."

"I don't want to go there and listen to her myths."

"They aren't myths. She's telling me the truth, who she was—"

"Arthur Miller and the Chelsea Hotel and all that? That's her version. The edited and shined-up story."

"How would you even know?"

"Mom was telling the truth. She doesn't own the house anymore. Mom and Dad do, and the mortgage is huge. I found one of the statements lying around. They owe so much money on it, they'll never be able to pay it back. As soon as she dies we're selling, we're gone. You and me and Mom will be living in some condo somewhere and—"

"Stop it, Ramona."

"I thought you wanted the truth?"

"Stop it."

She gives me the strangest smile. Not a smile, but a twisting of the lips. "In that case, I'll take the bus."

ii.

In my life, I've been called to the office numerous times, always for something good. The best, of course, was when I was called down and there was Mr. Tompkins waiting to tell me that his conference proposal, including the proof I'd done, had been accepted for the Math Around U conference.

So when Ms. Blythe finds me studying at a back table in the library and tells me I'm wanted in the office, I imagine what it could be this time: a scholarship, a summer math program, or maybe they'll tell me that I've been granted early acceptance to the college of my choice and can pack my bags right now. Not that I've made my choice. Not that I would leave Nonnie.

The secretary ushers me into the assistant principal's office. Ms. Pickering always dresses in these power suits, except on Fridays, when she wears jeans and high heels. Since it's Wednesday, it's a pink power suit. She smiles widely when I come in, and says, "Verrrronica," trilling out the *R*.

"Hi," I say, settling into the chair across from her.

Her face grows more serious. There's a vase of wildflowers on her desk, and she spins it a half turn, causing a few petals to fall onto her desk. "Your sister has been missing quite a bit of school."

Because really, my week isn't bad enough already. "Oh?" I try to sound neutral.

"Yes, three days last week, and of course she hasn't been in at all this week." She clears her throat. "She's missed more days than she's attended so far this year."

She isn't out. This morning I waited until I saw her board the bus, then cruised right by with the top down. "Yes, well, she's been feeling under the weather."

"Her attitude, too, seems troubling. Teachers report that she's listless in class. And she hasn't turned in any work. Of course it's early in the year, but this is not the best way to start off her high school career."

An accurate first impression: the best possible version of Ramona.

I look at the arrangement of things on her desk: calendar, clock, red stapler, a shallow bowl filled with paper clips. "Ms. Pickering, I don't know what to tell you."

She smiles. "You don't need to tell me anything, Veronica. I'm telling you. You're a great student, and I want to enlist your help in helping your sister. We find these things work best when the whole family is involved."

"Okay."

"To be perfectly honest, we don't normally go to siblings, but we've had some trouble reaching your parents." She pauses as if waiting for me to supply some information, but I do not. "I left a number of messages, but now it seems the answering machine has been turned off?"

"I'll check when I get home." The window behind her looks out into the parking lot. I can see Nonnie's car, and contemplate crawling out the window to get to it.

"That will be lovely, but the bigger issue here is Ramona. She could use your guidance."

"Well, like I say, she hasn't been feeling well. Maybe it's mono or something. I can take her to the doctor."

Ms. Pickering arranges the stack of papers on her desk. "I hope it's something so straightforward, I really do, but I fear there may be more going on. She seems to be disconnecting from her life."

Disconnecting from her life. Wouldn't that be nice, if you could really do it? Not like permanently, but just a little break for a while.

"We're thinking she might need some help."

"What kind of help?" My guess is Ms. Pickering isn't talking about a tutor.

"We have a school psychologist."

"She's not crazy."

"I didn't say she was crazy. I've heard your grandmother is ill. Ramona just might need someone to talk to, to process the situation. People grieve in different ways, and this could be Ramona's way of processing the stress of the illness."

For Nonnie's cancer to bother Ramona she would have to acknowledge it.

"You don't need to take this on yourself. Perhaps a family discussion about how best to handle the situation is in order."

"I'll see what I can do."

"Wonderful!"

Yes, everything is just wonderful. "Thanks for letting me know," I say as I stand.

"Veronica, there is something else I want to talk to you

about." I sit back down on the molded plastic char. Ms. Pickering's is one of those high-tech office chairs, sleek, curved, and black. "Of course it's not my practice to listen to idle gossip, I'm sure you know that. But every once in a while things bubble up."

Oh God.

"It's come to my attention that you've been spending some time with Dominic Meyers."

Actually I haven't seen him in two days; *he* is the one who hasn't been in school.

I look down at my hands in my lap—folded like two broken birds—and think of the last time I saw him, on Monday: after the parties, after Nonnie went to the hospital. On that day I acted like he was just some piece of loose paper that had blown up against me, something to be brushed away.

Ms. Pickering reaches out and again moves the vase, and another shower of petals rains down. "While I always like to see students breaking out of cliques, and of course you are free to be friends with whomever you wish"—she clears her throat—"I would never say that someone was not worthy of your friendship. At the same time, it's an important lesson to learn that you are judged by the company you keep."

"And?" If she is going to bring this up, she better go all the way.

"And." She shifts in her seat, rustling the power suit. "Perhaps how you want to be known, that is, perhaps you don't want to tie your reputation to Dominic's."

"Maybe he's tying his reputation to mine," I say. "If we're judged by the company we keep, wouldn't I be a good person to hang out with? You just said I was one of your star students."

"Yes, of course."

"So maybe instead of reconsidering my reputation, people should be reconsidering his."

"Well, yes, but it doesn't always work that way."

"If people trust my judgment, why shouldn't they trust my judgment of him?"

"Sometimes smart kids make bad choices. That's what I'm trying to avoid here. I don't want you to make decisions that have consequences that you regret."

"I have a lot of homework to do," I say. "I'll talk to Ramona."

Ms. Pickering looks like she wants to say something else, but in the end, she just nods, and says, "Thank you, Veronica."

iii.

Mr. Solloway sits on a stool behind his desk, holding up two pieces of thick white paper, looking from one to the other. He just nods at me as I enter, as if people go in and out of the art room all the time. There's a quiet hum of concentration and work. Every wall and flat surface seems to be covered with posters, student artwork, figure models, and art supplies.

This is where Ramona is supposed to be: sixth-period art. But as Ms. Pickering has said, she's not here.

Serena is working at an easel near the back. She looks up, sees me. Smiles. I take a deep breath. This is Serena, after all. She isn't someone you just stroll up to and start talking to. We've gone to school together for eleven years, and I've never once had a conversation with her.

You've got your friends and you stick to them.

I clench my fists and I navigate my way to her. She watches me as I walk to her easel but doesn't say anything when I arrive. "Um," I say. "Hello."

"Hello," she repeats. She says it with a slightly British pronunciation, *hell-oh* instead of *hel-low*.

"I just want to thank you. For English class, back on the first day of school."

"Sometimes Hunter just needs a reminder of common courtesy. And I meant what I said. I do like your grandmother's poetry."

I tug at the hem of my shirt. "She'd be glad to hear that."

I look at Serena's easel. It's a swirling painting of the night sky all in blues and purples with streaks of red. It looks dangerous. "That's nice," I say, and immediately wince. I know better than to call a painting nice. "I'm sorry. I've never been good at talking about art."

"That's okay. Neither am I."

When I first came in, all I could smell was the studio: paint, clay, that sort of thing. But now I can smell Serena. She uses a strawberry-scented perfume or lotion that is surprisingly innocent.

"It's supposed to be a self-portrait."

"You aren't going to have room for yourself in there," I reply.

"Maybe I'll make myself very, very tiny. Just a speck." She leans back and glances at a mirror that is set up next to her easel. "It's so much harder to see yourself than other people. I'd rather paint you in there. Your face has great angles." Serena points at her mirror and says, "I don't like looking at myself."

"But you're beautiful!"

"Yeah, sure."

"I saw the picture of you. The one from the high school art competition. It was gorgeous." Serena holds her brush above the canvas, and I look at her again. Hunter got rid of her freckles, and her smile. He made her eyes lighter and lips darker so she and Callie looked more alike. The picture doesn't seem so beautiful anymore. It wasn't really Serena. Or Callie. He'd turned them into interchangeable pieces.

She paints a few more brushstrokes. These are small and tentative, and I wonder if she's working up to painting herself, bracing herself, digging for the courage. And that makes me wonder how Nonnie did it, time and time again, pouring herself onto the page. When you write your own story, you're asking to be read. "It's poetry," she used to say. "You're meant to look."

"I might just paint over this one," Serena says. "Start again with my face."

I know she means she'll treat it with a solvent or sand it down and then paint over it with titanium white before starting over, but I picture the outline of her face over the swirls on her canvas.

"Sometimes you just need to step away from it and work on something else. Anyway, that's what my mom says. Not that she does it, but that's what she says."

"Is she a painter?"

I've always felt like everyone in town knew my whole lineage. "Yes. I remember her telling Ramona that once when she was stuck on a painting. 'Take it off the easel. Turn it around so you can't even see it. It'll let you know when it's ready for you.'"

"Ramona from this class?"

I glance around the room, but don't see her. "I thought she had art this period, but she's only a freshman, so I guess I got it wrong."

"No, this is her class. I don't think she's here today. She's good. Normally they don't let freshmen in this class." She points toward the front of the room, to a painting on an easel. It's a red rectangle on an off-white background. A Marcus Schmidt knockoff.

"I didn't realize she was your sister, but I can see it now."

It feels freeing that with Serena there are new things: I am discoverable. And I feel calm in the art room—much calmer than I did when I was actually taking art class and worried my GPA was going to plummet. Now it feels like I could come in and close the door on everything going topsy-turvy outside of it. Maybe I'll never leave. I'll just curl up on the floor to sleep, get people to bring me my food, and have teachers send me my work. Once the world gets normal again, then perhaps I'll come out.

Serena picks up a wider brush. "You're on the math team, right?"

I think about lying, but if she knows, she knows. "Yeah. It's kind of lame."

"I don't think so," she replies. She hesitates with her brush above the canvas to glance at me. "I used to be good at math, and then I guess I decided it wasn't cool or something, and then the ability just went away. It was like instant karma or something."

"The math gods are fickle," I say, and she laughs. I've never heard her laugh. It's low and throaty. I like it.

"Maybe if I prepare some sort of ritual sacrifice, I'll be able to pass geometry."

"I could help you," I say, too quickly. "I mean, if you want help, I wouldn't mind."

"That would be nice." I can't tell if she is really agreeing, or just being polite.

"Any time, just let me know." I take a breath so I will stop sounding like a puppy dog. "Anyway, I should go. I'm supposed to be in study hall."

"I'll grab you sometime for math help, all right?"

"Any time," I say again, before I turn to go. As I near the door, I glance to my right. Ramona's painting isn't a rectangle but a blanket—a red afghan that I recognize. The real, ratty one is draped across the back of the couch at home. That afghan was the roof of our forts, a magic carpet, the stretcher that saved Captain Honey-Dewdrop from a battle with the half-elf, half-troll warriors of the Western shore. It was the blanket we sat on at the outdoor pool, blades of grass pressing up in the holes. It is wrapped around our family memories. I want to go find Marcus Schmidt, grab him by the elbow, drag him here, and say, *This is how you do it so it matters.*

iv.

Ramona has taken her tie from her neck and wound it around her wrist. She tugs at the pointed end that flops down.

"Have a good day?" I ask.

"Yep."

"Classes were good?"

"I guess. Are we going to go home or what?"

"What did you have?"

She turns from staring at her tie to look at me. "Math, English—the usual."

"That's interesting because I was called down to Ms. Pickering's office and she told me you weren't here today. I guess there must have been some misunderstanding."

Just tell me the truth, Ramona.

"I guess so."

"Why are you lying to me? Where have you been? She said you've missed a whole lot of school. More days than you've been."

I know how I sound to her: my shrill voice barely muffled by the soft top of Nonnie's Rapier.

"You know, there are lots of programs at school—I mean lots of things in the arts. There's Drama Club and I think there's a literary magazine and I'm sure they're looking for people to help with that."

"I know."

It's like talking to a four-year-old who has decided she isn't going to eat her peas and carrots no matter how much you cajole.

"Where do you go?" I try to soften my tone and end up sounding like a preschool teacher.

She pivots in the seat to look out the window. "Around."

"I lied for you. I told her you weren't feeling well."

"Why'd you do that?" she asks, staring back at me.

"So you wouldn't get in trouble."

"I don't care if I get in trouble."

"Clearly. Now tell me where you've been."

"Can't we just go home?"

I do not start the car. I stare at her as she looks straight ahead. Her long hair is looking ratty—inches of split ends that needed to be cut off—and she has dark circles under her eyes. "Mom and Dad don't know," I tell her. "I think Mom turned the answering machine off."

"I turned it off."

"What? Why?"

"It was always blinking."

I turn the key in the ignition and back out of the parking space. When we're on the road home, I say, "All I want to know is where you go."

"Why?"

"Because you owe me one."

"I owe you one?" She says it slowly, as if she is contemplating it rather than being incredulous.

"Yes, Ramona. You. Owe. Me. One." I take a hard left onto our street, cutting it a little close to the oncoming traffic. Ramona doesn't flinch. "I sat in that office and listened to Ms. Pickering go on about looking out for you, like this was my fault, and I didn't sell you out. So I'd like to know what I was covering up. What I lied for. Why should I cover for you if you're not going to tell me where you were?"

"I never asked you to cover for me. I don't want you to."

"Fine," I say.

"Fine," she agrees.

I steal glances while I drive, taking in every detail of her disarray, from stained collar to her canvas shoes, which have a hole worn in the toe. She is evolving before my eyes. Sometimes when I look at her, it's like she isn't even there.

As soon as we get home, I march into the living room, where Mom is reclining on the sofa, of course, reading a book of Nonnie's poems, a cocktail in her hand. "Ramona's been skipping school," I announce.

"I know."

This stops me. "What?" Mom has always been kind of

flaky when it comes to school, not really buying into "the whole construct of children sitting in rows and reading from the same book and writing the same words," but she always played along.

"The school left like a hundred messages." She waves her hand in the air. "I'm sure she has a good reason for it."

"Mom, I got called down to Ms. Pickering's office. I got lectured."

"What's that saying?" she asks. "About siblings?"

"You can't pick them?" I suggest.

She takes a drink. "No. 'I am not my brother's keeper.' That one."

"So you're saying I should have told Ms. Pickering that it's none of my business? That she's not my responsibility?"

"I'm saying don't worry about it. There's nothing to worry about."

"Mom, there are laws about this. Truancy laws."

"Hear that, Ramona? You're a truant!"

Ramona giggles.

"Mom," I say. "This is serious."

"Serious as a heart attack," she says.

"She'll fail the ninth grade. She'll have to redo it."

"Well then, maybe I'll homeschool her. What do you think of that, Ramona?"

Ramona's smile falters. "I better go hit the books." And she walks up the stairs.

"Mom, you can't joke about this."

"Really, Very," Mom says. "Don't take this whole messed-up family on your shoulders. Live your life. Go have fun with that butcher boy. Go a little wild."

In my family, the whole world is inside out. Like everyone else got a memo that the usual rules do not apply. Except for me, still pottering along between the lines like a sucker.

v.

The wooden stairs are worn so each step has a divot as deep as a bowl. I hold on to the railing as I make my way up to the third floor of Peterson Hall. Mom was no help with Ramona, so I need to talk to Dad. I tried his office at home first. The dry cleaning was still hanging off the back of his desk chair, and there was bunch of junk mail and magazines piled on his desk, but no Dad.

When Ramona and I were younger, my dad had brought us to his office all the time. We'd sit on the couch he had, or on the floor, flipping through his magazines and entertaining the students who came for office hours. As we got older, though, he stopped bringing us.

Lainey, the music department assistant, greets me as I come into their suite of offices. She's worked there, behind the large desk, for as long as I can remember. "Very, how nice to see you! It's been forever and a day."

"You know how it is," I reply.

"Sure do! Your dad's in his office." She taps her fingers on her desk, one right after another, and looks at me meaningfully—though I'm not quite sure what the meaning is. "Been working away. He says he's really on to it this time." She smiles. "One of these days."

"Thanks, Lainey. I'll see you in a bit."

"Okay, doll."

When I push open the door to his office, Dad seems more distracted than surprised. He looks at me for a moment before saying, "Very."

"You busy?"

He looks at the books and computer printouts spread out over the desk. More stacks of books are on the floor, next to piles of CDs and albums, even a few cassette tapes. It is clear he is occupied, but he says, "There's always time for you, jelly bean. Come on in. Actually, maybe you could help me out." I sidestep a year's worth of *The Source* magazines to get to the chair on the other side of his desk. It, too, is full of magazines. He waves his hand toward the mess. "I'm working on a book proposal."

"The hip-hop history one?"

He wrinkles his nose. "No. Done with that. This is a thousand times better. I think this could be it, Very. It's got crossover appeal. It won't be just academic. It's going to be controversial. I'll be like the Malcolm Gladwell of musicology. Talk shows, NPR, the works."

"What's it about?" I ask, since I know that's what is expected of me.

"My thesis is that hip-hop isn't really a black art, it's a white art. Economically, sure, that's been talked about, and I'll go there, looking at where the money comes from and where it goes. You know, seventy percent of hip-hop is bought by white consumers. But I'm looking at the songs themselves, their antecedents."

I nod, but really I'm thinking, *What's the point?* Because I know my dad isn't trying to start some race war over music. He isn't trying to be the white supremacist of hip-hop. He is just trying to make a name for himself, to step beyond the world of academic publishing into the brighter spotlight.

"With this book, I can go anywhere. I'll be fielding offers from schools all over the country. NYU, UCLA. Who knows, maybe even Harvard, although I'd rather be at MIT if I'm going to be in Cambridge." His cheeks are flushed with excitement, and it hits me: he wants to get out. *I*, he said. *Me*. Not *us*.

Ramona knew.

As soon as she dies we're selling, we're gone. You and me and Mom will be living in some condo somewhere and . . .

It's a mistake, coming here for help. I see that but I press on. "Have you, I mean, how do you think Mom's doing?"

"Well, you know, as well as can be expected given the circumstances."

I wonder if it would be possible for him to spew out any more platitudes.

"I'm worried about her."

"Uh-huh." He picks up one of the printouts. There is girly

writing on it in green ink. The handwriting is so bubbly it looks like the *i*'s should be dotted with hearts.

"And I'm really worried about Ramona."

He reaches across his desk to pick up a Vanilla Ice CD. "Garbage," he mutters. "Still, I can't decide if I should talk about white rappers or not. Do they deserve a place in this or are they a special case?"

He isn't talking to me. Not really.

"There's something I need to tell you."

He looks over an article: Elvis Presley. God, at least he could choose a less obvious path. I mean, everyone already knows that Elvis made black music safe for white audiences. "I think Ramona needs your help."

"Uh-huh." He circles something with his pen.

"Dad," I say sharply.

He looks up. "I'm sorry, jelly bean."

"Are you even listening?"

"I get so caught up in this stuff. I don't want to lose my momentum. This is it. This is my big idea, and I don't want to lose it."

If it is such a great, big idea he shouldn't have to worry about losing it.

"Can this wait?" he asks.

The bobbleheads on his desk dance back and forth.

"I'm not sure." I don't really know what "this" is. "I don't think—"

His phone rings, and, after he looks at the display, he picks it up with a smile. "Hello, Kaitlin." He glances up at me and then immediately looks away. "Just working on the book proposal. Thanks for the articles, by the way. My daughter's here. Very."

I look down at the table. There is no one in the music department named Kaitlin.

I let my gaze travel around the room. The shelves are full of music theory books and mementos: framed concert tickets, a small drum, a signed Mos Def poster. There are, I realize, no pictures of us.

"Yeah, definitely," he goes on. "It wouldn't be a music book without Lester Bangs, would it?"

I tap my fingers on the table, and he looks up at me with pursed lips. Annoyed. He is annoyed with me. I came here to let him know that his wife and daughter are both losing it, and all he cares about is his stupid book idea. "I'm going," I say.

"Hold on," he says into the phone. "Very, this will just take a minute. Then we can finish our conversation."

"No." I shake my head. "You're busy."

"You sure?"

"Yeah."

"Thanks, Very." He goes back to his conversation, telling this Kaitlin person that he would love if she came over later to help him organize his resources. When I reach the door, he says, "Thanks for stopping by, Very. We'll talk soon."

"That'd be great," I say. I can lie almost as well as him now.

The one thing I was sure of was that he loved my mother. Another certainty slips away. I charge down the hallway and almost run right into Professor Winslow. "Veronica," he says. "You look like a girl who could use a butterscotch candy." He puts his hand on my back and guides me into his office, which I know well from my failed attempts at learning the piano. That same piano is still in the corner, its music stand holding one sheet of music.

Professor Winslow takes the top off of a glass canister on his desk and pretends not to notice as I wipe furiously at my eyes. He hands me two golden candies and then sits down on the piano bench. "These are hard days for you," he says.

I sink into an armchair, the same armchair where I always ended my lessons, and Professor Winslow starts to play a piece that I don't recognize. I am pretty sure it's in the minor key and it dances from scale to scale. I close my eyes and tilt my head back, and it is almost like I am little again, listening to Professor Winslow play at the end of our lessons, still believing that maybe someday I can play like that. The sweet, buttery taste fills my mouth as the candy dissolves.

The pace of the song picks up, like someone is dancing lightly in her shoes, spinning and waltzing, the notes tumbling the way Nonnie's poetry could.

I wonder if she knows he loves her. I would like to think not, but I feel certain she does. This kind man with his tweed hats and argyle socks and the—I'm imagining here—blue veins crisscrossing his calves. Professor Winslow would have loved her sweetly, would have taken care of her, bought the groceries, taken her for Sunday drives up the Maine coast. He would have read her poetry and filled her wineglass and told her she looked absolutely stunning and would have believed it—*meant* it—even as the cancer took spark after spark from her.

The music ends with one long note that he lets die out.

"That's beautiful," I tell him. "Who wrote it?"

"Original composition. I wrote it for your grandmother. It's based on one of her poems. And her."

I smile. It's the sort of thing she would love but profess to hate.

"She says I ought to play it at her funeral."

"I guess that's as close to a compliment as you could get from her."

He looks down at the keys of the piano. "It's hard being an old man giving advice to young people. It's always meant in earnest, but it can be so hard to believe." He reaches up and smooths the sheet of music. "I want to tell you that it will get better. And it will. But that doesn't make it any easier in the moment, does it?"

"No."

"Then I won't tell you that. But you see, the reason that we want to step in and give advice is that it hurts us—it hurts me to see you so in pain. I wish there were something I could do to make it lighter. And so we resort to words, which never carry all the meaning we want them to. Though perhaps Imogene would disagree."

"Could you play it again for me?"

"Yes," he says. He stretches out his fingers and looks at me with soft, pale eyes. "Yes, it would be an honor."

I tuck my legs up onto the chair with me and nestle my head on my knees so I am as small as I can be. I close my eyes again, and as I listen to the music, I feel Nonnie with me.

eleven

i.

THE GALLERY IS ALL lit up when I walk by, glowing against the gloaming sky. Marcus Schmidt's squares are like patches in a deconstructed quilt.

The door makes a sucking sound as I pull it open, and the older couple wandering around turn their heads to look at me before turning back to the pictures with intense inspection.

Maybe I remembered the paintings wrong, or hadn't paid enough attention. Maybe there really is some variation. Bleeding edges. Uneven paint application that will give a hint of the sideways message that Marcus Schmidt has to share. But no. I look at every single one of the paintings, and the only thing that changes is size and color. It's like he took paint samples from the hardware store and blew them up to one hundred times their original size.

And, I read on the gallery wall, he doesn't even sign his name. It's a stamp, applied in the same spot every time, "eschewing the

So I go back downstairs. I don't look at me. I don't look at the girls on the back wall. I look for something else.

A student from way up in the northern part of the state has a painting of a pig, its eyes bright as it turns on a spit, beer can shoved in its mouth. The hairs on the back of the pig stand up like thin wires. From this painting, I know this boy—far better than one could know me, or Serena or Callie, from looking at our portraits.

In the next cluster of art there is a sculpture of a dancer, a knockoff Degas, only the face has been replaced by a twisted clown's mask. Mom would call it shocking without a message. Nonnie would probably buy it and stick it somewhere prominent in our house. I'm imagining that alternate world—the one where Nonnie is healthy and she and Mom engage in an elaborate game of shifting the sculpture around the house—when I see an etching. The print is framed, and the metal plate used to make it is next to it.

It's the ocean. The actual ocean. Swirling and shining and *moving*. This life, that's what is missing from Marcus Schmidt's dull squares above.

I step closer and it's like being on the deck of a ship: the ocean in the print moves with me, catches me off-balance.

My eyes flick to the small white card that identifies the artist:

Our Ocean
Copper plate etching and print
Dominic Meyers
Essex High School

Proof:

STATEMENT	REASON
1. Dominic wrote the lyrics to "Veronica" on my locker.	Given.
2. The lyrics look like they are moving.	Given.
3. Dominic created the print of the ocean.	Given.
4. The ocean looks like it is moving and alive.	Given.
5. The sculpture on the house looks like it is growing and alive.	Given.
6. Therefore, Dominic created the sculpture on the house.	Transitive property, two times over.

There's no doubt anymore. Even Mr. Tompkins would approve of this one.

ii.

I'm certain I will find Dominic at his house, so I look up his address on my phone and just drive with the soundness of my proof carrying me. I need to tell him I know about the sculpture and to thank him for it. He'll be so pleased, I think, that I figured it all out, it won't even matter that I blew him off at school. I'll have a chance to explain that, too.

At his door, I hesitate before pressing the bell. *Our Ocean*, he called it. Who was the "we"? Who was the other person?

Shaking off the doubt, I ring the doorbell. A woman in a pink tweed suit answers the door. She has her hair pulled back at the nape in a way that is old-fashioned yet pretty. She must be a girlfriend of Dominic's father's. But no, that isn't right. Because, the thing is, she looks exactly like Dominic: same green eyes, same pointed nose. "You're back," I blurt out.

She blinks her eyes in confusion. "I'm sorry. Do I know you? Are you in one of my lectures?"

"Lectures?" Inside the house a grandfather clock chimes five times, as dull and final as a judge's gavel. "No, I'm a friend of Dominic's. He hasn't been at school the past few days, and I thought maybe you all had gone on vacation and now, you're back!" I speak quickly, rambling, feeling more and more like an idiot.

"He hasn't been in school?"

"Yes, well, at least, I haven't seen him. Maybe our paths just didn't cross or something."

"What's your name?" she asks.

"Very Sayles-Woodruff."

"Like the poet?" I nod. "Well, Very, this is the first I've heard of his not going to school."

As she speaks, I see him padding down the stairs behind her in white crew socks. "Like I say, it's possible we just weren't running into each other. It's a small school, but you'd be surprised how you can miss people."

270

"I see," she says, totally unconvinced.

"Hello, Very," Dominic says, not quite at the bottom of the stairs.

"Oh, hi," I reply, as if I've just seen him.

Mrs. Meyers looks over her shoulder. "Very just told me you haven't been in school."

"That I haven't *seen* him in school," I correct.

"Can we talk about this later?" Dominic asks.

"Oh, you can be sure that we will." She turns back to me. "It's been lovely to meet you."

We both watch as she walks away. He jams his feet into a pair of Vans. "Come on." He takes me by the arm and leads me outside. The evening has grown chilly, as if fall is whispering a teasing hello, and I zip up my jacket. We walk to the end of his driveway, past the recycling bin full of empty bottles of wine and organic juice, tin cans for hearts of palm, and the plastic clamshells for hothouse tomatoes, then turn and start down the road. "What are you doing here? I didn't realize I had another appointment with my peer counselor."

I kick at an acorn, my face hot. "I'm sorry. It's just that I'm having a hard time. And then I went to—"

"So what do you want me to do about it?" He stares past me.

"I'm sorry about the other day. I thought you would understand."

"That you were embarrassed to be seen with me. Who's too cool now?"

"Dominic, it's not like that, I just need—"

"Are you hoping I can hook you up? What's your pleasure? What kind of a girl are you, Very?"

I step away from him. "God, no."

"Of course not. Not Veronica Sayles-Woodruff."

"Jesus, Dominic, I just came here to talk." I am blinking so fast he seems to be moving like stop-motion animation.

"And fuck up my life."

"I didn't tell her you were skipping school. I told her I hadn't seen you around. And anyway, I don't know why you're being so self-righteous when you're the one who lied to me about your mother. What is she, a professor?"

"Why do you care?"

"I've been defending you at school, telling people to cut you some slack because they don't know what you've been through." I'd gotten all defensive with Ms. Pickering, but she had been right about him.

"Oh really?"

"Really."

"Because here's what I saw. I saw you backpedal away from me so hard you should have road rash. I saw you making a calculation—you're good at those, right—and you decided that what you knew about me had less value than the rumors."

"What I know about you? I don't know one solitary thing about you. Everything you told me was a lie."

"I told you what you needed to hear."

"So you could get in my pants?"

"Did I get in your pants? I don't remember that. I guess it

wasn't too memorable. Of course, with all the girls I've got it's hard to keep you all straight."

I stop where I am, tears in my eyes. "What the hell is wrong with you?"

"What's wrong with you? Showing up at my house like some kind of girlfriend or something."

"Why are you being so mean? Everything is messed up right now. Everything. And all I wanted was to come over and talk to you because I thought, that thing you made, I thought it meant something." The tears are rolling down my face now, and I know my skin is red and blotchy, and probably the snot will start flowing soon, but I just can't seem to care.

"Poor, poor Very. Game not going the way you want it? That's what this has all been to you. I'm just one part of your reinvention. Cut your hair, check. Retro car, check. Boyfriend from the wrong side of the tracks, check."

"You're not my boyfriend, and Essex doesn't have a wrong side of the tracks."

"That's right. I'm not your boyfriend. So, why aren't you at his house talking to him?"

I pivot and start walking back toward his house and my car.

"Fuck," I hear him whisper. I keep walking. I will not look back. The leaves are skittering across the street in front of me like spiders. I will not look back.

"Oh come on," he calls after me. "Come back, Very. I'm sorry."

The recycling truck careens around the corner. A man in a fluorescent green vest hangs off the back. He swings down like a gymnast from the uneven bars and scoops up the bin with one hand. He dumps it into the back of the truck, all of it crashing and cracking and slamming together. The man whistles as he jumps back onto the truck.

I'm nearly to my car now. The truck rumbles to the next house. Keep walking. Just a few more steps.

"Seriously, Very, we didn't even get to make out or anything!"

iii.

Dominic returns to school the next day. I know it before I even see him. Just as Ms. Staples says good morning, I glance up at him, and he mouths the words, "I'm sorry."

I look away.

"Welcome back, Dominic," Ms. Staples says. "We've been doing a group project getting ready to present a poet and her work. Everyone is partnered up, so you'll have to join a pair and make a group of three. How about you jump in with Britta and Very. They'll get you right up to speed."

"No," I say.

Ms. Staples looks at me with some surprise.

We've been working on this project for almost a week already. Admittedly, Britta has done the majority of the work. It seems unfair to tether another deadweight to her. "He doesn't even know who we've chosen. Shouldn't he be placed in a group based on the poet? Anyway, we've already done almost all the work. It wouldn't be fair for him to just jump in."

"I can join with someone else. No problem."

Ms. Staples, though, shakes her head. "Let me worry about the equity of work distribution. Dominic will join your group for the presentation next week." She shifts her focus from me to the rest of the class. "I'm going to give you some time to work on your presentation right now. So get in your groups."

Crap, crap, crap. Dominic walks across the room and pulls up an empty desk next to us. I stare down at my notebook. Britta takes over. Thank God for Britta. "We're doing Gwendolyn Bennett. From the Harlem renaissance."

"I know who she is," he says.

She flips open her notebook and shows him the outline we have so far. "So you've read her poems?"

"Yeah. I read the whole packet while I was out. I wanted to stay caught up."

Britta looks impressed. Even she hasn't read all the poems yet.

"We've started looking at her imagery. Lots of trees, for example, so we want to talk about that."

"Lots of body references, too," he says. "Hands, fingers, lips."

I flip through the packet like I'm trying to find something.

"That's not really one of our talking points, but if you want to go there, be my guest."

He laughs like falling leaves, and I finally allow myself to look at him. His eyes squint and his lips are chapped. I shift my glance out the window, where a bird is hopping along the windowsill, fluttering her wings without flying. I look down at my notes.

Britta says, "So we figured we're going to start by giving some background about her. Then highlight a few of the poems, talking about the imagery and the messages. You know, maybe compare the ones that are explicitly about race to the ones that are more universal. The love one."

"And the hate one," I say.

"And there's the 'artistic representation' piece." She makes air quotes as she says it. We have to do an art project that relates to the poems, which Britta thinks is not real scholarship and thus a waste of time.

"Sounds good," Dominic says. "Listen, Very, I'm really sorry about yesterday."

Britta snaps her head around to look at me. I glare at him. "Forget about it."

"I can't."

"Forget about it," I say again. "We need to break down who's going to talk about what. I've done a little research about her life, so I can take the biography."

Britta, recovering gamely, says, "I'll do the nature imagery."

"I think Very should do the art piece," Dominic says.

"What?"

"That's a horrible idea," Britta says.

"Why?" Dominic asks.

"Because we want to pass this course. Right, Very? Tell him it's a stupid idea."

They're both looking at me and it's like that story with the frog where both kids want it and can't agree and it's going to be pulled in two, and I'm the frog. "I'll do it," I say. "But then you need to do her biography."

Dominic leans back in his chair. "Fine."

"Can you handle it?" I ask.

"Yeah, of course."

"Are you going to be in class?" I ask.

He looks at the window, toward the now-still bird. "Yes, I'll be here."

"Because if not, just tell us now so we can be ready for it."

"I said I'll be here."

"Good," I reply.

Ms. Staples claps her hands together. "Okay, class, back into the large group."

Dominic drags his desk back to the other side of the circle, and I shift mine so I can't see him, but I can still feel his eyes on me.

iv.

I grab his arm in the hall after class once the crowd has dispersed.

"Very, hi, I wanted to talk to you, too." His eyebrows are knitted together over his eyes.

"You can't just come back and insert yourself into my life."

"I didn't insert myself, and anyway it's not your life. It's a school project."

"Same thing," I say. "I don't want to be in this group with you. I want you to leave me alone."

"I'm sorry, Very. I don't know what to say. I was out of line yesterday."

"You were," I agree.

"You weren't exactly innocent." He balls his hand into a fist and hits his own leg with it. "But I was way out of line. I do that sometimes, but I didn't want to do it to you."

"Do what? Lie? Insult people?"

He looks away from me for a second, and I wonder if maybe I've pushed him back over that edge. I tense my body, but instead he says, "I'm going to make it up to you with this project. I'm going to make the most kick-ass presentation ever. It will blow your socks off, set you on fire."

"You can't win me back through good grades."

"Did I ever have you, Very?"

My heart hiccups and I feel sure I have just revealed a secret to both of us. "Just do the project and do it well, or deal with the wrath of Britta."

"You don't have to worry. I might even dress up. I'll wear a dress, but don't be concerned, I won't come in with blackface or anything."

"Gwendolyn Bennett's life story," I say. "That's it."

"Life story," he agrees.

I leave him in the hall and make my way to my next class.

"Hey, Very," he calls after me. "I would take it all back if I could. Every word."

But he can't. Once words are out there, they can't be recalled. Nonnie taught me that.

v.

"So what is going on with you and Dominic?" Britta asks. She has met me in the coffee shop at the hospital, where I'm visiting Nonnie again. Mom's up with her now, though neither of them was talking when I left.

The table between Britta and me has a dull green laminate top, and our mugs land with a clunk each time we put them down.

"Nothing. Not anymore."

"What was going on, then?"

"I don't even know," I say.

She wraps her hands around the mug.

"Where's Grace?" I ask.

"Studying Chinese with Josh. Listen, I've been asking around, and your reputation is still good. People were confused by the perceived sudden breakup with Christian. But it's all blowing over."

"You've been doing approval-rating polls for me?" I ask.

"Just making sure no one's talking crap about you. You know, hanging out with Dominic Meyers doesn't exactly—"

"I kissed him. At that party." I lift my eyes to look at her face. "In the woods."

"I'd heard you'd gone. You could have asked us to go with you."

"I sort of tried when we were working on posters, and both you and Grace said it sounded awful."

"But if you had really wanted to go, we would have—"

"I didn't want you to go with me," I tell her.

"Because you were meeting Dominic."

"Yeah. I guess." I trace my finger along a crack in the table-top that looks like a bird's footprint. "But something more. I just wanted something different."

"Different friends?" She looks straight at me.

"Different me. Nonnie says you can write your own story." I rub my head. "It didn't work out so well. For either of us."

"Nonnie did all right for herself."

"She's dying alone."

"She has your family."

"She has me." I take a sip of the burned coffee. The taste lingers in the back of my throat. "Have you seen Ramona around school?" I ask.

Britta shakes her head. Her hair shakes around her shoulders.

"That's because she's not going. She skips practically every day, and my mother thinks that's just cool because Ramona's, like, too artistic for everyday rules. And my dad—my dad is otherwise occupied."

"Jesus," Britta says, letting the word slip out from between her lips. "I didn't know."

"I didn't tell you. God, this coffee is shitty. It's like because they have a captive market, they don't even try."

"Sugar and cream, Very."

The orderly who gave me the cigarette the other night comes in and orders a coffee. The woman working the counter juts her hip out and smiles at him—when she served us, I wondered if she even knew how to smile—and he laughs and leans on the counter. Lucky them.

"It hurts, you know," Britta says. "I mean, not to add to your tossed salad of disaster, but that you're going through all of this without us, without me, it feels crappy."

I shake my head. "I don't know what to say."

"You're supposed to give me some line about not wanting to burden me with your troubles. Or maybe tell me that Dominic was a way to feel more alive."

"And you'll say, 'Yes, okay. Makes sense. I'll forgive you'?"

The orderly nods at me on the way out, and I nod back.

"Please tell me that he's not another distraction," she says.

"He's my smoking buddy," I say.

"Good one," she says, but she doesn't smile. The fluorescent light above us flickers.

"I didn't want to burden you with my troubles. I didn't want to burden anyone. I didn't want to burden me by talking about them. And Dominic was, I don't know, an experiment."

"An experiment?"

"Can I be friends with a guy like Dominic Meyers? And the answer is no."

"Because he's not like us."

I look down into the shiny blackness of my coffee. "Something like that. I need to check back in with Nonnie. And finish that freaking artistic representation piece."

"I really wish the experiment or whatever had ended before you agreed to do that. I like my nice shiny A in English. A Ms. Staples A is like being granted knighthood."

"Sorry. I will try to make it as unsucky as possible." We pick up our mugs and carry them to the busing station, where they join a slew of other half-drunk cups. They're just distractions, these mugs of coffee. Just a way to pass the time until the time is over.

Britta hugs me and her bag bangs against my leg. I pretend it didn't. It's one tiny thing, a way to let her know she's still my best friend.

twelve

i.

MONDAY, HE IS WAITING for me after school. In my car. My previously locked car. I stand outside and just stare at him, his image crooked through the old glass. He stares back for a few moments and then leans over and opens my door for me. "Get in."

"This is my car."

"I know."

"You can't order me to get into my own car."

He sighs. "Would you please join me in your nice warm car?"

I frown but get in. "How did you get in here?"

"An old car like this is easy to break into. I had a cousin who taught me how to pick locks."

"Are you kidding?"

"No."

"Are you lying?"

He half shrugs. "Maybe about the cousin."

"This is not helping your cause, you know. This is stalker-ish. If you're trying to make some sort of, some grand gesture, this is not it."

"If you want me to leave I will. I just wanted to make sure I didn't miss you. Also, this is a nice car. Do you realize how nice this car is?"

"What are you doing here?"

"I want to apologize for how I treated you last week."

"You already did."

"But you haven't accepted." He runs his hand through his hair and looks out the window. "Let's go somewhere."

I should say no, but his suggestion surprises me. "Where?"

"I don't know. Ruby's."

I wrinkle my nose. "I went there yesterday." I'd stopped on the way home from the hospital since I knew there wouldn't be any food at home, and I couldn't stomach another meal in the hospital cafeteria. Plus it's open late. "What you get? Did you get a frappe?"

I shake my head. "Veggie burger."

"Veggie burger? Who gets a veggie burger at Ruby's? Was it at least slathered in cheese and pickles?"

"I need to get home."

"Come on, Very. I'm just asking for a chance to explain myself, and sitting here in your car, with people walking by—it's not the right place. We could go on campus somewhere, like that sculpture garden—"

"That's for dates and prom pictures."

He looks up at me through his flop of hair. "Fine. The beach, then."

"It's October."

"So no one else will be there. Let's go."

I look in my rearview mirror, but I don't really expect to see Ramona. Surely she's cut school again. I shift my gaze forward, passing right over Dominic. A shaft of sunlight hits a tiny dent in the windshield and the light splits and sparkles around the car. "I need to go see my grandmother tonight."

"Of course."

"And I have lots of homework to do. You might have heard about this English presentation coming up."

"English what now?" he asks. "Nah, I've got that done."

"So I can only go for a little bit."

"But you'll go?"

I look again at the dots of light and wonder how Nonnie might spin them into a poem, what they could represent for her. "I'll go."

ii.

We drive in silence. I can feel him watching me, but I don't return his gaze.

I pull into the empty parking lot, right up to the wall along the beach. We get out of the car and walk out to the sand. The wind is much stronger here than at school, and it whips across my face.

"I like the ocean in the fall," he says. "It looks more serious."

"It's just darker," I explain. "It has to do with the angle of the earth."

"Sometimes it's better not to have an explanation for everything."

"I disagree."

Our footsteps in the soft sand are erased almost as soon as we make them. I stare out at the breaking waves. It makes sense that people used to go to the ocean to convalesce.

"Let's sit for a while."

Sitting on the cold, silky sand, I pull my legs up to my chest and count the waves, trying to see if they come in a pattern. Three right in a row, then a pause, then two. Nature is supposed to be full of patterns, but I can't find one in the ocean.

"Why'd you come to my house the other day?" he asks. A seagull slides into a landing in front of us, then waddles, fat, across the sand. Dominic throws a shell at it before it gets too close to us, and it flies a few feet away, barely lifting into the air. "Do you want me to say I'm sorry again?"

"No," I say.

The seagull hops toward us and Dominic picks up another shell. "I want to explain why I acted the way I did. I know it wasn't right." He throws the shell into the sand and it lands upright like it's marking a spot. "It's just that I like you. I didn't realize that I would, but I do. I know I can be a real ass, and I like that you just come right back at me. And you can be funny in your own way. So I guess I thought, I don't know what I thought, but after we kissed, I didn't expect to come back to school and have you act like I was—like I was nothing. Like I was just some guy you cheated on your boyfriend with."

"I broke up with him."

"I know that now."

"But I didn't break up with him for you."

He picks up a handful of sand and lets it sift through his fingers. "That's fine. Really. It just sucks to feel the way I do and have you be with someone else."

"So that makes it okay—the way you talked to me, I'm just supposed to forget it because you were jealous?"

"I don't know. That would be the best possible outcome."

"For you."

"Yes. For me. Still, I know it doesn't excuse the way I acted, and so I am sorry."

"Okay."

"Okay."

I push my feet down against the sand, and watch it slip off like rats jumping ship.

"You said you were having a hard time. What's going on?"

The reasons are multiplying. Nonnie. Mom. Dad. Ramona. That day it had been Ramona. "Ramona's been cutting class. I don't know where she goes, but she just leaves school I guess. I don't know what's going on with her. I mean, I could talk to some of her friends, but I don't know who they are anymore."

"Your sister doesn't have any friends."

"Of course she does."

"Every time I see her, she's alone."

I think about it. I don't see her often at school—probably because she isn't there often—but when I do, she is always by herself. And even though she used to bring friends over, she hasn't this year.

"When do you see her?"

"In the art studio sometimes. She started saying hi to me after that day you came to see me in the grocery store."

"I didn't—"

"I'm just yanking your chain, Very. Anyway, sometimes she's there during lunch or her free periods. And she's always working, working, working. Like on this painting of the blanket. She doesn't really like to talk much. I tried. You Sayles-Woodruff girls have thick walls, you know."

"Is that meant as a compliment?"

"What do you mean?"

"In all those songs the girls put up walls and only the singer is able to scale them. It makes her dark and mysterious, and him special."

He picks up half of a blue-black mussel shell. "Your sister is dark and mysterious. Mysterious, anyway."

I sigh. Even Dominic thinks Ramona is more interesting than I am.

"You just don't want to make the wrong choice. And I can

see how I might come across as a wrong choice."

"Oh, you're wrong, all right. The wrongest of wrongs. Like, the radical of a negative wrong."

"Isn't that imaginary?"

"Little *i*."

"Didn't think I would catch that, did you?" He points at me with the mussel shell.

"You're full of surprises."

"Layers on the onion, right?"

"But what do you get at the center of an onion? It's all just onion." I pick up my own shell. A perfect small white one with a hole at the top, just the kind Ramona and I used to bring home to paint and then thread onto twine to make a necklace. "She must be going to see someone, right? Even if she doesn't have friends at school, she must have friends somewhere. Anyway, what am I supposed to do about it? She won't talk to me."

A big gust of wind blows at us from the ocean, and I shiver. He stands up and helps me to my feet—his hands are warm, but I let them go. We start walking again down the beach. The sand swirls around our ankles.

There is no one else on the beach. The coast could break off and it would be just the two of us. He bends over and picks up a piece of sea glass. "Blue. That's rare," he says.

"You can put it in your sculpture," I say.

"What sculpture?"

"The one at my house."

He shakes his head, looking confused.

"I thought . . ." I begin. "You didn't make it?"

"Honestly, I have no idea what you're talking about."

iii.

"That's amazing," he says. We've driven to my house so he can see the sculpture. "It's beautiful."

"And you had nothing to do with it?"

"Very, I swear I didn't. I know you might not think I'm the most trustworthy person at this point, but really, I only wish I had made this." He bends over and places the piece of sea glass in front of it. "Although, that would've been a little creepy."

"That had occurred to me. Then again, you are the one who just let himself into my car."

"I'm starting to realize that was a questionable decision."

We are silent for a moment, watching the sculpture and its subtle shifts with the light and wind. The copper flowers beat like castanets while the bottle caps seem to undulate. The bird is sitting in its nest, hopping and flapping its wings to warn us off.

It's warmer here than at the beach, like the air up on this hill is resisting the change from summer to fall.

"Are you going to invite me in?" he asks.

"What are you, a vampire or something?"

"Maybe." But he steps right into the house. He crosses the entryway and then pauses. I try to see the space through his eyes. The sunken living room seems dated, the bar cart comical. The exposed beams don't make sense in the Frank Lloyd Wright–style architecture.

There are books, CDs, and records in every room of the house, and I know he'll want to see them all. He'll comment on them. *This book is okay, but this record is simplistic, and this short-story collection isn't worth the paper it is printed on.*

Still, I want to show him every room, every book, album, trinket. I want to pick them up and hand them to him. I want to tell him the stories behind them. I want to hear his pronouncements and see his lips move as he makes them.

"Let me show you around," I say. When we step down into the living room, I notice that my mom is there. She reclines in her usual space on the sofa, drink in hand. Instead of reading, though, she has a dazed expression on her face. It takes her a moment to even notice that we're in the room. "Oh, hello," she says, propping herself onto her elbows. "It's the butcher boy."

"That's me," Dominic says gamely. "Very was just showing me around."

"Did you see the sculpture?"

"It's beautiful."

"It is. I'm feeling a bit under the weather, so—"

"Right," I say. Hastily grabbing his hand, I lead him out of the living room up three stairs and into the room we call the library, although just saying it makes me feel pretentious.

"My grandmother had the house built. It is kind of a joke. The house, I mean."

"An expensive joke."

The room is ringed with bookshelves. He crosses the room and begins to read the titles. His body twists to get a better look. He pulls one out: a thin paperback. "I'd think stuff like this would be hidden away in a bedroom somewhere."

The cover shows a woman in a low-cut dress, reaching across a desk for a phone, a knife in her other hand. "Nonnie loves pulp novels."

"Pulp novels and Moxie," he says. "I guess everyone has layers and layers."

"Some people more than others."

It feels like there is a thin wire connecting us, and each step he takes coils us closer. I watch the way his fingers linger on the books, gentle and reverent.

Nonnie lurks in every corner. There is a leather armchair scuffed around the edges. On the reading table next to the chair is an ashtray black with stains. In the window is a paper snowflake that Ramona or I made for her. Probably Ramona.

"Let's go," I say. "There's more to see."

I show him the sunroom, full of lush greenery. The spider plants, bamboo, and ivy are healthy and thriving. Someone has been watering and trimming them, maybe even cooing their silly names at them. But Dad hasn't been around enough lately. Mom would never remember to consistently water them. It has to be Ramona.

We cross back through the living room. Mom has disappeared, perhaps up to her bedroom to sleep it off. He nods toward the first set of stairs. "What's up there?"

"My mother's studio."

He starts to turn in that direction.

"We can't go up there. She doesn't like people to see her work until it's done." So I show him the kitchen instead. He nods approvingly at the stove. "Nice. You know I never did make you that French toast."

I look down, smile, blush.

Damn it.

He steps toward me and I back away. Right into the door, which swings open behind me. "We can go up this way." I lead him up the stairs of the turret Ramona and I share. Once at the top, there is nowhere to go but into my bedroom.

iv.

My bedroom is easy to see from his perspective. Matching furniture set. Matching pillowcases and flouncy bed skirt, all in periwinkle blue. A doll and teddy bear on the bookshelf. It looks every bit the bedroom of a little girl, and the blush that started on my cheeks spreads down my neck. I straighten a pile of books on my desk.

"A turret bedroom. If I come back at night, Rapunzel, will you let down your hair?"

I run my hand over my closely cropped head. "There'd be nothing to throw down to you."

"We probably don't want to be in that kind of story anyway."

The smile is gone, but his face is kind.

"Right. I mean, what if we get lost in the woods and I never find you to cure your blindness with my tears?"

"I think you'd find me," he says.

"Because it's our fated destiny?" I try to press a smirk onto my lips. I don't want him to think I'm serious.

"I was thinking more that as a newly blind man I'd be flailing and stumbling around the forest wailing, 'My eyes! My eyes! For the love of God, the witch has stolen my eyes!' There'd be no way for you to miss me."

"And when I found you, all I would have to do is cry. I'm not much of a crier."

"That's the thing about fairy tales, it's all metaphor."

"I'm not so good at that, either."

"You're probably selling yourself short, but in this case, it's how she feels about him. And there's all sorts of ways to show someone that."

The wire between us is coiling itself tighter and tighter.

He smiles. Just an upturn of the lips. I reach out and touch them. They are softer than I remember. And warm.

"You're so very solid," I tell him. "Not a fairy-tale prince."

"And I'm not going anywhere. I'm anchored to you."

"To hold me in place? Or do you mean like the poem? The Emily Dickinson poem about the ship in the storm?"

"Whatever you want me to be."

I don't know what I want him to be, but the idea of a still, calm night, a solid place to rest, that is appealing. And he is offering. So I fall toward him and my lips reach his, and we are kissing and lurching toward the bed. We stumble and my elbow hits his chest, but he just grips me closer. We kiss. And kiss. On the bed, and still kissing. His knee presses between my legs. His hand grazes my hip. Every place his body touches mine it's like he's flicking a light switch—*on, on, on*—until the electricity is sparking across my body. He puts his hands on my upper arms, pulls back, and looks at me. "Are you okay?" he asks.

"Yes," I say.

"Good." He pushes his hair out of his eyes and I want him to kiss me again. He makes no move, so I do, lifting myself up, and pressing my lips to his.

"You smell like the ocean," he whispers.

I could say I don't know what is going to happen next. I could say it is all his idea—his plan from the beginning even— and everyone will believe me. But I know what is going to happen. I want it.

He takes his shirt off.

He runs his fingers across my cheek and down onto my neck, then he helps me to sit up so I can take off my own shirt. "Are you cold?" he asks as he pulls the covers over us. I'm not. I am warm all over.

You'd think it is my first time the way my hands fumble over his body, not sure where to land. He thinks it is. "Have you . . . ?" He leaves the question unspoken.

"Yes," I say.

He pauses for a moment with his hands above the button of

my jeans and I nod. I watch his eyelids, as he undoes it, the way his long eyelashes flutter one two three times against his cheek. This close I can see every detail, the way his lashes cross over one another, and how the blue of his eyelids isn't consistent but mottled, light in some places, and almost purple in others, the way his lips have a tiny piece of skin peeling off.

"I have condoms. In the drawer by my bed."

I don't tell him why I have them, and he doesn't ask about this trace of Christian left behind. He reaches across me and I can smell him, and the smell envelops me and my body arches up so my face is in his chest.

The paper on the condom wrapper tears. We separate for a moment.

"Okay?" he asks.

"Okay."

And then his breath is in my ear, my neck, hot and sweet. There's a sharp pain, a hesitation—mine, his, ours—and then he is inside of me.

Now I know why my grandmother used such long metaphors for sex. You have to come at it sideways.

v.

After, we lie there. Still.

"You look pretty like that," he says. I sit up and pull my legs to my chest, then rest my head on my knees.

"Now you look sad," he says. He's lying on his side, holding his head up with his hand. With Christian, there was always a rush to clean up, to get back to our homework or a movie on TV. To act like it hadn't even happened.

"I'm not sad."

"You sure?"

"I wouldn't lie to you."

"Can I show you something?" he asks. "It's kind of cheesy. It might seem like a move—"

"You don't need to make a move. We already did it."

"True. But maybe I'm laying the groundwork for the future. Anyway, it's just something I drew."

He reaches down and grabs his messenger bag, and I pull my T-shirt on. He tugs a Moleskine sketchbook out; with it comes a small Baggie, and inside the Baggie are six neatly rolled joints.

We look at each other. "Do you . . ." I begin. "I mean, are these like, for sale?"

"You interested?"

I shake my head quickly, and he laughs. "Probably for the best. Minds like yours are few and far between and we wouldn't want to wreck it."

I pick up the Moleskine journal. "So what's this?"

"You can look through. It's mostly sketches."

As I flip through, I recognize people from school—Adam, Mr. Solloway, Ramona. He drew her looking off into the distance, her eyes wide and searching. Her long hair cascades down her back and almost seems to move. I notice her strong jawline and how it's so similar to my own.

"She was in the art room one day and said it was okay if I sketched her. She said she wanted to look permanent."

I flip the page and am surprised to see Christian. He stares out at me from the page with such open innocence, it makes me feel guilty and I turn the page. There are the lyrics to "Veronica," written not in Dominic's usual print, but in a shaky cursive.

I hold the page up and show him.

"Turn the page," he tells me.

I do and there I am. Beautiful. My short hair is sticking out in all directions. The bruise is a faded shadow of hash marks. With bright eyes I look up shyly. At him. Who else would I look at like that?

He sits up behind me now, his chest against my back. "That's what I wanted to show you. Do you like it?" he asks. "I want to make an etching of it. I sound like a total d-bag, don't I?"

"No." I shake my head.

"You don't like it, do you."

"I don't normally see myself that way. From that perspective."

"It's always interesting to see how someone else sees you." His hand settles on my ankle. "I haven't figured out how you see me yet, Very."

"We just had sex, didn't we?"

"That's just a thing any two people can do. It doesn't have to mean anything."

I turn my head away. It had been good sex, I thought, and

that seemed to be meaningful just on its own. Or maybe I was ascribing too much value to the physical. With Christian we were doing it because it was what we were supposed to do. This was different, and I liked it more. "Right—" I begin.

"No, wait. It meant something to me. What I can't figure out is what it meant to you. Why you did it."

I think of Ramona's words when we first saw the sculpture: *Why do people do any number of things?*

"Because I wanted to," I reply.

"I wish I could figure you out."

I look back down at the drawing. It isn't shyness, I realize, that he captured, but curiosity. I am trying to figure him out as much as he is trying to figure out me. I run my fingers along my eyes in the drawing.

"Tell me three true things," I say. "Three true things about yourself."

He scoots back on my bed so he's leaning against the headboard. "I have lived all of my life in Essex."

"I already knew that. Tell me the truths of the lies you told me."

He blinks. "Okay, well, my dad really did want to be a musician. He can play the guitar like crazy, and I think he's more than a little disappointed that I don't play. He does something really boring at a tech company. I don't even know what it is. Not cool technology, but, like paper pushing. He seems to like it. He does travel a lot. And when he travels a lot of times he goes to shows."

"And your mother?"

"Well, she probably should have left us. She's a professor at the college. Economics. She's brilliant, actually, and could probably get a job at a better school, but my dad's work is here. And she thinks she needs to 'be a mother' to me, quote unquote. Whatever that means."

"So why all the lies?"

"Is that my third true thing?"

"Yes."

"Because I was going to tell you something about you and your grandmother."

"Now you have to tell me both."

"Why?"

"My bed, my rules."

"Fair enough. I lie because it's easier than telling the truth. I mean, it makes the day easier to get through if you're telling a story about it rather than the actual day. Like my dad, I find him ceaselessly depressing when he's there listening to Eric Clapton and doing air guitar while he looks over quarterly reports. So I gave him a different life."

"A more depressing life."

"An appropriately depressing life."

"And me? And Nonnie?"

"I liked her first."

"I know."

"And that's okay?"

"Well, I liked her first, too."

"I just don't want you to think I was going after you because of her poetry."

"But you were."

"Maybe at first. But it was also what I said. I read all these poems and thought I knew her, and then there you were in front of me, and nothing like her at all, and I wanted to know why."

"I'm not like her, but she used to be like me. That's what she said."

"Now that I know you, I think you are like her. The good parts. Smart. Witty. Biting, but also kind."

I look down at my toenails. The polish I put on with Nonnie is chipped in places, and my nails have grown, so there are naked half circles at the base. "I have a truth for you." He slides over beside me so our thighs are touching. "Sometimes I wish she would die."

I wait for him to respond. To tell me I'm disgusting. That I'm some kind of a monster for wanting her gone.

"I bet she sometimes wishes that, too."

I bend my forehead to my knees, but he can still tell that I'm crying. He wraps his arms around me. "Remember how I told you it felt like people were trying to steal my memories of her? Now it's me. I feel myself trying to cut loose from her, trying to let her go, but I can't. I can't. And so I'm just in this stasis and I can't make one single decision. I can't decide where to go to college until I know if she is going to live or die. I can't decide anything. And I feel like once she's gone this veil will be lifted, and then the future path will be clear in front of me. I'll know where I'm headed."

We sit curled into each other like that so long that my back begins to ache. I stretch out my legs and slide down so I'm flat on my back and he's above me. He has his eyes closed, but I don't think he's sleeping, because his fingers are interlaced through mine.

It's what Ramona's been doing, too, I realize. She can't go see Nonnie because she's already letting go—maybe she's even already let go completely.

He opens his eyes. They are not solid green, I realize, but marbled with darker and lighter shades. It would be easy to dive into those eyes and forget. It would be just the kind of forgetting that Mom and Nonnie would want me to do. So instead of letting him speak, I kiss him again.

But I can't forget, not all the way.

We kiss for a while longer, until my lips are tingling and raw. He wraps his arms around me. "I should go," he says. "I'm grounded. I should have been home hours ago."

This makes me smile.

"What?"

"I just didn't think that Dominic Meyers got grounded. You're way too cool for that."

"I usually ignore it, but maybe this time I'll make an effort. I'm a changed man, Very."

"Sure you are. Do you need a ride?"

"I can walk. It's not so far."

"You sure?"

"Yeah. You look amazing right now, and I want to walk a while with that image in my head. I'll see you in school tomorrow."

I pause for a moment. "You promise?"

"It's the big presentation day, right? I've got my biography all written up and ready to go. Don't you worry."

I worry.

thirteen

i.

DOMINIC SITS IN ONE of the comfy chairs in the library. There's a floor lamp next to the magazine rack, and it casts its light down on him like he's some kind of angel, and I almost laugh because it's so silly and perfect and just the sight of him makes me giggle.

Britta asked Dominic to meet us in the library before school so we can make sure we're all set for our presentation. I sit down in the chair next to him, notice the small hole in the knee of his jeans. He smiles. Britta looks from me to him and back again. I don't care if she knows what Dominic and I did, but I don't want to tell her. The secret buzzes inside my mouth. Thinking about him last night gave me sweet relief from my fears about Nonnie. Sometimes things are just that simple.

"Everyone ready?" she asks.

Dominic pulls out a bulleted list of facts about Gwendolyn

Bennett's life. "Ready," he says.

Britta takes it and looks it over.

"I know this is last-minute, Dominic, but I was thinking maybe you could read one of the poems. You did a great job reading the one by Very's grandmother."

It feels like gears are sliding into place. I did my artwork after Dominic left. Britta's being nice to Dominic. Maybe everything will work out.

"'Song' is a good one," she suggests.

Dominic nods but says, "It's fairly long, though. And I'm not sure I feel comfortable reading the part that's like a slave song. I think I'd need to practice it so it doesn't sound like a stereotype."

"What would you prefer?" she asks.

I'm still glowing just watching them talk back and forth.

"'Secret,' maybe. Or the second sonnet."

"The love poems?" she asks. "That's not really what the Harlem renaissance was all about."

"Don't you think?" Dominic asks. "Wasn't it about raising their voices no matter the topic?"

Britta considers this, and I'm worried their conversation might go off the rails—although they are talking to each other without malice—so I unroll the poster I've made. It has my painting in the center, with copies of her poems around it.

"What's that?" Britta asks.

My stomach drops. "It's the art piece."

I'd painted trees on the paper, tall and still. They looked

more like those cell-phone towers designed to look like trees than the strong and regal ones Gwendolyn Bennett described. So I dug through the drawers of my desk to find, pressed way in the back, one of those kid sets of watercolors. Each circle a bright color: red, yellow, blue, green, brown, black, orange, purple. I always insisted on having my own set because Ramona always mixed the colors so each circle turned a dull gray-brown. Mine were still pristine. I got a paper cup of water from the bathroom, cleared a spot on my desk, and began.

I started with red and painted a square over the top of the leftmost tree. Then I moved more toward the middle to do another red square, as close to the same size as I could. I knew I needed to wait for the paint to dry before I could put another square on top or even close. I cleaned the brush, changed the water, and put a yellow square in the bottom right. Just one. Yellow might be too sunny of a color for these poems.

When I finished, my trees were covered with overlapping squares of color. The paper was curling and wrinkling a bit. It had been a long time since I'd painted with watercolors and I used too much water.

In the morning I glued it down onto the poster board before bringing it to school. I clear my throat. "I was just thinking about interpretation, how there are all these ways to look at a poem. How we take our own views sometimes and impose them on a poem. The colors represent the lenses we see the poem through. Like 'Hatred'—that could be about any two people, but because she's black, and the time period, we assume it's about the legacy of slavery."

"Or since so much poetry is about love, you might assume it's about a bad ending to a romantic relationship. But maybe it's just about friends," Dominic says.

"Right. The core is still there, what the poet wrote, but no matter how careful and precise the poet is, all these layers get put on top of it."

"It's kind of brilliant, Very," Dominic tells me.

"Thanks," I say. "The idea is that the trees are the poem, and the poet. The colors are the interpretation."

"Wow," Britta says. "Awesome job. Not that I ever doubted you." She grins at me, and I find myself grinning back. Neither one of us had thought I'd be able to pull off the artistic part of the assignment. Only Dominic had thought so.

We're all sitting there smiling at one another, and I guess I should have known that things were only going so well because something terrible was about to happen.

Ms. Blythe walks over, her kitten heels click-clicking on the linoleum. She stops beside us, takes a deep breath, and says, "The office just called down. Your grandmother, she—" Ms. Blythe shakes her head. "Your parents want you to go to the hospital right away."

I don't move. Don't shake. Don't stand. Britta and Dominic both put their hands on me.

"I can take you," Dominic says.

I shake my head. "I need to find Ramona," I say.

Ms. Blythe looks surprised. "She's not here today, Very.

She's on the absent list again."

Again.

"Okay," I say. "Okay."

I look at Britta and Dominic, who have the exact same expression on their faces. "I'm sorry; I can see if I can get back in time, or maybe Ms. Staples will let us—"

Britta squeezes both of my shoulders. "Just go, Very. Dominic and I will be fine."

So I go.

ii.

Nonnie is there but not there. Her body is still. Every once in a while her finger twitches. A machine fills her lungs with air.

In out. In out.

Mom's face is long, haggard, dark circles under her eyes. Dad is unshaven. That he is here at all is a surprise. I do not look at his eyes. I try not to look at his hand on Mom's, the plagiarist sign of love.

Ramona is not here.

There's a vase of day lilies next to Nonnie's bed, the scent sickeningly sweet, overpowering the smell of cleaner, of medicine. I want to take those lilies and rip off the petals, the dusty yellow stamen. I want to throw the vase out the window and wait, wait for the crash of glass as it smashes on the pavement below.

We sit and watch. Watch nothing happening. Watch life slipping out of her.

iii.

When visiting hours are over, Mom sends me home. I say I will stay, but she is already curled up in the extra bed next to Nonnie's.

Dad left an hour before to check on Ramona. His belated concern will likely prove useless.

So I go outside and get in the Rapier, which is smelling less like Nonnie and more like me.

As I drive home, a group of college students saunters out into the road. I rub at some crust in the corner of my eye, waiting for the seemingly endless crowd of pedestrians to pass.

In the pack of people there is someone who, for just an instant, looks like Ramona. The girl is shorter, and has darker hair, but she has on a pair of hot-pink tights with saddle shoes—an outfit that I thought only Ramona could put together.

For her eighth-grade graduation, Ramona wore a white dress with black polka dots. It was too short. It only went to her midthigh, so she had put on turquoise leggings that were woven through with silver. She had twisted her hair into what looked like dozens of tiny knots on the top of her head. And then she'd put on lipstick in a deep red-brown that she'd bought in the section of makeup meant for African American women, not pale white schoolgirls.

When she received her certificate, she did a curtsy and a pirouette. No one clapped or laughed. It was like they were collectively rolling their eyes at her.

And me. What did I do? I texted Britta and Grace: **Sister R continues to prove she is an alien changeling.**

But maybe I should have been paying more attention. Maybe that was the first sign that things were not right, that she was alone and lonely. That she was wrapping herself in a web so no one would want to get close.

I pull the car up into the driveway.

She is slipping away. I can feel it. These memories are hooks in me and as she falls away, they tug themselves free.

Inside, the house is near silent. I want to apologize to Ramona. I want to tell her that I should have played her games.

I jog up our stairs, and, without even knocking, push open the door to her room. "Ramona, I—"

She is crouched on the floor working on a drawing of a huge oak tree, like the one at the top of our driveway in which she spends so much time. Its branches reach out across the span of one whole wall, and she's pasted torn pieces of paper as the leaves. Apples—no, plums—are falling from the limbs. She is working on the trunk, sketching its texture. But as I step forward, I realize she isn't drawing, she is writing.

All the lines that made up the bark of the tree are words, tiny written words.

"What are you doing here? I didn't say you could come in."

"Ramona, what is this?"

"It's a tree."

"Well, yeah." I step closer still. "How long did this take you to do?"

"That's what you want to know?" Her body is tense, like the models of animals in the dioramas at the Museum of Natural History in New York. Frozen, yet still, somehow, ready to move. As if she might jump up and run past me and out of the house—or attack me.

"I doubt you'd tell me anything else."

Her body relaxes just a bit. "I don't know. A few weeks."

"Are you okay?" I ask.

"I'm fine."

"Are you really?"

"I said I'm fine."

Yes, she had. And she can say it over and over and over again, but I don't believe her. I watch her for a moment longer. She doesn't move at all. I can tell she wants to keep working but won't do it with me in the room.

I examine the tree again. The leaves. They aren't paper. They are pages. Pages torn from books—the library encyclopedias she'd been shredding. My friends told me she was fine, and I believed them, not because she was okay, but because I didn't want to deal with her.

I could have said something then, or tried to force her to talk to me. And if I had tried, then what? Then she would have pushed back harder. She was even less interested in receiving my help than I was in giving it. Still, I can't deny the pit of guilt that rests in my stomach. I could have done *something*. I could've taken Ramona to Ruby's when she asked, or to the library when she wanted to look up fairy tales. I could've done a stupid cooking class with her. All those times she asked, and I said no.

Some of the torn pages aren't from a printed book. They have handwriting across them. Nonnie's handwriting.

"Ramona, are those from Nonnie's notebooks?"

"Uh-huh." She smiles, pleased with herself.

"You had no right to destroy her notebooks!"

"I didn't destroy them."

"I came up here to try to talk to you like we used to and—"

"When?"

"When what?"

"When did we used to talk?"

I turn away, sharply. "That's not the point. The point is, you shouldn't have done that."

"I think she might like it."

"What do you know about it?"

She begins writing again. I move in so I can see what she is writing. It is the words to one of Nonnie's poems, which she wrote soon after Ramona was born:

> *2 little girls in pigtails and jumpers,*
> *fat thighs, round tummies.*
> *2 little girls with teeth not yet arrived,*
> *lips round and red as cherries.*

Someday hands will rake through that hair,
press over the thighs.
Hands not their own will travel
over the bodies,
a foreign land.
A land to conquer.
Plums to pluck
and devour
till the juices drip down
his chin.

Seeing the poem scrawled up on the wall makes me uncomfortable; I'd read it before, but back when I was far too young to understand the imagery.

"She used to come in and watch me sleep—she thought I was sleeping anyway—and just write and write and write. I can still hear the sound of her pen scratching the paper."

Nonnie never did that with me. Maybe I was just a deeper sleeper than Ramona. My thought is hopeful, but I don't believe it.

"She told me that I had the real talent. That I was finally going to make something of the Woodruff name."

"She told me that I was her practical girl." I reach out and touch the wall at the place where a page is pasted.

"It's like the godmothers in *Sleeping Beauty*, how they bless the baby with graces. It's like a twisted version of that. Like she thought she could tell us who we were. Like we didn't have a choice."

"Maybe we don't have a choice. Maybe it's just who we are."

"I don't accept that. I don't accept that this"—she waves her arm around—"is the only way I will ever be."

"What are you saying?" I step toward her, my hand extended.

"It doesn't matter. It just doesn't matter. Can you leave me alone now?"

"Okay," I say, but don't move. "If you want to talk, I—"

"Maybe later," she says, and picks up her pen.

I can tell her about Nonnie, how she's doing worse, but it won't stop Ramona from scrawling on the wall. It won't even sink in.

I go down into the kitchen but don't get anything to eat. I just stand there, staring out across the silvery-green lawn. It's the in-between time, when day is finally about to give way to night, and all I can do is sit and wait for the change. All I can do is react.

fourteen

i.

SHE SLIPS AWAY IN the night. The breath goes out and does not come back in.

ii.

I'd like to say I woke up in the middle of the night, shocked awake by the sudden loss, a ripple across the cosmos. I do not. I sleep a dreamless sleep and wake with sandy eyes.

When I come downstairs, Mom is on the couch. Dad is next to her, still pretending. They are both wilted flowers with red-rimmed eyes. Mom's hair is tousled; Dad sports the shadow of a beard. And it is in that moment, when I see their eyes, that I know.

I shake my head to keep them from saying it aloud, but

they do anyway. "Very," Dad says, his voice even. "Last night Nonnie—it happened last night."

"Don't tell me," I say. I do not want to hear the words from him.

"She's gone," Mom says, her voice hoarse. "She's gone away."

There's all this language we use to avoid saying the truth, to avoid calling it what it is: passed, passed on, passed away, gone away, gone to a better place, left us. It's as if death is one big road trip and the rest of us are left behind.

My mind should not be spiraling out like this. It should be focused. I should be focused.

"Okay," I say. Then again: "Okay. I understand. I'm going back to bed."

iii.

I sleep. Deep beneath blankets, pillow over my head, I sleep. I do not dream. And when I wake it's like learning the truth all over again.

Nonnie is gone.

iv.

Outside the sculpture glints like broken bottles on a summer sidewalk. The pipes that made the flower stems are now entwined, snaking around the bottle caps like the ivy that grows on the buildings of the college. The bird's nest is empty, one lone feather fluttering in the breeze.

It will have to be removed. Now that Mom will want to put the house on the market, the sculpture will have to be removed. Maybe there's a way to take it all off in one piece, to preserve it.

You always were my practical girl.

The words come unbidden. This is not how I want to remember Nonnie thinking of me. I want to think of our conversations in her room, painting her nails, driving around town. I want to think of her teasing me, not cursing me.

But maybe there is no escaping her words, because my next thought is: I will have to plan the funeral. Mom isn't able to. Dad will find a way to abdicate responsibility. So it will fall to me. I will have to find a funeral home. Unless they have already sent her body to one. Is it in the hospital morgue? Do hospitals even have morgues or is that just the thing of movies?

I don't know where Nonnie is.

I don't know where her body is resting, and I don't know where she wants it to be.

I hope she has a will with all the details laid out. She always was so particular. Yes, a will. Leave the decisions to someone else.

A breeze blows across the front of the house and the sculpture sighs.

fifteen

i.

MOM HAS THE RED afghan over her feet and calves. She's wearing a sleeveless silk blouse that has faded from black to gray, and I can see small pinpricks of goose bumps on her arms. It's like she has taken up residency on that couch. I wonder if she even sleeps in the bedroom anymore.

I sit down next to her and pull the blanket over both of us.

"Going to school?"

"I don't think so." I had thought about it, but when I texted Britta and Grace to let them know about Nonnie, Britta said I should take as much time as I needed, and it made me feel like going was the wrong choice.

Mom laces her fingers through the holes of the afghan. "It could be something to keep your mind off of things."

Things. Nonnie would hate that we're using such an imprecise word to describe her passing away. Her death.

"You know what the last thing she said to me was?" she asks.

I shake my head, the semipermanent lump in my throat re-forming.

"She said she hoped I didn't dissolve. She said, 'Don't dissolve, Annaliese. Those girls need you.'" She untangles her fingers from the afghan and wipes at her eyes. "'Those girls need you,' she said. Not even a moment to let me grieve. Did she think I wouldn't grieve?"

"It's not like that. She said the same thing to me about Ramona, about how I would be okay, but Ramona would struggle. I think she wanted me to watch out for her."

"You are not your sister's keeper. How many times do I have to tell you that?"

I glance toward the bookshelves. The books are more tumbled and out of order than usual, as if Mom or someone has been looking for something. And perhaps she has. Just the right book, just the right words to erase the ones that Nonnie left for her. "Those were her last words?"

"To me. Her actual last words were 'Rage, rage against the dying of the light.' She must have planned that, don't you think?"

"Maybe."

"Definitely. The question is, how long did she know? When did she choose it?"

"I don't know," I say. One of the ice cubes in her glass cracks.

"You need me?" she asks. She looks at me. Her bangs are swooping down toward her bloodshot eyes.

"We do."

"It's all just so jumbled up. Life is just a big jumble and we can write and paint and never make any sense of it."

"I have something to show you," I tell her.

"Can you bring it here?" she asks.

"It's up in Ramona's room."

Maybe learning the truth about Ramona is too much to throw at her right after Nonnie's death, but it's too much for me, too—too much for Ramona. I can't carry it myself anymore, and Mom is all I have.

She unfolds herself from the sofa and follows me up the stairs. When we get into the room, she stops and stares, her eyes shifting left, right, up, and down as she takes it all in. She puts her fingers up to her lips, and relief swells over me like the tide in the bay. I'm not going to have to take care of this on my own.

We are still. In front of us is the tree. Behind us is the chaos of Ramona's room.

"I tried to talk to her about it, but, well, you know," I say.

Mom sits down roughly on Ramona's unmade bed.

"She ripped all those pages out of Nonnie's notebooks and encyclopedias at school. I caught her doing it one day. I should've said something." I nestle close to her on the bed, like I did when I was little. "She's going to be okay, right?" I've been silly to keep it from her for so long. Parents make things better. Even sad, damaged parents. They put the Band-Aids on and kiss your head, and sure, Ramona is probably going to need more than that, but at least Mom is involved now.

"She's brilliant," Mom replies, shaking her head. "I thought

I . . ." Her voice trails off.

"This isn't brilliance, Mom. She's writing on the walls like someone in an insane asylum."

"You don't understand, Very. It's not your fault. Your mind isn't wired like ours."

Focus on Ramona. Just focus on Ramona. "I think that she's depressed or something. Like she's, I don't know—she's there but not there."

Mom shakes her head. "That's her creative space, the place she goes. There's this line between madness and creativity. If you can walk it, that's genius." She points at the wall. "She's walking it. Her message, her impact—so precise." She stands up, forgetting me, and walks around the room, letting her fingers linger on the wall. "I have to go," she says.

She flees from the room, and I follow her downstairs. She crosses the first floor and flies up the second set of stairs to her studio, where I know I'm not supposed to follow. So I just stand at the bottom of the steps, looking up, waiting to be invited when I know I won't be. After a few moments, the crashes start.

ii.

Years ago I put glow-in-the-dark star stickers on my ceiling. I tried to peel them off, but they just left marks, so I let them stay. Now I stare at their uneven pattern, listening to the sounds from my mom's studio. They are muffled, but I can still hear them: two crashes, then a pause, then three loud bumps, one after another.

A particularly loud crash makes me shudder. Then the noises stop, and I think maybe I can go see her. It's true she's made it clear that she doesn't want us in her studio, but everything's changed now, hasn't it?

So I climb the stairs.

Of course I shouldn't be surprised by what I see, not after all of the commotion. It is as if every inch of floor is covered by torn canvases, their frames splintered. She smashed some of the glass jars she uses for paints. The floor sparkles with the shards.

"Don't come in," she says. "Your feet." I'm not wearing any shoes. But I can't leave, not with the room like this. I sidestep shards of glass and splinters of wood. Mom stays by the window, looking out. Canvases are piled in the middle of the room. Picking one up, I smooth out what I can: it is Nonnie. A portrait made with heavy oils, the colors off so that her skin has a green hue, her hair almost purple, but there is no doubt who it is. Her eyes flash just right, as if she is composing a poem—or a quip—in her mind.

Another painting is bent in half, but I recognize this one right away, too: it is me. My skin is rosy—too rosy—and she has made me more beautiful. My hair is smooth and pretty—still long—and I purse my lips in a seductive manner. When I pick it up and see the lower half, I see that she has dressed me in a top with a plunging neckline. It is like she painted me the way she thinks I ought to be. I put my portrait on top of the one of Nonnie.

Digging through, I next find a Ramona painting. Mom has captured her younger than she is right now—probably eight or nine. She is laughing with her head tilted back, face bathed in the light of an unshown sun. That's the way Ramona used to be.

Then I find Mom's self-portrait. The colors are dark, ominous almost. You nearly can't see her face because of the shadows. But she is gorgeous. There is no doubt of that. And it is the most realistic. The jawline is absolutely correct, the fleck of gold in her eyes. I realize then that not all the glass is from the paint jars. Some is from a mirror. She studied herself to make this painting.

The other canvases are in various states of completion, but they are always of the four of us, and always playing the same rolls: Imogene grotesque, me glamorous, Ramona in the sun, and Mom overshadowed.

"Mom, these are beautiful."

"Don't lie to me."

"I'm not lying."

She smirks. "Derivative. David Hockney did it first and better."

"Well." I have no idea who David Hockney is. "There are only so many ways to do a portrait, right?"

"The thing about art is, it needs to be an original thought. Your grandmother had her words. I thought I had . . ." She shakes her head. "Your sister, she's an original thinker. The way she sees the world. If I could just get in her head for a day, an hour."

Ramona doesn't need anything or anyone else inside her head. "I think she's breaking down."

Mom tilts her head back and closes her eyes. "That's just what I was trying to say. All the best artists were a little crazy, a little depressed. Hemingway. Van Gogh, of course. Emily Dickinson. Plath; your grandmother. Your sister is lucky. If only I had been more touched."

"Are you serious?"

"What do you even know of art? I didn't want them to be beautiful. I wanted them to be true."

"But they aren't true at all."

Damn it.

"That's not what I meant," I say.

"It is. And you're right." Mom crosses over to a sink and begins washing her hands, roughly rubbing them with the paint-stained bar of soap.

"Mom."

Scrubbing, scrubbing, scrubbing until her hands are pink.

"Mom!"

"What?" She turns, sprinkling water out around her like a fan. The sun coming in the window catches it and it refracts the light into a hundred rainbows. We both stop, breathe in, as we watch it.

"What is so important now?" she demands.

Everything, I want to say. Everything is important. "You painted us how you want us to be. That's its own truth, isn't it?"

"What are you talking about?"

"Well, me sexier than I am. More like you. And Ramona, you kept her young, so she isn't a—" This time I stop myself from saying the word: *threat.*

Mom dries her hand on an old dish towel. "And Nonnie? Tell me, what secret is hiding in those paintings?"

"I'm not trying to be mean, Mom. I'm trying to help."

"So help me, Very. Oh, please do. Tell me what you see."

"I see Nonnie as someone who shaped you, and, well, you're always painting yourself in shadows, so I guess you think she overshadowed you."

"You think I'm that literal?"

"I don't know, Mom. You know I'm no good at this."

She throws the rag onto the counter by the sink.

The sun is pounding through the windows that circle the turret. I have to squint my eyes against the glare and I start to sweat. "You can't change us by changing how you portray us."

"Oh, can't I? What do you think Imogene did with me, Smart One? Trotting around her beautiful daughter. Using me to get into parties when no one wanted her there anymore? 'Taste the wine, Annaliese. Tell them about the modeling you're doing, Annaliese.' Did she ever tell them about my painting? How do you think I ended up like this?"

"Like what?"

"For a smart girl, you miss a lot." There's a small cosmetics bag near the sink, and she pulls out a tube of lipstick. She puts it on without a mirror, perfectly in place. Her gaze flits about the room, looking at everything but me.

"Not as much as you think."

She raises her eyebrows.

"Anyway, right now, I don't really care about the problems you had with Nonnie. Nonnie's gone. Ramona's still here."

Mom throws up her hands. "That's the problem, isn't it!" she cries out.

"What do you mean?"

Her body stills. She opens up the toiletry bag and pulls out a compact. Moving it around, she looks at her eyes, widening them, then narrowing them.

"Mom, what do you mean? You can't tell me you're jealous of Ramona?"

"Me? I was talking about you!" But her voice has lost her fire. I know I have caught her out.

She snaps the compact shut and drops it back in the bag. "I'm going," she announces.

"Where?" I ask.

"I thought you had everything figured out."

She strides past me and down the stairs. A few moments later I see her car driving down the driveway way too fast.

iii.

So I am alone in the house. The weight of it presses down on me.

I run out into the evening air. I want to be anywhere but here. I pull my phone out of my pocket. Dominic's number is there in the missed calls. I could go to him. The phone is warm in my hand. Then it starts to vibrate.

How's it goin?

The text is from Christian. I just stare at it. I don't know how to respond. It would be pretty hard to sum up in a text message: **My lifes fallin apart. Nonnies gone. moms losin it. Ramona's craz, 2.** Not exactly my style. So I type: **Fine.**

Almost immediately, he responds: **Workin on chem. Want 2 come over?**

My fingers are on the keys typing **Yes!** and **Getting into the car now.** I will just go to his house, lie down on the floor of his furnished basement, and we'll spread out our books. I'll correct his math, he'll explain the reactions in a way that makes sense when it never does in class. Good and warm and comfortable. I can practically smell him—the Right Guard he uses and his cinnamon toothpaste.

I drive over there with the music off and the top down. The cool air cyclones around me, chilling my fuzzy head, and I don't think about where I'm heading and I don't think about what happened with Nonnie or what I did to Christian. I don't think about any of it.

When I get there, he is waiting for me. He smiles, cheeks pink, and I follow him to the basement. He turns and looks at me over his shoulder, still grinning ear to ear.

He doesn't know, I realize. He doesn't know that Nonnie is gone, and it's like a time warp, jumping back to when she was still alive. My heart races as if it could be true.

Downstairs, Christian has his chemistry book out, and a bowl of potato chips. "I thought this part might be hard for you."

"Gee, thanks," I say.

He punches me lightly on the shoulder, like we're old football buddies or something. "You're just better with the practical than the theoretical."

He is right. I've been struggling with this unit, though I ascribed the problem to everything else going on in my life. He looks over my shoulder at what I am writing. "See, you're off to a bad start."

He explains the problem to me with his hand flat on my notebook. I stare at the veins in his hand, the torn cuticle on his ring finger. Maybe Christian doesn't make me as happy or excited as Dominic does, but he also doesn't make me as angry. And he is here. He is always right here.

"You're not listening," he says.

It's true; all of his words passed me by. "Sorry."

"Things, I mean, with you, your things—" It is unlike Christian to be so bumbling.

"There's a lot going on," I say. I do not want to tell him, do not want to break the spell and jump forward in time.

"I'm still— You can still talk to me."

"I know."

He pushes his book away, but I still stare at the pages. I don't want to talk to him about whatever Ramona is doing in her room. I don't want to talk about the dark side of my mother that flashed up when she saw Ramona's work. I can't talk about

Nonnie. I don't want to talk at all.

"I'd rather just sit here doing homework. I'd rather things be normal."

"Normal." The word seems to get stuck on his lips.

"Normal," I confirm.

"I can do that."

And that's why I love him. Except that is the whole problem: I don't love him. Not the right kind of love anyway. It's the way a person loves their first puppy, but of course that is something I could never tell him, even though at this moment that straightforward relationship is the most valuable one in my life.

Straightforward until I confuse it.

I try to focus on what he is telling me, but all I can do is look at his skin. I know how soft his forearms are, and how rough his palms. It's my fault. I blamed him, but it is my fault we stopped being physical. I stopped seeing him like this, noticing every detail. I reach out and brush my hand against his, like I did in the beginning when everything was new and every touch mattered because the touches could still be counted.

Nonnie and Mom, they always seemed so glamorous, but their glamour was just that—a magician's trick. It was as flimsy and frail as a fairy house made of sticks. I can't live that way. I don't have the mind to create that magical glamour of a world. I don't have the stamina.

Well, Very. I suppose I was just like you.

And so I will stay myself. I will build my house of sturdier things, of numbers and college acceptances. I will not be that girl made otherworldly by an artist's hand. I am the girl in Christian's sketch, eyes down, concentrating. That is me. To be otherwise is pretending. This haircut is pretending. Dominic is pretending.

I turn my head so I am looking at his face. Yes, it is just like at the beginning, when every bit of him triggered one of my senses. I lean forward, my head tilted. Our lips brush, and then he rocks back.

"I'm sorry," he says quickly.

"No, I . . . I shouldn't have."

"It's just too soon."

"I never meant to hurt you," I tell him.

"I know. But you did."

He can't look at me. I look down, too. His hand is off of my notebook. "I'm sorry," I say. "I never should have come."

"No, look, it's nothing. It doesn't matter."

Each word stings more.

He goes on, "Let's just focus on the chemistry. You want a distraction, right? To not think about your problems? So let's just get this set done."

"I have to go."

"Very."

"I have to go," I repeat while I shove my things into my bag.

"Very—"

"She's dead, Christian."

He doesn't say anything else, but I feel his eyes on me as I run up the stairs: his stupid, stupid girl running away again.

iv.

Dominic was always the one trying to get my attention, but now I'm the one throwing rocks up at his bedroom window. I hope it's his window. There's a light on and I can see a computer screen glowing. A moment later there's a face behind the glass. He sees me, gives a wave, then disappears. A moment later he's outside in an old T-shirt and pajama bottoms.

"Hey," I say.

"Hey back," he replies. "Are you okay?"

I nod.

"I heard about your grandmother. Britta told me. I tried calling, but—"

"I know."

"Let's get away from here. My mom has the place on lockdown since she found out I was skipping school."

We hold hands as he leads me through his neighborhood. I shouldn't be holding his hand, considering why I've come to see him.

All the houses are dark, though each seems to have its porch light on, winking through the oak and maple leaves. We round a corner toward the old soccer fields. There's a small playground there. Just a couple of slides and a swing set. He sits on the bottom of the wide metal slide and leans back to look at the sky. There's room enough for me beside him, but I don't sit down.

"I know it's late," I say.

"Hey, you can show up under my window anytime." That wolf grin, the not-really-him grin, is there. "You know I've always wanted to fool around in this playground."

"I'm sorry about the other day. The sex."

"You're sorry we had sex?" He lifts his head to try to see me better in the dark.

"You asked me what it meant. What it meant to me. And I couldn't tell you. I didn't know. I shouldn't've had sex with you if I didn't know."

"Hey, Very, things aren't always so simple." He reaches out toward me, but I stay rooted.

"But I know now. I know I can't be with you."

A bat careens across the night sky.

"Can't or won't?" He sits up.

Sometimes it's easier to tell someone the lie he believes rather than the truth. Dominic told me that himself. So I don't tell him that I'm confused and that I still don't know if I can trust him. I don't tell him that I want everything and nothing from him. Instead I say: "You were right about me. Mostly."

"What part was I mostly right about?"

"I thought I could handle this—the ways we are different, who we each are—but I can't."

He draws his eyebrows together. "Is that so?"

"I just thought you deserved to know you didn't do anything wrong."

"It's not me, it's you?"

I look toward the swings, which hang still and straight as anchors. "Yes. It's me and my hang-ups."

"Look, I know we come from different groups, but it doesn't matter."

"Dominic, I—"

"I can be an ass, I know that. Trust me, I know that. And if that's why you don't want to be with me, then I guess I can accept that. But if it's because of what everyone else thinks of me—"

What everyone else thinks of him: that he's a screwup, a bad seed, dangerous. He is and is not these things, but that's not what's keeping me from him. But that's what he thinks, and therefore what he will accept. "I wish it were different."

"Then make it different."

"I have to go. I just wanted to tell you. I'm sorry." And then once more, as if repeating it will make it stick: "I'm sorry."

I leave him sitting on the edge of the slide. I hope he looks up at the stars. The clouds are passing over them, shifting and changing, and it's just like the ocean's movement that he loves so much. *Our Ocean.* Maybe there wasn't a specific someone. Maybe he was just looking for someone to share it with.

v.

I fall asleep on the sofa with the red afghan over my face, spider-webbing the world around me. When I wake it is morning, and Ramona stands beside the couch. "Are you going to school?"

"Where's Mom?" I ask.

"Asleep upstairs."

"Are you sure?"

"Yes. I heard her come in last night. After you."

I tug the afghan down off of my face. "I'm sick. Take the bus."

She shrugs and goes out the door. Whether or not she goes to school I have no idea.

I lace my fingers through the holes of the afghan as my mother had done the night before. Who made it, I wonder. Certainly not my mom or Nonnie. Nonnie said she'd learned how to knit for that poem, but never very well. I couldn't imagine either Mom or Nonnie buying it, though.

Ramona could make an afghan. She'd just sit down and do it like it was nothing.

And then she'd probably rip it up.

I want to fall back asleep, but I can't.

I turn my head and see the bar cart. There are crystal decanters with different-colored liquids at various levels. Mom likes the clear stuff, gin and vodka. Nonnie prefers the browns. It has never before occurred to me that this is unusual knowledge for a girl to have about her family.

Cocktails in the afternoon. Parties all the time. But Mom has just been hiding, building up this wall of a perfect life, when inside she is atrophying. And Nonnie is . . . Nonnie was. Nonnie is gone.

I wish my mind would stop its whirling.

I could get drunk. It would be a balancing act. Tipsy might be okay. It could lighten my mood, perhaps. But if I push it too far in the state I'm in, I'll surely end up morose, and might make a terrible decision like calling Christian. Or worse, Dominic. I'm letting go of that false life, the one Mom and Nonnie were trying to write for me. So no drink for me, no moment of forgetting.

I walk to my parents' room, knock softly, and get no response. Using both hands, I push the door open. Mom is spread diagonally across the bed. Dad is already gone for the day, back to his office to work on his book, as if nothing at home has changed. Maybe he is reworking his résumé, cruising college sites for job listings. Maybe he is having office hours with that Kaitlin girl. I close the door as gently as I can.

Unlike Ramona, I call the school.

"We really need to hear it from the parent, Very," the attendance secretary tells me.

"My mom's still asleep. She's really struggling with . . . things. I wanted to call before first period."

She pauses. "Okay, just this once. You've never been in any trouble."

I hang up before she can ask if Ramona will be out, too.

I don't know what to do next. I've never skipped school before. I don't want to stay home, I know that much. Mom will wake up eventually, and I'll have to talk to her. Only I have no idea what to say.

So I put on sneakers and head out through the garage, where I walk past Nonnie's car and instead pick up this creaky bike of hers. It's an old-fashioned kind, like the one the witch rides in *The Wizard of Oz*, before you know she's the witch, with a wicker basket and everything. I take off toward town. Most of Essex is just beginning to rise. There are kids waiting for the school bus. The air is warm, but fall is here. I breathe in deeply and smell it.

I ride through campus into town. At an intersection I watch all the people walking by. Students in their ratty jeans and fleece jackets. Professors dress the same, only they wear khakis. Everyone looks like they are from the L.L.Bean catalog, and I wonder if they even realize how much the same they look.

I swerve among the acorns in my path like it is some sort of obstacle course, letting my weight steer the bike toward Main Street. I park the bike in a rack and now I'm just standing on Main Street watching the people go by.

I can smell the food from Ruby's and realize I'm hungry. Inside, I take a seat at the counter, where I order a muffin from an older woman with orange hair. Not bad orange, but clearly dyed. It's poofy and doesn't move when she does. Yet despite all its orange poofiness, it actually seems to suit her.

The only other person at the counter is an older man with a trucker-style baseball cap and an old down vest. The waitresses all wear polyester pants, polo shirts, and ruffled aprons. Most of them are old, but there is one younger girl bustling around in the back room. I bet she hates those polyester pants.

"Here's your muffin, hon."

I turn around and there is the orange-haired lady, smiling at me and holding the muffin. As she puts it down she says, "You're Veronica Woodruff, aren't you?"

"Yes," I say, and then add an unusual-for-me "ma'am."

"I was so sorry to hear about your grandmother. She was

a nice lady. Used to get frappes in here some Fridays with her students. Or alone. We've got a postcard," she says. She takes a few steps over to the counter and grabs a postcard off a small spinning rack. It's a picture of the town from above and it says, "Essex Is Woodruff Country."

"It actually sells pretty well. You can have that one if you want. On the house."

"Oh. Okay. Thanks."

I pick at the bottom of my muffin; I like to save the sugary tops for last.

"I went to high school with your mother."

"Really?" The woman looks a good ten years older than my mom. And not just because my mom looks so young: this woman looks ten years older than my mom's thirty-nine years. I check her name tag: Allison.

"Uh-huh. You look just like her, hon. That's how I knew who you were. The spitting image except not as splashy."

Not as splashy. Somehow I know this is meant to be a compliment.

"I voted for her for prom queen. Some of the girls wouldn't. They said it didn't make sense to vote for someone so new, but I knew they were just jealous. Anyway, she was always nice to me. And she was pretty. And popular. Pretty, popular, and nice— that seems like the perfect combination for prom queen to me."

Allison and the man look at me, so I agree.

"She didn't win," Allison says. "I don't think she even went to the prom."

"So you knew her?" I ask. "My grandmother?"

"Oh sure, both of us did, me and Henry," Allison tells me. "She used to scribble ideas on napkins and then ball them up and throw them away."

"I kept one of 'em," Henry said. "I figured it might be worth money someday. I can't say that I understood it."

"I don't understand a lot of her poetry, either," I confess.

"Well, I think it's beautiful." Allison leans forward. "I like to read it in the bathtub."

"Now there's an image!" Henry says.

She swats at him. "I got her to read one to me once. I know she didn't like to, but it was my birthday. Her voice was different when she read. Deeper, you know, and more slow. It was like, I don't know, like she picked me up and carried me with her."

"Now don't you go trying to write poetry."

Everything they say is kind, but I just want them to stop because it seems like they are piling all of their memories on me and weighing down my own. I dig through my wallet to find the money, and push the plate away, muffin top uneaten.

"You have a good day, hon," Allison calls to me from the far end of the counter.

"You, too."

"Don't forget your postcard."

I had left it beside my plate. "Right. Thanks."

I exchange nods with Henry, and then as I walk out the door, I look at the back of the postcard. There is a line of her poetry printed at the top: *a spot so lovely, like the moon.*

The moon of Jupiter.

And so I cry the whole way home.

When I get there, Mom is back in her usual place on the sofa in the sunken living room. She has the afghan pulled up over her, and a drink in her hand. The ice has melted, or maybe she just forgot ice altogether, and there is only clear liquid left in the glass. She is reading *The Bell Jar*, which she left on my bed the previous year, claiming it is a book that should be read by every adolescent girl, but only by adolescent girls. "Once you get out of your twenties, it seems more self-indulgent than profound." She said the same thing about *The Catcher in the Rye* when I read it in ninth-grade English. So, what it means that she is reading Plath again, I'm not sure. Britta would say it means she is regressing. Nothing seems so obvious with my mother anymore.

She barely moves when I walk down the three stairs into the living room, and doesn't look up. I sit down on the chair next to the sofa and regard her. There are crow's-feet around her eyes, and wisps of wrinkles around her lips, like smokers get, though as far as I know she was never a smoker. She blinks slowly, but frequently, her hazel eyes disappearing and reappearing. She lets me watch her for several minutes, the in and out of her breathing, before she finally says, "So."

"So," I echo. "I met an old friend of yours today. Allison."

"Allison who?"

"I don't know. She's a waitress at Ruby's."

"Allison Wooster. Wooster Rooster. She's been doing that

dye job since high school. I remember she always claimed she was a natural redhead."

"She voted for you for prom queen."

"I didn't go to prom."

Outside a herd of sparrows lifts up and flies past the window, squeaking and squawking. They dance together and apart like someone is choreographing them.

"You have to forget everything I said last night. All of it. Everything I said and did." Her eyes are glassy. "Come sit with me, Very." She draws up her legs so there is space for me on the couch. When I don't move she says, "Please, Very. Please. Forget."

I sit down on the edge of the couch with a pillow on my lap.

She lolls her head toward me. "I don't expect you to understand." She gives me the sad smile again. "You've got your numbers. That's what speaks to you. You're steady. And I'm glad you are. But there are some things your sister and I share, as artists, that don't fit with your worldview. It makes me a terrible mother," she says. "But it doesn't make me a terrible person."

My mother has summed herself up in a single sentence: not a terrible person, but perhaps a terrible mother.

"Maybe. But you *are* her mother first and foremost."

This makes her wince. "I'm your mother, too. You're my little girl. You were my baby once. You used to coo and brush my eyebrows. I don't know why you did that. I'd be holding you in my arms, and you'd reach your fat fingers up and brush the hair of my eyebrows. I'd move them around and you'd laugh and laugh and laugh. I could get drunk on baby laughter back then."

340

"Ramona needs help," I tell her.

"Now, Ramona was not a cheerful baby. She would cry whenever you put her down. She always wanted to be held. I ended up getting a sling and tying her to my back like the women in Africa. It was the only way I could get any work done. Do you think that's why she's more artistic than you? I always thought it was genetics, but maybe it was being up there with me, soaking it all in."

"I don't know, Mom, but right now, right now she's really struggling."

Mom takes a long sip from her drink. "That, I think, is a matter of perspective. If her goal is to get through high school, then maybe. But perhaps she has higher aspirations. You shouldn't mess with the artist's temperament."

"Well I'm not just going to sit by and watch her collapse," I declare.

As if a switch has been flicked, she sits up, her hair wild and mussed, staring at me wide-eyed. "What are you going to do?"

That is the twenty-million-dollar question, isn't it? What am I going to do? That's why I went to my father, and to her, because I simply don't know. "I guess I'll have to figure it out on my own."

My lack of confidence soothes my mother, and she sinks back into the couch. "Very, love, don't get involved in matters you don't understand. You aren't prepared."

It's true. Walking the straight line, doing what I am asked, it hasn't prepared me for this.

sixteen

i.

THIS IS WHAT I know: I need things to be stable. To be the same. And so today, sixty-odd hours after Nonnie died, I decide to go to school.

I have jeans and a T-shirt picked out, and then I remember that today is the Math Around U conference. I'm supposed to go present with Mr. Tompkins and then meet Professor Singh. So I dig a skirt out and pair it with a short-sleeved sweater. My new haircut has the unexpected benefit of being easy to care for, and so I call this good.

Easy. Normal. I can do this.

But then I can't find Ramona. I wait for her first in the car, then back in the house. Then I go upstairs and her bed is still covered with CDs pilfered from our dad, dirty laundry, Magic Markers, and a stack of notebooks. She didn't sleep there. She left for school or wherever she went the day before and I haven't seen her since, which means she could have been missing for twenty-four hours. Isn't that the baseline for filing a missing-person report? That's how it is on television anyway.

I go to school by myself, and park in my usual space. As I shut the door behind me, my mind clicks: Ramona is missing and I am the only one who knows.

Telling myself that this is nothing new, that this is what she's been doing for weeks, I try to stop my brain from imagining ever more dire scenarios. Kidnapping. Rape. Walking into the ocean with stones in her pockets. She wouldn't even need the stones. The water is so cold, that alone would kill her so long as she let herself slip under. If that is her intent. Which I don't know if it is. I don't know what she is thinking at all.

In homeroom Mr. Tompkins gives me a sad smile, which I wonder if teachers practice the way that Dominic practiced his rakish one. Is it part of teacher training? He puts his hand on my shoulder. "It's okay, Very. It's all going to be okay."

Grace stands beside me and squeezes my hand.

"Are we going to drive over together?" I ask Mr. Tompkins. "Or should I meet you at the conference?"

"The conference, Very? Are you sure?"

"Yes."

Push Ramona down. Push Nonnie down.

I can do this.

"Good." Mr. Tompkins's smile relaxes. "I went back and forth but never actually canceled with Professor Singh. Truthfully, after all it took to set up the meeting, to convince her to meet you, well, I was a little scared to cancel even under the circumstances. But I know you're such a rock, you would rally for this."

Rock and rally. "Sure thing."

"Great!" He's positively beaming now.

Push it down.

"I have to go to English."

"Of course, Very. Meet me here after fourth period. We'll drive to campus together."

When I take my seat in class next to Britta, I say, "Ramona never came home."

Her eyes widen, but before we can talk about it more, Ms. Staples comes in and starts class. Dominic isn't here.

Britta writes on the corner of her notebook: *When did you see her last?* Her handwriting is straight and firm.

Yesterday.

When yesterday?

In the morning.

Where do you think she is?

No idea.

She looks up at me from the paper. I've been managing to keep a cap on my panic, but seeing it in Britta's eyes cracks the seal. I bite my lip hard, just shy of making it bleed.

"Ms. Staples, Very's not feeling so well. I'm just going to take her down to the nurse."

Ms. Staples looks at us, and says, "Of course."

Britta leads me out of the classroom. "I'm sure Ramona's

fine. Really. I mean, there's a lot going on for you guys right now, but she's always been a little flighty, you know? Remember that time when we were in fourth grade, so she would have been, what? In first, right? And your mom and Imogene brought us to the beach, and she wandered off? We were all going crazy looking for her, and she had found some other family and was just sitting down on their blanket."

My hands are shaking. "She was eating their sandwiches."

I rub my eyes, and Britta pulls me into a hug. "It's going to be fine," she says. And I believe her. I want to believe her. "I just think we should go to the office and let them know and then they can help. Okay?"

I nod.

When I open my eyes, I see Christian standing behind us, concern across his face. "Are you all right?" he asks. "I was in class across the hall and saw you guys come out. I got a bathroom pass." He holds up a giant wooden board that says, *To the LOO, no B.S.*

I don't want to say it out loud. I mean, maybe Britta is right. Maybe it is nothing. But if I say it out loud, then Christian will react. He will go into protector mode, trying to console me, and the only person I want is Britta.

"Ramona's missing," Britta says. "We're going to the office. It's all under control. But thanks anyway."

"Okay," he says, but his voice isn't sure. He swings the bathroom pass. "I can send some texts around."

"No," I say. "We'll find her."

"Okay," he says again, like he's one of those dolls that talks but only has a certain number of phrases. *Okay. You look nice today. I love you. Why'd you break my heart?*

"Actually," he says. "I know this isn't a good time right now. I mean, of course it isn't a good time. Duh. But once you find Ramona, maybe we could talk. I just want to let you know, I mean, we haven't had a chance to talk about the other night and—"

"Please let's just not talk about it."

"I just want to let you know that it's okay. That I understand. You just lost your grandmother, and something is clearly going on with Ramona, right?"

I nod.

"We should go," Britta says.

Christian doesn't seem to register her words. "So it's okay. We can just forget about it for now."

"Thank you."

"It's not that I didn't want to. I mean, trust me, I want to."

This is decidedly not not talking about it. "Okay."

"It's just that if we get back together, I want it to be about us, and not about, you know, the other things going on in your life."

Getting back together? The full force of my mistake hits me.

"And I guess we'd need to talk about those other things."

"Okay," I say again. What else is there to say?

"We're going," Britta says as she pulls me down the hall to the office. "Sister, when this is over, you've got a whole lot of talking to do."

Before we make it to the bend in the hall, someone calls my name. "Very!"

I turn around and there is Dominic. He's walking right past Christian. Mistake one and mistake two.

He trots to catch up with us. "I need you to come with me."

"And good morning to you, too," I reply.

He stiffens his back, but says, "Why, good morning, fair Veronica. How are you this fine day?"

I shake my head. "Not today, Dominic. Ramona is missing."

"That's why I'm here."

"Very, is everything okay?" Christian asks as he strides up to us.

"I've got it under control," Britta says.

"It's nothing," I say.

Dominic scoffs.

Christian turns to him. "Very's been under a lot of pressure lately, so—"

"I think I know what's going on with Very, thanks."

I feel like a fire hydrant between two dogs.

"You boys just settle this among yourselves. Very and I are going to the office."

"I know where Ramona is," Dominic says. "Let's go."

"Right now?"

"Yes, right now."

"You want me to cut class?"

Stupid, stupid. Why would you say that?

"I'd think you'd want to see this."

"Is she all right?" Britta asks.

Christian is still swinging that bathroom pass.

"I don't think so," Dominic says.

I look toward the stairs. Britta squeezes my hand, but I don't know if it's a *let's just go to the office* squeeze or a *go with him* squeeze. Before I can answer, he gives up on me.

"Fine, you know, forget it." His face has grown red, and his lips are set in a tight, thin line.

"What?" I demand.

"You can't take even the slightest step off the path, can you?"

"Hey now," Christian says.

I can speak for myself, though. "I don't know what you're talking about."

"Your sister is in trouble, but you're too concerned about your perfect reputation to help. You said it yourself. You care too much what other people think."

"That's not fair."

"Then prove me wrong."

Proofs—that's something I'm good at.

ii.

I expect sneaking out to involve subterfuge with a rendezvous point and synchronized watches. Britta says she'll make up a cover story for me, but I don't even need her help. Dominic and I walk right out the front door and no one stops us. We get into Dominic's black beater of a car. I move some perhaps dirty napkins off the seat before sitting down. I watch the school as we pull away, feeling liberated and strange.

"So where are we going?"

"It's on the edge of town."

That isn't an answer, but I don't push it. If he wants to have his super-dramatic moment, then fine. I just want to get back to school in time to meet Mr. Tompkins for the conference.

"Are you sure she's there?"

"I saw her on her way this morning."

I watch him as he drives. When he's not making his wolf smile, his lips are both full and long, almost too big for his face. There's a cut right in the corner, sharp and red.

"So that's what a knight in shining armor looks like," he says, eyes on the road.

"Drop it."

"Steadfast and reliable, that's for sure. And a demon with a bathroom pass."

I squeeze the edge of my seat. "God, what is your deal with Christian? Would you just let it go?"

"I could say the same thing to you. Do you love him?"

"That's none of your business."

"Do you?"

"Why do you care?"

He doesn't have to ask the question again. Just raises his eyebrows.

"No." I look at the pile of junk on the floor of the car: paper coffee cups, an old paperback without a cover, and three pens, none with caps. "No. I thought I did, but I guess I'm not sure what that feels like."

"It's not neat and clean and easy, if that's what you expect."

"Let's not have this conversation again."

"You're the boss."

I shift in my seat. It's a sunny day, and the car is getting warm. I push the button to lower my window, but it doesn't do anything. I don't want to ask him to do it for me. I don't want to ask him for anything.

Dominic turns onto a road that I've never been on before, strange in this small town. It winds around a number of curves and up and down subtle hills.

After a few minutes he turns to the right and I see the sign: *Town of Essex Transfer Station.*

iii.

Dominic drops the car into coast as we approach the guarded entrance to the transfer station. Beyond the gate I can see heaps of organized garbage: wood in one pile, tires in another, metal scraps, plastic, pallets, appliances, computer monitors—all the detritus of our lives neatly categorized like a hoarder's museum.

"This is where she is? The dump?"

He nods.

"But why?"

"I don't know. We don't have to go and see her. Maybe it's just enough for you to know?"

I stare at him like he's gone as far off the rails as Ramona, and he starts the car rolling again.

We pull up to the gate, and Dominic puts down his window. Before he can say anything, the man in the booth says, "You here with that other girl? For the school project?"

"Yes, sir," Dominic says without hesitation. "We're in the same class."

"Starting late, aren't you? She's been here all semester it seems."

"She's an extraordinarily dedicated student."

The man nods. "Park over by the truck."

Dominic does as instructed. I reach for the door with my right hand just as he places his left hand on my arm. His smile now is unlike his normal sly grin.

"I'm fine," I say, and turn my body away from him.

That's when I see her, right at the periphery of the scrap-metal heap.

Ramona.

Stooped and fragile, she holds a long pipe in one hand like a staff. She has a pink feather boa wrapped around her neck that flops from side to side as she moves. She hears me coming and looks up. Her face tightens like a prune. "What are you doing here?" she demands, but her voice lacks force.

"School project. You?"

She bends over again, and picks up something glinty and

silver, which she drops into a large bag she has slung over her shoulder. I step closer. "Ramona, is this where you've been coming instead of school?" I try to make my voice sound soft and calm, but I can't get rid of the edge. It makes her shudder. I take another step.

"Leave me alone," she says as much to the ground as to me.

"Ramona."

She stands up and starts backing away. "Why do you even care?"

"Ramona, please. Of course I care. Just tell me what's going on."

She looks over her shoulder at the various piles of trash behind her. "You wouldn't understand."

"Try me." I want to run to her, grab her, and shake her out of whatever funk she is in. And she can tell. She keeps backing away from me. "Come on, please. We can go get a frappe at Ruby's or something."

"You're talking to me like you think I'm crazy."

"It's the sculpture, isn't it?" Dominic says from behind me. "You're the one making it."

She looks past me at him, and her posture softens. She nods and tugs on the feather boa.

Of course. *Of course.*

I was so sure it was Dominic—so wrapped up in that drama—that I missed it.

I keep walking, slowly, until I'm right up beside her. "I thought—" I began. "I thought you didn't care. I thought—"

She shifts the weight of her bag on her shoulders.

"Why didn't you say anything?"

"About what?"

"That it was you, I mean. Why didn't you let anyone know?"

"I didn't want anyone to know. It was between me and Nonnie."

"Why did you do it?"

Her body tightens again. She leans on the long pipe and it seems to be holding her up like a shepherd's staff. "For Nonnie. It's what I needed to do. It's like it's a part of me, to give to her, and if I don't take care of it—" She stops herself as if she's afraid she's revealed too much. She turns her back to me.

Dominic moves up so he is standing by my side. "Come on, Very." He puts his hand on my upper arm.

"Ramona, please let's just go home." She bends over and picks up another small piece of metal and drops it into her pack. I don't think there is any chance we will get her to leave, and so I turn to go with Dominic.

"Okay. We can go home." Her voice is soft. I hear her put down the pipe and she follows us to the car.

She crawls across the backseat to the driver's side, leaving the front passenger seat of his two-door tilted forward. It is almost an invitation—the only one she's given me recently—so I climb in back with her.

Ramona's hip digs into mine as every slight bounce seems to jostle her.

When we turn onto School Street, "Veronica" comes on the radio.

After the first verse, Ramona turns to look at me. "This is a crappy song."

"Yeah," I agree.

"To be named after, I mean," she clarifies.

Dominic's eyes lock with mine in the rearview mirror. "It's not so bad," he says.

"It's better than being named after a children's book character."

"You're not named after that Ramona," I say.

She picks at dirt I can't see on the back of Dominic's seat. "Yes," she insists. "You named me after the books. Mom says."

I shake my head. I hadn't even been a fan of Ramona—always getting in trouble; I found her bratty. I definitely related more to older sister Beezus. I wanted to name Ramona Charlie, after a boy in my swim lessons, but then she was born a girl. "Dad named you after the Ramones," I tell her.

She frowns.

"Think about it," I tell her. "I was only two when you were born. I wasn't reading Beverly Cleary yet."

"Whatever." She stares out the window at students kicking a soccer ball back and forth as part of gym class. I can see Adam Millstein, with his Ronald McDonald hair. Ramona doesn't seem to see anything.

iv.

Ramona practically climbs over me to get out of the car. Her feather boa falls off. I pick it up off the ground, as Dominic gets out of the car. He walks around and tucks his head into the backseat, then extends his hand to help me out. Once I'm standing, he doesn't let go, so I tug my hand free. "I should go," I say. "I need to get back to Ramona. I'm going to take her home."

"Of course."

I look over my shoulder and see her sitting in my car. The top is down, and the wind dances her hair around her head. "She looks like a fairy. Not that I ever believed in them. She did. Not me."

"Well, they aren't real. You can't fault yourself for not believing in them."

"I could've pretended."

"She'll be all right."

"Ms. Pickering told me I should bring her to the school psychologist. Maybe." I shake my head. "I guess maybe I should." Then I laugh. "And maybe I should go, too."

"Maybe," he says.

A crow circles above us, then lands on the power line. Immediately after another joins it.

"Dominic, I'm—"

"Sorry. I know. You said that. Several times."

"I lied to you the other night. You're right. It was easier than the truth."

"What is the truth, then? Tell me the truth of your lie."

"Maybe someday—" I twist Ramona's feather boa in my hands. One of the pink feathers slips out and twists toward the ground. Dominic bends gracefully and catches it in his hand.

"I don't operate in somedays, Very."

He turns his head and looks across the parking lot. I turn in the opposite direction, toward the school. So we stand there like birds on a wire, staring away.

He speaks first: "Here's what it comes down to: I like you. A lot. Neither of us knows what's going to happen, so you just have to make the best of every moment, and for me the best possible moment is with you." As he speaks, he rolls the base of the pink feather between his fingers. "I don't want to be that guy, you know, pestering you after you said no, but I guess part of me still thinks I have a shot."

The first crow caws and a third crow joins them. They balance on the power line as it sways in the breeze. Do they feel unsteady up there? Or have they gotten used to life on that slack line?

"Why do you use that smile?" I ask. "The fake wolfish one?"

His eyes look up from beneath the blue-veined lids. I think for a moment that he's going to deny it, maybe even flashing the wolf smile while he does so. "I guess you're not the only one trying to write a story about yourself."

"It's not a good story," I tell him.

"It's not."

"None of your stories are. The one about your dad. Your

mom. But you, actual you . . . Hope is the thing with feathers, right?"

"I guess."

I unfold his hand, where the pink feather is now lying matted and crushed. "Hope," I say.

"Veronica Woodruff, did you just use literary symbolism?"

"I'm not entirely sure. And it's not a promise."

"I know. It's hope."

I watch his feet walk away from me. Sand falls out of the treads of his Doc Martens in faint footprints. His car door opens. Shuts. The car starts. I could wave my hand, and he would stop. He'd throw open the door and I could run across the parking lot and jump into the warm, sweet-smelling car. We could drive away without looking back.

I don't, of course. I know I have to take Ramona home.

v.

We don't talk the whole drive. We are each waiting for the other to do something. Ramona waits for me to question her; I wait for her to make a confession. I feel her glancing at me, a shift of the head, and then a shift right back. And I peek at her, too. But neither of us manages to say anything.

I park the car right in front of the sculpture, we both sit still for a moment, staring at it. I leave my hands on the steering wheel and look at the instruments below, as if the odometer could tell me not only my distance but also how to talk to my sister. Instead I hear the click of her unbuckling her seat belt.

"Thanks for the ride," she mumbles.

"No problem."

She stares out the window. The air between us is growing warm, stale. I want to tell her that I understand, even though I don't, and that I'm there to help.

"I'm going to take it down," she says.

"What? Why?"

"It's ruined now."

"No it's not. It's beautiful," I tell her.

"Mom doesn't like it."

"Mom loves it." That's the problem, although I don't tell Ramona that.

"I thought we could have, you know, something nice here. I thought it would make us happy." I notice then that she is crying. She wipes at a tear with her wrist.

"It did make us happy."

Her hand is still on the door handle. Dirt is packed in around her nails. Her hair, too, is greasy, and I wonder when she last showered.

I watch her go inside, and check my clock. Plenty of time to get to school and meet Mr. Tompkins. I can just drive back and stroll into the building as easily as I went out. Unless they stop me. Today isn't a day that I have class at the college, and so I have no reason to leave campus. I tap my fingers on the steering wheel. I need a good excuse, and I've been working the Nonnie one too hard. If I go in and get my graphing calculator, then I'll have a plausible story.

I'm halfway up the stairs to my room when I hear a thud from my mom's studio.

If your mom trashes her studio, and you pretend not to hear it, does it make a sound?

I can't just leave. I want to. I want to get in my car and go back to school, find Dominic, and maybe get some French toast sticks from the cafeteria before I meet Mr. Tompkins and head to the conference. But instead I pivot and make my way to her staircase.

I hear three more thuds before I reach her studio, low and hollow.

With a deep breath, I press open the door. The studio is spotless, no trace of her outburst, not even one wayward shard of glass. She's by the window stretching canvas over a frame and hammering it in.

"Hi," I say.

"Hi, yourself," she replies. She has nails in her mouth, pressed in her lips, but she takes them out and tucks them into the pocket of her denim painting apron. Her eyes seems clearer than they have in weeks, but they're surrounded by dark, sleepless circles. "So I'm starting again," she says. "Again and again and again."

"On the portraits?"

She shrugs. "Maybe I'll do something more abstract. Reinvent myself. A series on the body that shows a square of flesh or a strand of hair, all out of context."

"Good. I'm happy for you."

"Don't be. It's not like I have a choice. We begin again. That's what we do. Over and over, even though we know it's going to be another disappointment. Boats against the current and all that."

"It doesn't have to end the same way."

"That's what your grandmother always said, and look how it wound up for her. She made something new, and it disappointed her even more than her first life."

"She wasn't—" I stop myself, shaking my head.

"I'll paint and I'll hate them and then I'll paint again. You're lucky, you know." She bends over to grab another canvas and I see gray streaks at the roots of her hair. I didn't even know she colored it.

"I brought Ramona home. She's sick." My voice is flat.

"But you're leaving?"

"Yeah, I just needed to bring Ramona home. I'm going back. I have—I have this thing with Mr. Tompkins."

"Oh, don't go down that road, Very. He's a handsome man and all, but don't go down that road."

"I'm not." I stop myself from lobbing an insult at her. *I'm not like you, Mom. Not like you. Not ever.* "Ramona's sick. Let her sleep."

Mom smiles wanly.

The canvas and the wood make the studio smell more like a workshop than usual. Mom tucks some hair behind her ear.

"This weekend we're going to need to have some conversations. Family conversations." She forces a chuckle. "Maybe you and Ramona can make dinner again."

"I don't think so," I say. I don't think Ramona will be up for much of anything for a while.

"We need to talk about the house, and—"

"You've already made up your mind, Mom." Maybe it's not entirely fair to say this. If Ramona's right, Mom and Dad won't have much of a choice: they can't afford the mortgage payments. "Will Dad be there?"

She touches her fingers to her temples. "We need to talk about the house and where we're all going to be going. Dad has some ideas of his own."

"You do what you need to, Mom—"

"Come on, Very. Enough." Her voice cracks with exasperation.

I step farther into the room so I'm standing next to a butcher-block counter where Mom usually keeps her paints, but there are none on it. No paints or brushes. "I'm not being bratty. I've got seven months left of school, and then I'll go to college. I'll figure it all out."

Mom shoves her hands into the pocket of her apron. "You always were our practical girl. Nonnie and I would watch you, you and Ramona, and we'd say, 'We can run off, run back to New York City. Very will take care of it all.'"

So I guess I was Ramona's keeper all along.

"I have to go, Mom."

"Date with Mr. Tompkins, right?"

"Mom. It's a math thing."

She picks up another frame. "It's that math conference, right? Mathematics and You?"

"Math Around U."

"Close," she says. "Bet you didn't think I remembered."

I look past her, out the window. The leaves of the oak tree wave in the wind. I catch a glimpse of Ramona sitting on the branch, and then she's gone.

Mom takes a nail from the pouch in her apron and starts pounding nails into the stretched canvas, holding it to the frame. She already has a stack of seven canvases ready to go, but her paints and brushes remain packed away.

"See you later, Mom."

"Not if I see you first."

coda

WHEN I COME OUT of the house, the sun is shining right into my eyes, like walking into a solar flare. I am being blasted clean, shaking off what happened with Ramona, the conversation with Mom.

I step forward, and the glare fades.

"Will you take me to the beach?" Ramona is leaning against the front of Nonnie's car. My car.

"What? Now?" It's ten thirty. I'm supposed to meet Mr. Tompkins for our presentation in an hour, and then my meeting with Professor Singh. It's twenty minutes to the beach, and that's pressing it.

"Never mind." Ramona's hair falls in front of her shoulders. There's a huge tangle in the back. She used to howl so much when she got her hair combed that Mom would throw up her hands and walk away. Only Nonnie could do it. She'd use her fingers, and they would sit together singing songs while Nonnie untangled her snarls.

Your choices don't shape you, they shape people's perceptions of you. But maybe that's not the whole story. Maybe your choices can shape how you see yourself.

"We can go."

We drive out of town and over the bridge. Ramona stares out the window as we pass the malls and Chuck E. Cheese's, where we both had birthday parties as kids. Mom stayed firmly planted at one of the tables, sipping a Diet Coke with her fingers pressed to her temples, willing away the noise around her. She wouldn't let us go in the ball pit because she said kids peed in it. I wonder if Ramona is remembering these things, too. I turn to ask her, but her eyes are closed.

I ease into the traffic circle, gripping the steering wheel more tightly, still nervous about rotaries. We drive past the motels and then onto the winding road that leads to the ocean.

I keep driving to the parking lot at the beach. I'm not sure if she just wanted a ride, or for me to come with her. She doesn't move to get out of the car. We can hear the ocean but can't see it over the concrete wall. Still she stares out in that direction, tugging on a ratty lock of hair.

"You can't just take someone's name away from them," she declares.

"Excuse me?"

"It's like pulling the foundation out from under me. I always thought I was named for one thing and now you tell me it's really another. That's not fair."

"I'm pretty sure that's not what rocked your foundation," I mutter, and instantly regret it as she turns silent again.

I try to really look at her, then, to take her all in, but my eyes fixate on a small tear in her jeans around which she has drawn teeth, so it looks like some weird inverted mouth.

She shifts in her seat, which makes a rustling sound.

"Are you still with Dominic?" she asks.

I consider saying that I never was with Dominic, but that isn't exactly true. "Maybe."

"He found me. He did that for you."

I wonder if this could be an opening, if she is inviting me to talk about what has been happening with her. I trace my finger along the steering wheel. There are so many questions, so many places to start. I don't want to mess it up. "What are you trying to say with it? The sculpture, I mean."

She looks straight ahead through the windshield. Her head, I realize, almost touches the fabric ceiling of the car. She's taller than me now. She seems to consider the question for a while, or maybe she is just zoning out. Finally she says, "I didn't know what else to do." She won't look at me as she speaks. "I was angry and sad and scared and it was like if I didn't do something or make something it would just overtake me."

"You didn't seem sad."

"How do you seem sad?" she asks. "I was. I *am*, and you and Mom and Dad knew just how to act, but everything I did was wrong."

I suck in my lower lip.

"I know that everything I did was wrong, and you looked so disappointed, but I didn't know what was right. And it was, like, itching me. And then I saw those bottle caps and there were the Moxie ones, and I thought of Nonnie—those were *her* bottle caps. She was dying, but they were still around. And I thought how the house is like her, and I wanted to put them on the walls. So I did."

That never would have occurred to me. Not in a million years. I would have picked them up and put them in the trash where they belonged and that would have been the end of it. If I had been the one to find the bottle caps first, maybe none of this would have happened. We'd both be home in our beds snug and happy.

But of course, nothing is that simple.

"So why'd you start going to the dump?"

"We weren't throwing away the things that I need."

Of course. I mean, really, no sarcasm: of course. If you're building a statue with trash, then you go to the dump.

"At first it wasn't about her poetry. I just did what I thought was right, but then I read some of her poetry, and I had more ideas. So I had to start getting stuff to make them. I had to skip school because the dump isn't open the rest of the time. And anyway, the art seemed more important than anything we were learning. I couldn't concentrate."

People grieve in different ways, that's what Ms. Pickering had told me, and I thought she was stupid to make such a banal statement, especially when she didn't know anything about our family—only what she thought she knew. But in the end she was right, wasn't she?

"It really wasn't about 'Detritus'?"

"The bottle cap poem? I hadn't even read that one when I started working on it."

"But it's exactly like the poem. Everyone says so."

"People always see what they want to see. What they need to see. They take the pieces that they can understand and match it up to what they think they know and then they decide what the art is all about."

I think about patterns in math, why I like them, because you need real evidence. But maybe I was just fooling myself. Maybe it was just what I thought I knew, just like with the sculpture and Nonnie's poetry and even Nonnie herself. Everyone thought they knew exactly who she was, even me. Even her. She had toiled over her words, trying to get them just right. In spite of it all, though, people still didn't know her. *I* didn't know her. Or maybe she had been different people for different audiences, a kaleidoscope that shifts as it passes from hand to hand.

Maybe we are all like that. We are all grotesque, glamorous, sunny, and shadow. We are all pixies in polyester nightgowns and plums to be plucked. We are all of these things. Maybe none of us can be pinned down as easily as a butterfly in an insect collection—or Nonnie's lightning bug.

"What about the poem tree in your room?"

Her whole face, it's like the life drains right out of it. Her lips purse, and I figure that is it. I've blown it. She isn't going to talk to me anymore. So I turn my head and look at the stand that sells sodas and ice cream in the summer, and wonder how

369

long I have to wait before I can suggest we go home. There is still a chance I could make the conference and the meeting with Professor Singh. Then she says, "It's messed up. It's messed up that she used us like that, that she took that from us."

"Took what?" I ask. But I know. Our virginity had been offered up for discussion to the public before we even had a chance to realize what it was for ourselves, to decide what we wanted to do with it. But it hadn't been that way for me—I hadn't been plucked like a plum, or conquered, or anything remotely close to it. We had fumbled awkwardly.

My head snaps around to look at her. Had she—? As if reading my mind, she blows air out slowly. "I'm still a virgin. Don't worry."

"I'm not worried about *if.* I'm worried about how and who and where. And why."

"Well, you don't need to worry at all." She seems disappointed by this fact. I want to tell her not to be, to wait. I want to explain how you could never tell how it was going to be—boring or exciting or clumsy or lovely. You can't foretell that.

She looks so tired—dark circles under her eyes, chapped lips. And thin. Frail. I want to wrap her up in something—a blanket, my arms. When I was four, I started calling her my baby. I helped her get dressed every morning and tucked her in at night. My mom had laughed at how charming it was. I want to do that again, to be for her what our parents cannot. But I can't.

"Let's go," she says. She pushes open the door, and the cool air pours in, like breathing life back into a corpse.

I check the clock. Eleven o'clock. Still time to make it back.

She runs from the car, and I run after her. Up the stairs, over the wall, and down onto the beach. Our feet grow heavy in the sand. She tumbles forward, not even trying to stop herself with her hand, just rolling forward and onto her back, looking up at the blue sky. I jog to catch up with her, then sit down beside her.

"It's a water buffalo," she says, pointing up. I look up at the sky, expecting to see a fluffy cloud in the shape of a water buffalo, but there is just a bank of gray clouds.

"I love the sculpture. And the tree in your room. I love them. They're beautiful. And honest. And you know I don't know how to talk about these things. I don't have the words to say what I mean, but the way I feel when I look at them, it makes me hopeful." As I say the words, they become true. Because I know now that she created the art, and it all clicks into place for real, and makes sense. She does miss Nonnie. She hated her and loved her, and she misses her.

She sits up with her knees drawn into her chest. Her breath scratches in and out.

"I'm sorry," I say, and I wonder why the words we have are so weak. "I haven't been a great sister."

"You've done your best."

"I didn't know—I didn't know anything."

"I didn't tell you. I wouldn't tell you. I don't want it to go away, you know?" She waves her hand in a circle as if that explains what she means.

A seagull soars over the water, and we both watch its trajectory.

"It's like I go and go and go and I get an idea and I can't stop and so the other days I need to rest." She looks up at the sky and digs her fingers into the sand as if holding herself down. "I just want to be even. Like you."

"I'm not always even," I tell her.

"Yes you are. I always feel like I'm walking on the deck of a ship in a storm." She shifts her gaze from the sky to me. "Do you ever feel that way?"

I have to tell her the truth. "No."

She nods and then her body seems to curl in upon itself, like she is morphing into a spiral shell. Her face is between her knees, and her shoulders move up and down with each breath.

Her breaths fall into a long, easy pattern. Perhaps she is sleeping. Her hair tumbles forward, and I reach out to brush it back. She lifts her head. "Come swim with me." She stands up, and starts pulling off her oversize sweatshirt.

I don't like going in the ocean in the summer anymore, let alone the fall. "Are you crazy?"

She laughs. "Evidently." She beams down at me, and I can't help but crack a smile. But I'm not going swimming. We'll get hypothermia. She starts shimmying out of her jeans. I shiver looking at the gooseflesh on her thin legs. "Come on, don't make me go alone."

She is down to her mismatched bra and underpants. Her hip bones press against her skin. She gives me another pleading look, then starts running toward the water. "Ramona!" I call.

"Ramona, wait! It's too cold."

Her thin frame rocks in the knee-deep water. When she shakes, it is like she is wavering in her very existence. Like everything else in my life that I thought I had, she could just fade away and disappear. Nonnie died—that is the simplest and hardest of all. Dad will leave once he can figure out how. And Mom. I've always thought she was so alluring, so above it all, but disappointment and envy have hollowed her out. It's like you go through your whole life thinking you know your family, and then you wake up and a curtain's been pulled back to show you that you don't know anything.

But there is one thing I thought was lost that I can get back. So I start stripping off my clothes. She looks back, sees me, and grins. Jumping from foot to foot, she waits for me.

My skin puckers with goose bumps almost immediately, and I run through the lapping waves to meet her.

She pulls me on into the water. It is like walking through ice. She pulls me so fast the water seems to be overtaking us.

Then we dive. It takes my breath away, the cold. I come up gasping, my lungs tight. Blinking my eyes, I see her laughing, the spray from the ocean hitting her face. She turns that sunny smile on me, and I laugh, too. Her fingers slip from mine, but she is okay. She isn't slipping under. And if she does, I'll be here. I'll always be here.

I turn to her and shout it. "I'm here!" She jumps up through the crest of the wave, water drops spread out around her, as if she's transformed herself into a mermaid. "I'm here!" I yell again, and feel the weight of it as a small pit in my stomach.

She turns to me, floating down through the water. "I know," she replies, so softly I can't hear her above the surf; I have to read her lips. "I'm here, too."

The sun slices through the clouds, just a thin line, and just for a moment, but for that time, we are illuminated. Hand in hand as the water laps against us. Her fingers are thin and slick, and I'm afraid she is going to slip away. But then she grips me, just a little tighter.

ACKNOWLEDGMENTS

Thank you to early readers for your insight and support: Manda Goltz, Deva Fagan, Saundra Mitchell, Cheryl Renee Herbsman, and Lisa (L.K.) Madigan. Thank you to Sarah Pikcilingis for talking with me about math and the ways in which it is beautiful.

I am grateful to everyone at HarperTeen, starting with Alexandra Cooper: you saw what I wanted to do and helped me to get there. Thank you to Alyssa Miele for your thoughtful comments on the manuscript, and to Rosemary Brosnan for signing on to this book. Erin Fitzsimmons and Kate Engbring, thank you for the lovely jacket design.

Thank you to Sara Crowe for always being a champion for my work and looking out for me.

Thank you to my family, immediate and extended: the Frazers, the Blakemores, and beyond. Nathan, Jack, and Matilda—endless gratitude.

And finally thank you to Larissa, Cara, Jen(n), Jessie, Sarah, and Lindsay. You're the best at being you.